Flipping the Scales

Pete Tarsi

ISBN: 1502999102
ISBN-13: 978-1502999108

Cover by Vila Design
www.viladesign.net
Beach by Hydromet | Bigstock.com
Girl on left by kobayakov | Bigstock.com
Girl on right by kohrhzevska | Bigstock.com

This book is dedicated to my three daughters.
You have flipped my life upside down and turned it into
the greatest adventure ever.

~ Chapter One ~

"We should *not* be doing this." Marina brushed away wet strands of blonde hair that had clumped together in front of her eyes.

Her friend Lorelei danced ahead along the boundary between the ocean and the shore, and her long, wavy red hair streamed behind her. "Running on the beach, Marina. No other experience like it." Her outstretched hand held a piece of some translucent material, which rippled in the air behind her like a pennant blowing in the breeze. In the early morning sunlight, it shimmered with almost every color of the spectrum. When she stopped running and started twirling, her teal sundress billowed in the breeze, and while she fluttered her arm up and down, a rainbow appeared to circle around her. "Look at the sky from out here!"

Yellow and orange filled the panorama as the morning sun slowly revealed itself through the wispy clouds streaking the sky. Waves rustled as they gently rolled onto the island beach, and seagulls squawked as they glided above the water. The air was warm but breezy, filled with the light aroma of ocean salt. It may have been as close to a perfect summer day as possible.

Marina lagged behind her friend and kept one arm at her side against the damp yellow sundress, even though it was already clinging to her thighs. Clasped tightly in her other hand was a similar iridescent piece of material, but because she held it close to her with her back to the sun, it wasn't sparkling. "Lore, are you sure we should do this? The others—"

Lorelei looked over her shoulder at the ocean stretching to the horizon. "The others have not come this far north yet. My father knows we are here, so there is no reason to worry. He has allowed me to do this before."

"I know *you* have, but I have not. We should be back in the—"

"You *almost* did that one other time. Little steps, Marina." Lorelei turned around and saw Marina walking tentatively over the sea foam towards her. "Today is time for bigger steps. Come and catch me!" Then Lorelei skipped off in the opposite direction.

Marina ran as quickly as she could, but by the time she reached her friend, she was breathing heavily, almost hyperventilating. "You move…much quicker than I do…out here."

"Can you feel that?" Lorelei pointed at their bare feet. "The way the wet sand squeezes its way between your toes? *Between your toes*, Marina! There is no other experience like that feeling."

"Lore, please listen to me."

"Try it." Lorelei grabbed Marina by the shoulders and then pointed down at their feet. "Do it there with those toes! Oh, there has got to be a better word to describe this sensation. Scraping, but crunching the sand—scrunching! Yes, that flows. Scrunch the sand between your toes." Lorelei swiveled her hips, which dug her feet deeper into the moist sand.

"I do *not* want to scrunch sand. I want to go back."

"One day, Marina. It will be like no other experience."

Marina sighed. "What if I think otherwise?"

"Give it a chance." Lorelei pranced around her friend, who simply stood there with her arms and the translucent pennant folded across her chest as the tide rolled in and out at their feet. "Simply feel the water on your feet. Your *feet*, Marina! And the bottoms of your legs. If that is not one of the flowiest feelings ever, well, then what is?"

"Lore, you know I trust you, but what if—?"

"You know what I always say, Marina. Sink or swim." Taking Marina's hand, Lorelei tried to lead her friend away from the water.

After a few steps, Marina hadn't budged. Letting her arm flop back by her side, she said, "I choose swim."

"That flows, Marina. Today is going to be an adventure like no other." Lorelei continued ahead while she babbled to herself about the day's plans.

Marina turned toward the water and started smoothing out the object in her hands until it separated into two layers. Once Lorelei realized she was walking alone, she turned and saw Marina opening the material into one continuous tube. Dashing back, she snatched the coarse material out of Marina's hand and said, "You promised me."

"Please give it back to me," groaned Marina.

"Not until you promise me that you will not put it back on." Lorelei held the sparkling object high above Marina's head. "Please share the day with me."

"Lore, be careful with that." Marina tried to stretch as much as her legs could, but she felt like her feet were firmly stuck into the ground.

"Do you know what really flows?" Lorelei glanced down at Marina and giggled. "I did not expect my head to be so much higher than yours."

"This is *not* funny, Lore." Marina wiped tears from her eyes. "If anything happens to my—"

"Nothing will happen. You have got to come out of your shell sometime."

Marina's shoulders slumped as she sighed. "Not going to let this one float, are you?"

"Of course not." Lorelei grinned broadly. "So which is it? Sink or swim?"

Marina hung her head in the knowledge that once Lorelei had her mind on an adventure, there was no convincing her otherwise. As she was going to give her answer, Marina noticed that the wet sand had swallowed her feet and ankles. "Sink," she replied.

"Sink? Not swim?" Lorelei frowned. "Please join me for the day, Marina."

"I mean I have sunk in this stuff."

Lorelei crouched down, her eyes following Marina's legs from the knees downward until she saw Marina's ankles and feet buried in the over-soaked sand. A wave broke nearby, and foamy water rushed toward them. Some splashed against Marina's legs, which sprayed and tickled Lorelei's shins. As the wave receded, the ground underneath Lorelei shifted as it got softer. "I never knew that would happen." She looked up at Marina. "Now I see why our heads were at different heights. See all the things you can experience out here?"

"One day," said Marina, holding up one finger. "Now get me out of this."

After Lorelei hopped up, she returned the shimmery skirt to Marina and took hold of her free hand. Together they counted to three, and then Lorelei pulled Marina out of the wet sand and away from the water. They took off quickly, but Marina's footing gave way as the terrain changed, and she tumbled onto the sand.

"The ground is different here." Marina sat up and sifted some sand through her fingers. "What is it?"

"Dry sand. And it gets *everywhere*." Lorelei helped Marina back to her feet. "Now come on. Today will be a wondrous adventure."

Marina held up the translucent skirt. "What do we do with these?"

"Hide them."

While walking away from the water, the girls scanned the area. A sign stated that it was a private stretch of the beach, which Lorelei insisted would be better for them because fewer people would be around during the day. Of the three houses in view, she focused on the one in the middle because it would be the easiest to recognize later. While the other two stood only one story, had expansive back decks, sliding glass doors, and many windows, the middle house looked more old-fashioned and welcoming.

Less sprawling than the others, probably because it had a second floor, it was a small cape-style cottage, though the girls didn't know the specific architectural names. It was painted red, making it stand out to them more prominently than the bland shades of white and gray of the two more modern-looking houses. After a few wooden stairs upward over the line of large rocks that served to stop stronger waves from reaching the houses, a small footbridge led to the yard behind the house.

Lorelei ran up the steps and then lay down across the length of the bridge. Carefully, she inched forward until her head was underneath the lowest crossbar of the railing. She peeked underneath the walkway and fiddled around with some of the boards.

Meanwhile, Marina was a little further down the row of rocks, cautiously climbing over them. Each step was difficult, especially while barefoot, and she found herself holding on tightly to some of the protruding stone edges just to keep herself steady. Between two rocks, she saw a space barely wide enough to fit her arm. She reached inside and explored the nooks and crannies. It was a dry place and out of direct view, and since getting there required balancing skills, she deemed it the perfect hiding spot. After a quick check to both her left and her right, she stashed the piece of material deep into the crevice and then slowly climbed back down to the sand.

"Are you ready?" Lorelei had unexpectedly appeared beside Marina and startled her.

"Yes. Now will you please stop bobbing up and down so much?"

Lorelei bounced one more time and flailed her arms. "Wait, you have got to see this! It looks much better from some distance." Lorelei put her arm around Marina to face her toward the water. "That way is south, from where we came. Now look this way."

They turned to the left where the sun had made its full presence known in the eastern sky. The ocean water reflected the sunlight and caused the crests of every single ripple to sparkle.

"Beautiful. Would you agree?" asked Lorelei.

Marina nodded her head, having never seen the sun so large and magnificent. As she basked in its post-sunrise glow, she took a deep breath, a little anxious about whatever Lorelei had planned for the day.

Lorelei took Marina by the hand and led her to the footbridge. "First, we find shoes, so we do not injure our feet. There are so many wonderful things we can do with them." She clapped her hands and then hopped off the other end of the bridge onto the cool green grass. "Later, we get ice cream."

"Ice cream? Does it flow?" Shaking her head, Marina knew the exact answer Lorelei was going to give her.

"Flows fastest."

They swiftly made their way past the red house, hoping not to wake the sleeping residents inside. As they headed down the road to begin their adventure, Marina hoped that her stay on land wouldn't last too long.

~ Chapter Two ~

Sitting on one side of a booth near the snack bar on the enclosed middle deck of the ferry, Meredith took her eyeglasses off her short brown hair and slid them back onto the bridge of her nose. She opened her paperback novel to the bookmark about midway through it and continued reading. On the table in front of her was an opened single-serving carton of orange juice and a plate with a cranberry muffin, both untouched since she sat down.

"I can't believe you and my mom ganged up on me." Her best friend Jill plopped her face and chest down on the table. Jill's mane of uncontrollable dark hair sprawled all over the place. "I thought you were my best friend."

"I am your best friend." Without taking her eyes off the book she was reading, Meredith moved her plate to the side before her muffin was attacked by untamed hair. "But your mother made a logical point."

The second ferry for the island left at eight-thirty in the morning, and without traffic it was almost a thirty-minute drive to the terminal. Walk-on passengers were recommended to arrive at least a half hour prior to departure in the event that the ferry reached vessel capacity on busy weekends and holidays. The nearest holiday was July Fourth, over a week away. Though it was the start of summer, it was early in the morning on a Thursday. An authority on schedules and timetables, Jill's mother had correctly assured them that the boat would be nowhere near full and that they'd have more than enough time to buy their tickets.

"Seven-thirty in the morning, Merri. You convinced her to

leave the house at seven-thirty in the morning!" Jill clutched the tall cup of coffee beside her and raised her head to look across the table at Meredith. "That means we had to be up earlier than that. During summer vacation. That's just wrong." She sat up and took a gulp of the hot liquid.

"Just because you do drama in school, it doesn't mean you have to be a drama queen right now." Meredith took a sip of her juice. "Besides, shouldn't you be excited? We're going to visit *your* cousin, after all."

School had been out almost two weeks, and the girls would be spending three weeks on the island with Jill's family: her aunt, uncle, and cousin Hailey. It was an annual summer trip for Jill, and in exchange, Hailey usually spent a school vacation week in either February or April off-island with Jill and her parents. Jill's older brother Jeff usually came to the island also, but he had just graduated high school and was spending his summer working both a full-time and a part-time job to save money for college in the fall.

"That's right!" blurted Jill. "My cousin's cottage on the beach. A private beach. I don't see why *you're* not more excited about it."

"Oh, I'm excited." Meredith turned the page of her book. "A private beach means that there will be very few people around to disturb me."

Meredith's parents had left the day before to go on a two-week African safari for their twentieth wedding anniversary. When they had planned the trip, they asked if Meredith wanted to join them, but she told them that she was planning to spend the summer studying and researching colleges. With a mother who was a surgeon and a father who was a mechanical engineer, it was a foregone conclusion that she'd study science—a subject she both enjoyed and excelled at—but which precise field or career goal, Meredith wasn't entirely sure.

"You're seriously going to sit there on the beach and read all summer?" Jill groaned and swung her head back and forth.

"You're also taking AP Lit. You have to read this book

too."

"Yeah, like a month from now. After we get back. How can you study on the beach? On an island? With all that beautiful sunlight?"

"I don't tan; I burn." Meredith broke off a piece of her muffin and popped it into her mouth.

"All that water?"

"I don't swim."

Jill rolled her eyes. Apart from being a straight-A student, Meredith was on the student council at school, and she played varsity field hockey in the fall, where she was one of the regular starting players during their junior year and was named a co-captain for the upcoming season.

Though Jill admired Meredith's commitment to her education, it seemed to be at the expense of free time. Jill occasionally asked if those extracurricular activities were mainly to pad her college applications, but Meredith denied the accusation and insisted that she actually liked what she did. Jill observed Meredith's dedication to the sport and student government, but not passion for them like Jill had for theatre. Whenever confronted further, Meredith said that she wanted to make her parents proud above all else. At their respective high schools, Meredith's mother played field hockey and was homecoming queen, and her father was class president and pitched for the baseball team.

"Forget swimming." Jill was tapping her fingers on the table. "What about just playing in the water? Splashing around?"

"Bathing suit."

Jill sighed and swept her hand through her hair, sending it all to her left side where it draped over her exposed shoulder. "Merri, how do you think you're going to attract any boys?"

"I'm not." Meredith hadn't yet looked away from her book.

"It's the best place to meet boys. No strings attached. Flirt with 'em and then leave 'em at the end of the month. Summer lovin', nothing more." Jill started singing about it as her character had in the school's spring musical.

While Jill was engrossed in the song, Meredith inserted her bookmark into the crease of the page she was on and stashed the book in the backpack hanging from her shoulder. Quickly finishing her orange juice and muffin, she grabbed the trash and slid out of the booth.

"Where are you going?" asked Jill.

Meredith reached down and grunted as she lifted her heavy suitcase. "Upstairs."

"Is it my singing? Well, my volume, I mean. Because if it's that, I can sing quietly."

"Not the singing. Not the volume. And we both know you're rarely quiet." Meredith headed for the door and thrust herself into opening it, which revealed stairs heading up to the top deck of the ferry.

Her flip-flops thwapping on the floor, Jill darted after her friend. "You liked that song, remember? You were in the chorus after I got you to audition this past spring."

Meredith started up the stairs. "Yeah, I remember."

After returning to the booth to get her suitcase and, more importantly, her coffee, Jill went back to the staircase, but Meredith had already gone out to the upper deck. She stood there for a moment, feeling guilty for upsetting her friend. All because boys were mentioned.

Jill knew that Meredith hadn't gone on many dates yet, despite being interested in a boy or two over the years. Meredith had asked one of them to the junior prom but was turned down, not because the boy wasn't interested in going with her, but because he had already asked someone else to go with him. So Meredith went alone, mainly because her parents encouraged her not to miss the event. She wore a full, frumpy dress, hiding her figure. Jill couldn't understand why since Meredith was somewhat athletic and far from unattractive.

But Meredith wanted a boy to be interested in her for who she was, not for how she looked. Maybe the boys at school were intimidated by her because of her intelligence or her involvement in so many activities. Her parents would tell her there'd be time to date after high school, after college, and once she was fully immersed into her career. Plenty of time.

"I'm sorry," said Jill when she came outside onto the upper deck.

Due to the breeze from the ferry slicing through the ocean and air, Meredith could only barely hear Jill's voice. She turned to find her friend, standing there by the door. Wearing a pair of denim shorts that gave an accurate definition of the word *short*, Jill's legs seemed to extend forever. Meredith knew Jill stood six feet tall, but she imagined her friend in high heels, towering over her like an Amazon princess. Add to that image a flat stomach, and Meredith wasn't surprised that she'd never had a boyfriend when she compared herself to Jill.

Meredith zipped up her gray hoodie as the chilly New England air rushed by. And to further hide her average body compared to the figure of her supermodel-like friend.

Jill trudged over to the railing where Meredith was leaning and looking out to the ocean. "We don't have to meet any boys if you don't want to. This vacation can be about we girls."

"About *us* girls. Objective case of the pronoun after the preposition."

"Yeah, yeah, yeah, whatever." Jill twirled her fingers in the air. "School's out. No grammar lessons. And no boys, if that's what you want."

Meredith muttered, "More for you and your cousin then?"

Chuckling, Jill swayed her hips and gently bumped them into Meredith. Meredith smirked and returned the hip nudge, but against Jill's thigh.

"I'm not going to stop you from meeting boys, Jill." Meredith looked up to the clear blue sky and shook her head. "They're going to want to meet you whether either one of us wants them to or not. I'm sure they'll show off for you any way they can."

"Oh, you ain't seen nothing yet. Some of the guys out here

actually grease up their chests. Lots of shirtless hotties on this island in the summertime."

Meredith looked over and up at Jill, whose eyes were practically bulging out of their sockets. She was smiling broadly, and her hair was blowing in all directions. "You really do have a one track mind, Jill. You know that, right?" Meredith was trying her hardest not to burst out laughing.

"You sure you don't want to change your mind? Live outside your comfort zone; shed your skin for a few weeks. We can find you a guy with rock hard abs who can't seem to keep his shirt on."

Meredith turned her head away from Jill and down towards the water. She watched the long streaks of white-capped waves left in the wake of the ferry. They stood there against the rail and stared out to sea in silence for a few minutes until Meredith noticed the island in the distance. "Only if he quietly serves me lemonade on the beach while I read my book," she mumbled.

"Nice to look at, but doesn't speak much?" asked Jill, holding up her hand for a high-five. "Girl, I like the way you think."

~ Chapter Three ~

The ferry ride lasted just over an hour, so the girls disembarked shortly after nine-thirty. At the bottom of the gangplank, Jill squealed and started running, weaving her way through the line of slowly moving passengers ahead of her. Standing immediately beyond the entry gate, her cousin Hailey was jumping and frenetically waving her extended arm.

Meredith trudged behind, dragging the suitcase along on its rickety wheels. She watched the two cousins hugging and bouncing and shrieking at each other. Their mothers were identical twins, and it was obvious that these two girls were related not only by their strikingly similar appearance, especially in their faces, but also by their similar behaviors.

Hailey was almost as tall as Jill, and they more or less had the same slender build. Maybe Hailey was a little slimmer. They both had long, dark hair almost halfway down their backs, but where Jill's was curly and wild, Hailey's hair was straight, the last six inches or so tinted with hot pink streaks. And they were dressed similarly, denim short shorts and cropped tees, Jill in white and Hailey in pastel pink.

"Hello, Hailey," said Meredith when she finally passed through the gate. "Good to see you."

"Come here, Merri, and gimme hugs!" Hailey didn't wait for Meredith to come to her, instead rushing ahead to inflict a claustrophobic squeeze upon her. "I think it's so cool that all our moms went to school together. We're gonna be like B-F-Fs these three weeks."

Hailey led the way to the parking area, which was a single row of twenty or so spaces. "Check this out." She pressed the button on her keychain, and after a series of boops, the trunk of a red convertible popped open.

"Sweet, you've got the top down!" Jill bounded ahead, tossed her suitcase into the trunk, and hopped over the closed door into the front passenger seat. "Your parents actually let you drive this thing?"

"F-Y-I, my dad is off-island for work until right before the Fourth," started Hailey, who then continued to speak rapidly without coming up for air. "And my mom made plans to get a ride to the library where she works while you're here, so O-M-G, the car is ours during the week!"

"Now, Merri's never been here before." Jill had turned around and kneeled on the front passenger seat. "So we're going to show her everything and take her everywhere. Oh, remember that time…"

Meredith tuned out their conversation and feared there would be many more like it to come. She knew that Jill and Hailey were close cousins, so she expected to be somewhat of a third wheel for a good portion of the vacation. Since she was already planning to read and prepare for the next school year, Meredith didn't mind if they left her alone.

Jill's suitcase had landed haphazardly in the center of the trunk, leaving limited space for anything else. Meredith stood hers upright and started rearranging the trunk's contents to make room.

"Let me get this for you," said Hailey, reaching for the handle of Meredith's suitcase. Not expecting it to be so heavy, she nearly lost her balance. "Whoa, W-T-H do you have in this thing? Bricks?"

"Schoolbooks," called Jill, checking her make-up and priming her hair in the mirror on the backside of the visor. "Someone wants to study. Think we can do something to change her mind?"

"Absolutely!" Hailey heaved the suitcase into the trunk and slammed it shut. "This island has a way of changing people."

With that, Hailey opened the rear driver's-side door for

Meredith, and then she climbed into the driver's seat. After buckling her seat belt, she adjusted the rear view mirror and lowered her sunglasses from her hair to her eyes. Turning the ignition as she turned to the others, she said, "Hold tight."

The car jerked backwards out of the parking space, lurching Meredith forward until the seat belt restrained her, but launching her eyeglasses off of her face.

The ferry dock was on the northern coast of the island, but Hailey lived with her parents along a private beach on the southern shore. There weren't any divided highways on the island and only a few major two-lane roads. Since the island wasn't much more than twenty miles across at its widest, the shortest route to Hailey's would take at least half an hour. Still early enough in the morning and with so much free time ahead of them, Jill suggested that they take a more scenic route around the island to show Meredith the sights.

The car moved slowly in the traffic when they reached the first public beach, which already had visitors at it, though not anywhere near full capacity. "This is nothing," said Hailey, one hand on the steering wheel and the other pivoting one way then another as she spoke. "Wait till the Fourth. O-M-G, this place will be, like, totally packed."

"I'm sure it gets very crowded." Meredith found herself having to shout over the bustle of pedestrians and other slow-moving, horn-honking traffic.

"Some of the people don't like it," explained Jill. "Too many tourists taking up space, not taking care of the place, littering, and so on. They forget that people do live here year round."

"I'm sure their presence bolsters the island's economy." Meredith squinted to read the high prices printed on the sandwich-board sidewalk menu outside a seafood restaurant. "Especially at those costs."

"Whatevs," said Hailey. "I like the tourists because, I-M-O, off-island guys are usually hotter than the ones who live here. And I know all the guys here 'cause there's only one high school."

15

"It's like I told you, Merri." Jill turned to look at her friend in the back seat, and then she hummed the melody of her musical number.

A pair of boys sitting in the back of a parked pick-up truck called for Hailey and whistled. She identified one them as a big jerk who dumped his girlfriend because she wouldn't change her online relationship status to mention him.

Then, the driver of an open jeep going the opposite direction honked her horn and waved at Hailey. The male passenger had his arm around the girl, but he leaned in front of her and lowered his sunglasses to see the girls he didn't know in Hailey's car. "Nice," he said, smiling and bobbing his head as he checked Jill out.

"Four-one-one, Jill," said Hailey when the convertible had moved forward away from the jeep. "He's also dating a girl on my swim team, but I don't think either of them know about it."

"Hi, Hailey." A tall, muscular, shirtless boy smiled at them as he walked by on the passenger-side sidewalk.

Jill leaned over the door to examine him from behind. "Please tell me there's nothing wrong with him." Jill's tongue was practically hanging out of her mouth.

"Great guy," said Hailey. "Sweet guy. I dated him for a bit."

"But?"

"Kisses like a fish."

Meredith wasn't entirely sure what Hailey's comment to Jill even meant, so she chose to ignore it. She took her novel from her backpack and tried to read, but due to the jerky, stop-and-go motion along the beach, she couldn't focus on the printed words without starting to feel the nausea of carsickness. So she had no option but to listen to Jill and Hailey. Even though she didn't swim, falling off the ferry and swimming home appealed more to Meredith than the possibility of listening to incessant boy talk for three weeks.

Once they got away from the beach, Hailey could drive faster without having to stop as often. However, the air rushing by the open convertible rippled the pages while Meredith was trying to read. She wasn't going to be obnoxious and ask Hailey to put the roof back up. After all, it was a sunny day, warm but with a nice ocean breeze. Perhaps too sunny, thought Meredith, so she removed a tube of sunscreen from her backpack and lathered a generous amount on her arms, neck, and face. Then she offered the tube to Jill.

"Thanks," she said. "Now would you look at all the cool places to explore here, Merri?"

"I live here all year long, and I still think it's the coolest place ever." Hailey pointed to a tall, red-brick lighthouse, standing solitary atop a cliff with white-capped waves of the ocean beyond it. "S-W-I-M? Isn't it gorgeous?"

"I don't swim." Meredith leaned forward to look, but then slumped back into her seat. "Especially not at a dangerous place like this."

"No, not *swim*. S-W-I-M. See. What. I. Mean. See what I mean?" Hailey giggled.

Meredith sighed and shook her head in disbelief that it required a translator to understand the language of the island natives. "Yeah, I see, but why would you spell it out? It's two fewer syllables to say the words than the letters."

"It's less letters when texting, though."

"But we're not texting."

"I could say *dubs* for W. Let's see: S-dubs-I-M." Hailey shook her head and stuck out her tongue. "Nah, doesn't sound right."

Quickly changing the subject, Jill reached across her cousin to point at the water. "Hey Hailey, isn't this the place where you thought you saw a—"

"T-M-I, Jill. Only family knows that." Hailey glanced at the rearview mirror to see Meredith looking away. "I think the Fourth of July fireworks would look great here, but they're on the other side of the island."

Hailey's tour around the perimeter of the island continued until they were back where they started. Hailey parked the convertible, and they got out and walked to Jill's favorite fried clams stand. They bought their lunch and sat on the beach wall across the street to eat. Throughout the meal, Hailey and Jill finished each other's sentences while they told Meredith stories about previous summers on the island.

"I'm thinking we can check out some shops here first," said Hailey, when they were throwing away the trash from lunch. "Then drive back to my house and…"

"…do the beach thing there," continued Jill, without skipping a beat.

Convinced that the two cousins had telepathic abilities, Meredith shook her head.

"Fewer people, more fun. What do you say, Merri?" Jill put her arm around Meredith. "And before you tell me you don't swim, we'll barely be wading."

"No bathing suit," said Meredith. "I didn't bring one."

"W-D-Y-M you didn't bring one? Beaches everywhere." Hailey's body shook as if in shock. "I could lend you one."

Shaking her head, Meredith eyed Hailey—about four inches taller and almost rail thin. "I appreciate that, Hailey, but I don't think so."

Clapping, Hailey bounced up and down, and then she took Meredith by the hand. "I know the coolest little shop."

Across the street from the beach, the sidewalk was lined with all sorts of stores. They passed ice cream stands, an arcade, several restaurants, a bicycle rental lot, and various souvenir stands selling shirts emblazoned with island images.

Outside a gift shop specializing in aquatic-themed artwork, figurines, and other such knick-knacks, two barefoot girls gawked through the window as if in a trance. "Lore, why do you suppose they picture us that way?" asked the blonde-haired girl.

"I am not sure, Marina," replied her friend with red hair. "Though it is curious what they believe."

"But they have our lifestyle all wrong. How can you enjoy it here if they clearly misunderstand us?"

"Their misunderstanding does not make them any less

interesting. Maybe one day, they can learn the truth. That could be a wonderful experience for them."

Marina looked around at the passersby, all seemingly oblivious to each other and in some cases to their own surroundings. "They seem to be in too much of a rush even to stop and look around. I doubt any of them could ever—"

"It takes only one." Lorelei noticed the girl with the short brown hair who lagged a few steps behind the two taller girls. "If one understands, others may follow."

When they finally reached the shop, Hailey skipped away from Jill and Meredith to rifle through the racks of swimsuits.

"I don't know, Jill." Meredith shuffled her feet. "My parents only gave me so much money to spend. I don't want to waste it on something so expensive."

"Consider it an early birthday present from me." Jill waved her arm towards the corner of the shop. "You can even go over there and not look at what I pick out, so it will be a surprise when you open it later at Hailey's."

"Fine, but nothing too…well, you know."

Squeezing Meredith's shoulder, Jill said, "Trust me. It'll be tasteful, and you'll look great."

Meredith was afraid of that.

~ Chapter Four ~

"Come out, Merri." Jill knocked once more on the door to the guest room in Hailey's house. "I'm sure it looks fine."

From beyond the door, Meredith called, "I'm only doing this for you."

The door opened, and Meredith emerged wearing a blue two-piece bathing suit with a tankini top. Jill, in her black halter-top two-piece, applauded and said, "See, told you it wasn't that bad."

"When in Rome." Meredith shrugged in partial agreement. Though the top covered her well, and there was only a thin sliver of exposed midriff, the bottom piece revealed more of her thigh than she was comfortable showing. But it was more modest than what Jill was wearing.

Wearing the hot pink string bikini she had just bought, Hailey quickly closed her bedroom door behind her when she entered the hallway. Meredith turned away, embarrassed to be looking at how it contrasted against so much of Hailey's lightly bronzed body. The two of them dwarfed her, and as Meredith crossed her arms in front of her chest, she couldn't help feeling inadequate next to them.

"We'll totally hit the big beaches Saturday," said Hailey, emphasizing each word with her hands. "There'll be lots more guys then. Hot guys. Just the two of you and me tonight."

Meredith was about to correct Hailey's grammar but thought better of it when she saw Jill shaking her head and glaring at her. Instead, Meredith meekly said, "Girl power?"

"Girl power, L-O-L." Then Hailey actually did laugh out

loud.

They went out the kitchen's sliding door onto the back deck, and then across the yard and over the wooden footbridge. Leaving the three beach towels hanging over the railing, they made their way to the water. Jill and Hailey ran ahead, and Meredith dawdled behind.

It wasn't that Meredith had anything against the beach, only the portion of the beach that accumulated everywhere— sand in her hair, between her toes, in her shoes—and followed her home. And it wasn't that Meredith had anything against the concept of swimming; she simply wasn't that good of a swimmer, and she detested not being good at something. And it wasn't that she had anything against being in the water; pools were fine to have fun in, but the few beaches she had visited back on the mainland were infested with seaweed. She hated the feel of slimy things unexpectedly brushing up against her.

For the sake of her friend, she would give this beach a chance. It was private, and there was no one other than the three of them there. The sand granules were finer than at those other beaches, and they didn't seem to clump and collect like coarser sand. The water looked crystal clear, almost inviting. *When in Rome*, she reminded herself as she jogged ahead to join the others.

The ocean was warm and calm, with steady waves that weren't very high. Displaying her skills from her team, Hailey quickly swam away from them until she was chest-deep in the water. After Jill had joined her, they rode the waves back to the shallower water where Meredith was staying. All the while, Jill and Hailey described different places on the island they wanted to show Meredith and different activities—like hiking, biking, or even parasailing—they could do. Some of it sounded interesting to Meredith, maybe even fun, but it frustrated her that neither of them had asked her what she wanted to do. She wanted some freedom to schedule her own time, even if it would be for studying.

Eventually, they got out of the water, and Hailey wanted

to show them this one spot further up the beach where they could see directly into her cute neighbor's weight room. It was nearing his usual workout time. They smoothed over their wet and windblown hair—Jill clumping hers together and letting it hang in front of her left shoulder—before heading towards the house on the left.

Jill and Hailey were already several steps ahead, but Meredith didn't care. She preferred the alone time rather than listening to them drone on about boys or hair or clothes. She didn't need to or want to be part of that conversation, so she headed for the footbridge and her towel to dry off. The wind had blown the towels off the railing, scattering them along the wall of rocks.

Meredith gathered the two that were closest to the stairs and then went to get the third. She cautiously climbed onto the wall of rocks, and as she reached for the towel, she saw something sparkle inside a crevice. She carefully reached inside so she wouldn't cut herself if it was a piece of sea glass, and she pulled out an object that looked like a rumpled piece of fabric.

Wanting to examine it closely with empty hands, she returned the towels to the railing. She shook the material to let it unfold, and despite being compacted and crumpled, it was free of wrinkles. Though it appeared smooth, it had a coarse texture. Its shape was an irregular trapezoid with a leg perpendicular to the two parallel bases, one of which was a few inches shorter than the other. It was sheer and translucent, and when she held it up, the sunlight made it shimmer.

As she held it at different angles, it sparkled vividly through every color of the visible light spectrum from red to violet, though orange seemed to be the most dominant. Without her glasses, she squinted and held it up to her face as she tried to find any threads or fibers. There was a faint crisscross pattern as if the material consisted of two layers, each one refracting the sunlight in a different direction. Static friction kept the two halves clung together, and Meredith struggled to separate them.

When she laid it on her lap, her damp thighs twitched as if receiving a light electric shock. She wondered if the material had scratched her, but it felt curiously smooth when she spread it across her legs. The two layers easily slid apart to reveal that it was one continuous piece of fabric, almost like a skirt, but she couldn't find a seam.

The waves rolled gently onto the shore, and their sound calmed her. Suddenly compelled to try on the skirt, Meredith stepped into it and pulled it up past her hips, where it fit snugly even without an elastic waistband. The longer end hung almost to her right knee, and she was pleased that it covered the bottom of her bathing suit.

The cousins were further down the beach behind Hailey's neighbor's house, but Meredith didn't want to show them her find in case they didn't think it was fashionable. Drifting toward the water, she was overcome with an inexplicable desire to go swimming.

Upon entering the ocean, Meredith noted that the water seemed colder than it had only minutes earlier. Shivers coursed up her legs, and though the feeling was mildly uncomfortable, she stood there knee-deep in the water and watched as goose bumps erupted all over her thighs.

She knew something wasn't right, so she turned around to get back to her towel and back to the cottage. A slightly larger wave struck her from behind and knocked her down. Bracing her fall with outstretched hands, she found herself keeled over in the shallow water, submerged up to her chest.

Suddenly, there was a sharp pain around her waist, as if her stomach muscles were constricting. Fighting the aches inside her, she elevated herself to a kneeling position. The translucent skirt was drenched, having absorbed plenty of water, and it appeared to have contracted around her.

Meredith tried to remove the garment, but she couldn't wedge her fingers between the skirt and her body. She tugged on the fabric wrapped around her waist to no avail; the skirt wouldn't budge. However, as she gave one more yank, she knocked herself backwards and heard something tear.

Hoping she had pulled off the skirt, she stood, but in her hand was a partially shredded piece of blue fabric that matched her tankini. Quickly, she reached around herself to the small of her back and felt it was bare. She had torn the bottom of her swimsuit completely off her body, but the skirt was still covering her.

She panicked upon remembering that it was made of see-through material. She squeezed her thighs together and kneeled back in the water up to her stomach to preserve her modesty. But when she looked into the clear water, she saw that the skirt had become completely opaque and iridescently orange.

Her skin underneath felt like it was burning, and her legs were itchy and prickly, as if they were falling asleep. Slowly, she stood but found it difficult with her thighs sticking to each other. She reached down to pry her legs apart, but gasped when she felt the skirt. When she ran her fingers down its length—which somehow had elongated to her knees—the material felt smooth and slippery. But when she retracted her fingers upward, the material was jagged, even sharp.

"What is this thing?" she asked aloud.

The skirt seemed to have been activated by the water, so she hypothesized getting to drier land would reverse its effects. Unfortunately, with her knees bound, all she could do was waddle. Whatever the orange-red stuff was, it was now skintight and creeping further down her legs, wrapping around them like she was an Egyptian mummy. She took short hops forward, but ultimately lost her balance and fell over.

Meredith landed face first into the salty water. She couldn't see what was happening to her, and she wasn't sure she wanted to look. The prickling of the pins-and-needles sensation reached her ankles, making it difficult for her to separate them from one another, let alone stand. She tried pushing down on the soaked sand to lift herself upward, but she could only raise her upper body. Everything beyond her waist remained immobile, the numbness feeling like her legs were no longer there.

Her face clenched as she wailed, and her feet were overcome with a new, excruciating pain. It was as if a steamroller had landed on her ankles and was slowly moving toward her toes, flattening her feet and sprawling them outward.

When the pain and numbness finally subsided, Meredith devised scientific explanations for her symptoms. An allergic reaction could cause her legs to become unusually bloated. A jellyfish sting could explain the aching of her feet. Still having difficulty moving her lower body, she craned her neck to examine her condition.

But a wave washed over her and obscured her view. Water thoroughly soaked her hair, and she had swallowed some, the taste of saline lingering on her tongue. Oddly, her gag reflex didn't kick in, and she simply spit out the water left in her mouth and throat. Finding out what had happened could wait, as getting out of the ocean became her top priority.

Her legs and feet wouldn't cooperate, so she dug her elbows into the wet sand and dragged herself forward. No longer numb, her lower body was exceedingly heavy as she hauled it along with her.

Once she could feel dry sand on her stomach, she heaved herself over onto her back, closed her eyes, and took a deep breath. The next wave rushed up to her ankles, which she flexed up and then back down, hearing a loud *thwap* upon the foamy film of ocean water.

Her eyes popped open. Curious about what had made the sound, she repeated the movement at her ankles and could feel her wide, flattened feet smack against the wet sand.

Another wave approached as she raised her upper body. Again, she flexed her ankles, hearing the sound and seeing water splash upward.

Meredith stared at her chest and stomach, which were still covered by the tankini top. As she let her view drift downward, she lifted the bottom edge of the bathing suit to reveal her navel. Just below, her pasty pink flesh started blending with glimmering oranges that reminded her of the translucent skirt. The garment had vanished, replaced by a cocoon that secured her legs tightly into a single mass, which was covered with thousands of thin discs in different shades of orange, all glistening in the sunlight like sequins. Wide at her hips, the shape of Meredith's lower body gradually tapered to a considerably narrower width at her ankles.

The water from the wave receded and revealed the shape of her now singular, flattened and expanded former feet. Upon viewing her full form for the first time, Meredith shrieked.

Jill and Hailey heard the noise and looked toward the source. At the edge of the water behind Hailey's house, Meredith sat with her back to them. She was rocking back and forth, her arms holding the sides of her head as her screams continued.

The two cousins sprinted across the sand. As they got closer to Meredith, they could see that she was trembling and could hear that she was whimpering.

"Merri, what's wrong?" called Jill.

Meredith craned her neck to the side and saw them approaching. "I…I'm…I don't know what…how…but I'm…I'm a…" She turned away and buried her face into her hands.

Jill and Hailey decelerated and slowly circled around Meredith until they could see what had happened. They stood there, their lower jaws slowly dropping in a mixture of awe and confusion.

"O. M. G." Hailey turned to her cousin. "You never told me you were B-F-F's with a mermaid. That. Is. So. Cool!"

~ Chapter Five ~

Jill turned to Hailey and sternly said, "My best friend isn't really a mermaid."

"R-U-K-M, Jill? Look at her!" Hailey pointed down to where Meredith's legs weren't. "Cool sparkly fish tail."

"Yeah, but it can't be real. There's got to be an explanation. Meredith, you aced science class. What happened?"

"I...I..." Meredith's stutters continued as she stared in disbelief at her lower body. Slowly she brought her hands away from the sides of her head until they hovered about an inch above the...whatever it was. She didn't want to identify it as a tail, and she was afraid that if she touched it, it would become more real. And it couldn't be real. Mermaids weren't scientifically possible; they were folklore. But she was persuaded otherwise when flexing what should have been her ankles moved the orange flipper.

"I'll tell you what happened." Hailey's hands gyrated as she explained. "Don't you know simple mermaid rules? She got her legs wet, and it made her tail appear."

After considering the explanation for a moment, Jill shook her head. "Then why didn't a tail show when she was in the water with us?"

Hailey quickly opened her mouth as if to answer, but then closed it. She leaned forward and opened her mouth again, but again didn't speak. Eventually, she said, "I-D-K."

"I'd expect *you* to dress up as a mermaid, Hailey, but not her." Jill kneeled down and put her hand on Meredith's bare shoulder, which startled her. To avoid frightening her further,

Jill spoke slowly. "Merri, when I said shed your skin, this isn't what I meant. Where'd you find this costume?"

"Costume?" muttered Meredith. She glanced at Jill and then back down to her whatever, and then her eyes bulged. "The weird skirt."

"What weird skirt?" Jill looked around for a skirt, but the only odd piece of clothing was the torn bottom of Meredith's swimsuit floating in the water. "What are you talking about?"

"It got wet. If it gets dry, then maybe—"

Hailey thrust her pointed finger forward and shouted, "That's right! Dry a mermaid's tail and the legs come back. I'll go get the towels." Hailey took off towards the footbridge.

A wave crashed on the shore, and water rushed up the beach. Meredith squealed as she soon found herself sitting waist deep in the water. As the wave withdrew, Jill started tying up her hair so it would stop blowing in her face. "Hailey, come back! We should move her to somewhere dry first."

Hailey froze in her tracks, but before she spun around, her eyes fixated on the house to the right of hers. In a panic, she ran back to the others and said, "F-Y-I, Mr. Dobbins next door will be home any minute. He'll come outside with his shirt off—eww!—and then he's gonna check out the beach before he takes a nap on his deck. He's really nosy and I-M-O kinda creepy."

Turning to each other, she and Jill scratched their heads and shrugged, nonverbally communicating with each other that neither of them knew the proper way to transport a mermaid. But there was no time to waste, so they instinctively each reached under an arm and dragged Meredith away from the water, leaving a tailfin-wide path of packed-down sand in their wake.

When they reached the wooden stairs, they grabbed the towels and wrapped them around the tail to cover it up and start the drying process. Not wanting to give Meredith any splinters, Jill lifted Meredith from her underarms at the same moment that Hailey lifted where Meredith's knees would have been.

"This would be easier if your brother was here," said Hailey. "O-M-G, she is so heavy."

Jill was carefully backing herself up the stairs. "That was rude, Hailey. Meredith is not fat."

"Didn't say she was."

"Well, you inferred it."

As if by reflex, Meredith said, "Implied."

"Whatever." Jill grunted as she stepped onto the top step and could move backwards a little more quickly.

However, Hailey was still ascending the stairs, and her grip on Meredith was sliding towards where her ankles would be. "Slow down, Jill, she's slippery. Kinda slimy, too. Eww!"

"How can it be slimy?" asked Jill. "It's just a costume."

"I don't think it's a costume." Meredith's voice sounded deflated. "I can't feel my legs or feet. I don't think I have them anymore."

"We'll get them back for you." Hailey had a better hold on the tail once they were hurrying along the footbridge. "Once we're inside, we'll dry you off."

Inside the house, they managed to get Meredith upstairs to the guest room. They laid her down on one of the single beds and rested her head on the pillow, but the full length of the tail extended beyond the edge of the mattress. While Jill knelt by the bed and wiped Meredith with the beach towels, Hailey raced out of the room to close all the shades and curtains. She returned with an electric hair dryer, which she plugged in, turned on, and started waving high over the mermaid tail.

All Meredith could do was lie there. Even if she wanted to, she wondered where could she go and how she could go there, since it was clear that until her legs reappeared, there was no way she could walk anywhere. She didn't want to watch. She just wanted it to go away. She started turning to the side, but her lower body turned with her, and she felt awkwardly twisted, especially down at her other end. So instead, she chose to lie on her back with her head turned to the side. She focused her attention on the glowing display of the alarm clock, located on the nightstand beside the other bed.

Five minutes passed. Then ten minutes. Though Meredith appreciated that Jill and Hailey hadn't given up, Meredith didn't need their diligent efforts to tell her there had been no change. She could feel it herself. Because the bed was shorter than the—she still was denying that it was a tail, that it might even be *her* tail—she could feel it drooping, and occasionally she flicked it upwards. She controlled its movements, as if it was her actual appendage. Why didn't it go away?

"W-T-H, this always works in movies and TV shows," said Hailey, turning off the hair dryer and kneeling beside her cousin. "Maybe we need more power. We could, like, bring her to a tanning salon."

After quickly dismissing Hailey's crazy idea because they'd have to transport Meredith there and sneak her by the employees, Jill turned to Meredith and asked, "Merri, how did this happen?"

Meredith sniffled and wiped her eyes, and then she described the events from the moment she found the strange translucent skirt to the moment it came in contact with the water. It was the skirt that caused the transformation, she insisted, but the skirt didn't seem to exist anymore. She tried to prove her statement by showing them that there was no pouch or gap at her waist, like there would be with a regular skirt or even a pair of pants. Her hands slid over the smooth human flesh along the sides of her waist down towards her piscine hips. As soon as her fingers felt them, and the scales—*her scales*—felt the tips of her fingers, she pulled away in shock. And her tailfin abruptly launched upward and then flopped back down, thwapping itself loudly on the mattress and front edge of the bed.

A voice from came downstairs. "Girls, are you up there?"

"Mom!" shouted Hailey as she looked at Jill, who had simultaneously turned to her and shouted, "Aunt Susan?"

Jill and Hailey both hopped to a standing position and started yanking the bed sheet out from under Meredith like a magician impressing his audience by removing a tablecloth quickly enough without breaking the dishes atop it. Newton's First Law of Motion, as Meredith fully recalled it, stated that in the absence of external forces, an object at rest would tend to stay at rest due to the object's inertia. Though Meredith knew the mass of her tail gave her plenty of inertia, she could also tell that her friends weren't trained magicians. Or they didn't know their physics.

When Jill and Hailey yanked a second time, they had done so forcefully enough to remove the bed sheet and flip Meredith over. Once again, the tailfin smacked down loudly upon the mattress.

They threw the bed sheet over Meredith, but even with it untucked from the bed, it didn't completely cover her tailfin. Hailey collected some other blankets to finish the job while Jill bent over to bring her mouth close to Meredith's ear. "Pretend you're asleep," she whispered.

Turned the other way, Meredith was facing a window with its shade pulled down. With not much to look at, she followed Jill's instruction and closed her eyes.

Jill opened the door, switched off the lights, grabbed Hailey by the hand to pull her outside, and then closed the door behind them. Coming up the stairs and turning the corner to greet them was Hailey's mother, wearing her signature librarian-style glasses. She was slender with dark hair like her daughter, but a few inches shorter.

"Hi, Mom," said the two girls in unison. When Hailey and Jill were younger, being the children of identical twin sisters, they often mistakenly called the wrong sister Mom. The family in-joke eventually stuck, and even as teenagers, they still did it.

"I see you've been on the beach, Hailey." She glowered at her daughter's skimpy swimsuit before hugging her niece. "And it's so good to see you, Jillybean."

Jill rolled her eyes. At some point over the years, her Aunt Susan added the "bean" to her name because she was sweet like a jellybean and had grown tall like a beanstalk.

"One. Two." Aunt Susan pointed at the girls as she counted. "Where's Meredith?"

Without hesitation, Jill answered, "She's sleeping. Well, we woke up early this morning. The ferry ride over was bumpier than expected, and it made her kinda queasy. Then we were in the sun all day, and I don't think her lunch agreed with her. We thought it would be best for her to lie down, and we just checked on her. She's asleep."

"Poor girl." Aunt Susan passed by the girls and quietly opened the door to the guest room.

Hailey was smiling broadly and nodding her head as she gave Jill a thumbs-up signal, but Jill shook her head and put a finger to her lips to keep Hailey quiet.

There were slow, rhythmic sounds of breathing coming from one of the beds, where the contours of a body under the blankets could barely be seen in the darkened room. The only part of Meredith not covered by sheets or blankets was the brown hair on the top of her head. Not wanting to disturb Meredith's rest, Aunt Susan closed the door and said, "You two are good friends. Now, I understand pulling down the shades makes it easier for her to sleep, but you didn't have to do it for the entire house."

She started down the stairs, but turned around and came back up. "Oh, my book club meets tonight, so I'm heading out soon. I'll call to have some pizza delivered for you two, and Meredith if she wakes up hungry. Toppings?"

"Just cheese is fine with me," answered Jill.

"Me too," said Hailey, who then giddily perked up and added, "Meredith likes anchovies."

Hailey's mother nodded skeptically. "Really? Okay." She headed down the stairs, muttering, "One cheese pizza. One pizza half cheese, half anchovies."

Jill put her hands on her hips and turned to Hailey, who looked up and asked, "What?"

"Seriously?" said Jill. "Anchovies?"

"They're little fishies, right?" Hailey shrugged. "What other pizza topping would a mermaid eat?"

Jill rolled her eyes and groaned. "I'm in my school's drama club, so from now on, let me handle the improv."

They walked back into the guest room. Hailey switched on the light while Jill knelt beside the head of Meredith's bed. "You did great, Merri," she said softly. "We've got Aunt Susan covered at least through tomorrow morning. We'll figure this out."

But there was no reply. Meredith had actually fallen asleep, with the hope that when she woke up, changing into a mermaid would be nothing more than a dream.

~ Chapter Six ~

As they climbed out of the motorized vehicle, Lorelei thanked the driver for his kindness in transporting her and Marina across the island and returning them to the red house. Just as Lorelei had assured Marina several times throughout the day, they were able to influence some of the land-dwellers to show them kindness and generosity. She wasn't sure how or why, but she enjoyed the experience and how the ability enhanced their adventure.

"Did I tell you? Or did I tell you?" asked Lorelei between licks of mint chocolate chip ice cream.

"You told me. This stuff really flows." Marina felt some of the cold white liquid trickle onto her hands. "It flows all over the place. Onto my fingers. Down my hands. To the ground."

"You are supposed to eat it before it...before it...I am not sure what word they use to mean turn to liquid." Lorelei bit off a chunk of the ice cream and allowed it to liquefy in her mouth and slide down her tongue. "Never mind. What flavor is that again?"

"They called it vanilla." Marina's arms and neck contorted as she tried to eat without dripping any more ice cream on herself. "It tastes good, but it is runny and sticky. Will the ocean wash this stickiness off?"

"It will. Next time, try a flavor with more color. And sweet things mixed in it."

"Speaking of next time, there will not be one for me. Now it is almost sunset, and we need to get back."

"Let it float, Marina." Lorelei lowered the sunglasses from her eyes, looked around, and smirked. "Besides, we are here."

Standing before the red house, Lorelei surveyed the terrain while taking her first bite into the sugar cone. All the doors were closed, all the shades were drawn, and there wasn't a vehicle in the driveway. She watched patiently for a few more moments, crunching away at the cone until it was gone. Occasionally, Marina would say something, but Lorelei would politely shush her while she listened to the sound of the neighborhood: the soothing rhythm of the ocean waves and birds calling each other in the distance. Other than the two cats that trotted by and hissed at them, there weren't any signs of people nearby.

"Now!" shouted Lorelei, and then she ran across the gravel driveway and towards the wooden footbridge.

Startled, Marina dropped the soggy remains of her cone and chased after her friend. When she reached the stairs, Lorelei was already sitting on the bottom step, removing the sandals she had been given from her feet. "I am going to miss these. What are they called again?"

"Flip-flops," replied Marina, who turned at the bottom of the stairs and started walking along the edge of the wall of rocks.

"I will bring you with me to show Father." Lorelei was talking directly to the shoes, and as she laid them beside her, she started to address her feet. "I am going to miss both of you, too. Until next time, pretty legs."

Lorelei reached underneath the footbridge and retrieved the garment she had hidden there after sunrise that morning. After unraveling the translucent tube of material, she inserted one leg into it, followed by her other leg. As she stood, she pulled the tube up under her sundress until it fit snugly around her waist. She picked up the flip-flops and looked around. The only person in view was a shirtless older male, lying asleep on a deck chair at the gray house next door to the right. Even if he woke up, she figured there was no way he'd see what she was hiding under her sundress. She would make it to the water, and her secret would be safe.

"Marina, meet me at the sunken yacht where we found

these coverings!" Lorelei tugged at her sundress to indicate what she meant. Then she sprinted towards the water, right down the middle of the track of flattened sand, her footprints effectively obscuring the path where Meredith had been dragged back to the house.

"I will be right there," called Marina, precariously walking along the rocks and trying to locate the correct crevice.

When she reached the damp sand, Lorelei stopped and stood there for a second, allowing the cool sea foam to run over her toes. Tingles ran up her legs, making her giggle, but when the water receded, the sensation dissipated. The feeling was intoxicating, and when the tide returned, she recognized the tingling as the ocean beckoning her to return to her true form.

Finally finding the correct pair of rocks, Marina reached into the opening and felt around. The edges of the rocks were jagged, and her hand collected granules upon granules of sand, but that was all. She leaned her body against the adjacent rocks so she could reach deeper inside, but as her elbow disappeared into the crevice, she knew she wouldn't find what she had hidden there. At sunrise, she hadn't stashed it so far inside, or at least she didn't think so, and she feared that something terrible had happened.

"Lore!" she called, twisting her neck to see her friend at the shoreline. "Lore, I need your help!" But the crashing of the waves was too loud for Lorelei to hear Marina's cries for help from so far away.

Lorelei was walking much more purposefully now, step by step into the oncoming waves. Though the water offered more resistance as it deepened to her knees, Lorelei wore a large smile on her face as she continued forward. The intensity of the tingles had increased almost to the point of a pleasant numbness, but she kept heading homeward.

A wave surged towards the shore, and the level of the water rose to Lorelei's waist. As soon as the ocean came in contact with her shimmery skirt, she could feel it contracting around her hips and expanding down her legs. She lifted the hem of the sundress so she could watch the transformation happen.

Turning back to the land, Lorelei saw Marina still rummaging among the rocks. She cocked her head to the west. More than half of the sun had sunk below the horizon, painting the sky a beautiful combination of orange and red. "Marina, hurry up!" she shouted. "Time is running out!"

Tears welled in Marina's eyes as the muscles in her arm strained from being extended into the crevice almost all the way to her shoulder. She would have tried to reach further inside, but there was no more room. Her fingers were pressed flat against the far end of the cavity, and all she could feel was abject terror with the realization that what she was looking for was no longer there.

"It is gone, Lore. What do I do?" Marina withdrew her arm and climbed down off the rocks. She charged toward the water, waving her arms frantically and calling out Lorelei's name. "Come back and help me, please!"

In the water, Lorelei felt her knees go numb as they were fused together into one. She glanced down and could see faintly iridescent scales appearing where the shimmery skirt had been, all the different shades of green returning to their full brilliance. Though the process amazed her every time she witnessed it, she was more concerned with Marina swiftly approaching the shoreline and trying to get her attention.

Sensing that something wasn't right with Marina, Lorelei wanted to swim or even walk closer to her distressed friend, but neither option was working. She couldn't walk correctly because her feet had flattened and started stretching into her fluke, and she couldn't swim effectively until the fluke had fully formed. All she could do was tread water.

Marina saw how slowly Lorelei was moving and knew it meant she was in mid-transformation. "I cannot swim out to you, Lore!" she called. "I have no idea how with these two feet!"

"Where is your tail?" asked Lorelei.

"It is not where I left it! What am I going to do?"

Suddenly, moving through the water became easier for Lorelei. Her fluke had grown to its normal size, and she propelled herself halfway to Marina. "I cannot come any closer," she said. "I cannot risk getting washed ashore. What happened?"

"I cannot find my tail." Marina was weeping. She lumbered into the ocean towards Lorelei and cringed as water flowed back and forth around her legs. Though she was accustomed to complete submersion, standing on the odd appendages in the waters of home felt so strange. So awkward. So wrong. "I need my tail, Lore. What will happen to me?"

"It will be all right." Lorelei reached up and took Marina's hand. "I will swim home and ask my father. He will know what to do."

Marina clutched Lorelei's hand with both of hers. "Please do not leave me alone!"

"It will be for one night only. I promise I will meet you right here at sunrise tomorrow."

"What am I going to do until then? I know nothing about being out of the ocean! Today was my first time." She paused and looked down into Lorelei's eyes. Then she jerked her hands from Lorelei's grip, letting Lorelei's hand drop and splash on the water's surface. "This is your fault."

"Marina, what are you talking about?" The outer points of Lorelei's green tailfin poked their way up through the water's surface. "I did not see where you hid it."

"I would not have come up here without you convincing me to join you. I would not have had to take my tail off if you did not make me come up here!" Marina's volume increased and her body trembled as she cried more and more. "And I would never have lost my tail if I had kept it on!"

"Calm down, Marina. We will fix this."

"I do not think it can be fixed. Without my tail, I am no longer...no longer..." Marina got herself all choked up to the point she could no longer speak.

"This is a private beach, young lady!" called a male voice

from the houses. "What's going on out there?"

Marina's crying and screaming had woken him up. From his deck, he saw her standing alone and knee deep in the ocean. He noticed her blonde hair, unlike the teenage girl who lived next door to him, so he stepped off his deck to investigate. "You don't belong here," he said.

Lorelei flexed her tail to hide her fluke under the water. "I must leave now, Marina. If he sees me—"

"You cannot leave me alone!" Marina reached for Lorelei's hand, but the mermaid pulled away.

"Sunrise tomorrow. I promise I will be here. We will figure this out, sink or swim."

With that last comment, Lorelei dunked her head into the water, turned herself around, and started flipping her fin. Marina watched her friend's long and lithe form swim away from her, farther and farther, and deeper and deeper, until her silhouette was no longer visible.

"Sink," muttered Marina as she ran out of the water and then along the beach in the opposite direction of the man that was approaching.

He called for her, but she kept running westward. Looking ahead, she watched the last sliver of the sun sink below the edge of the water.

~ Chapter Seven ~

Hailey knocked lightly on the guest room door four times—the secret signal—before slowly opening it. "Mom's all Z-Z-Z," she whispered as she entered, and then quietly closed the door behind her. She saw Jill first, lying on the other bed and keeping a constant vigil for her friend. "How's she doing?"

"Still the same." Jill gestured towards Meredith. "See for yourself."

Meredith was lying on her stomach under rumpled bed sheets. In her sleep, she had tugged at the covers, gathering them closer to her head and shoulders. And the additional blankets had fallen to the floor so her tailfin and about half of her tail were exposed.

"Her tail has pretty shades of orange." Hailey sat cross-legged on the foot of Jill's bed. "Looks kinda like a big goldfish."

"How can you say that?" Jill clutched her pillow and sat up. "What if she can't change back?"

"She's gonna change back. We just gotta figure out which mermaid legend this is."

"What do you mean *which* legend?"

"Seriously, Jill, don't you know who I am? Haven't you seen my room? I was brought up watching princess movies in a place surrounded by water." Hailey was wildly gesticulating as she spoke. "My friends and I played mermaids all the time. B-T-dubs, I wanted a pink tail."

"I'll gladly trade this tail for your legs, Hailey," said Meredith glumly.

Jill leaned forward. "You're awake? How long have you

been awake?"

"Long enough to know that I still don't have legs." Meredith heaved her torso upward and swung one shoulder to the side, which caused her to roll over. The effort needed to do so left her short of breath, so she lay there on her back. "And unfortunately long enough not to be catatonic about it anymore." As she propped herself up to a seated position, Meredith scooted backwards to lean against the headboard, which slid the tailfin fully onto the mattress. Sighing, she said, "That's better. It was feeling numb down there hanging off the bed."

"Did I hear you right?" asked Jill. "So what you're saying is that you can actually feel your...I mean the..."

"You can call it a tail, Jill. And the fin at end can be called a fluke. Whether I like it or not, I've got to accept that's what it is. That's the only way I can cope with this and try to figure it out." Meredith closed her eyelids and inhaled slowly, hoping that breathing in air would also pull back the drops of water welling in the corners of her eyes. "And to answer your question, yes, I can feel it like it's any other part of me."

Still somewhat groggy, Meredith yawned. As she stretched her arms, her fluke lifted off the mattress, curled, and pointed towards her.

"Whoa!" Hailey jumped to her feet on the other bed. "O-M-G, that was awesome! Did you do that? How did you turn it like that?"

"I'm not entirely sure, but it's like I had curled my toes when I yawned." Meredith further explained that though she could sense that her body no longer had legs or feet or toes, she could also sense that her brain and nervous system knew the corresponding muscular motions. She demonstrated by flapping her fin up and down, pivoting it to the left and then to the right, and curling the tips inward and then back to fully spread out. All the while, she described for them what she thought her brain would be telling a complete human body to do: bending her knees, then twisting her ankles, and wiggling her toes.

"Oh, I wish I had this on video." Hailey was hyper, zipping all over the room. "Can I take a photo with my phone?"

"No way, Hailey!" Meredith held her hands out in front of her in a stop gesture. "Terrible things could happen if someone got a hold of that photo."

But Hailey wasn't listening. She was kneeling at Meredith's bedside with her hands clasped. "Please? Please? Just one for me? Please? P-P-S-O-T?"

Utterly baffled, Meredith and Jill gaped at each other until Hailey translated, "Pretty please with sugar on top."

"Here you drop the W?" mumbled Meredith.

Jill chuckled. "Even when half your body is a fish, all of your brain is still Meredith."

Her back ached against the headboard, so Meredith tried to reposition herself on the single pillow. Noticing her discomfort, Jill offered one from the other bed. Then Hailey volunteered to get a few more from her room but promised not to get a camera. Before Hailey left the room, Meredith asked her for a drink of water. Her mouth and throat were unusually dry.

"B-R-B," whispered Hailey as she opened the door and tiptoed into the hallway.

"Hailey's harmless," said Jill as she crossed the room. "A little wacky maybe, but I'll keep her under control. No pictures of you."

"Thanks." Meredith slid a little closer to the wall to make space for Jill to sit beside her. "I'm sorry if this puts a damper on your vacation. I didn't mean to ruin—"

"You didn't ruin anything." Jill sat, swinging her legs onto the bed parallel to, but not touching, Meredith's mermaid tail. "If nothing else, it's going to be a memorable vacation. And if anyone can figure out a way to change you back, it's you. You're the smartest person I know. Look at this as one big science experiment."

"Yeah, but if I passed this in as my AP Bio summer research project, I doubt Mrs. Rosenberg would ever take me seriously again."

Imagining the stodgy teacher's reaction, they snickered, but the laughter faded into silence. Jill leaned against Meredith's shoulder and could feel her quivering. She glanced up and saw that a few tears were trickling down Meredith's cheeks.

"Merri, just think." Jill's eyes scanned the room, and eventually settled on where her feet rested in comparison to Meredith's tail. "Hey! For the first time in your life, you can actually say you're taller than me."

There was no immediate reaction. Jill had failed to break the tension. She hoped that maybe commenting about the color of the tail would work, but then Meredith muttered, "Longer."

"What?" Jill asked.

Meredith wiped her eyes. "I can't stand straight up right now, so, technically, you'd have to say I'm *longer* than you."

They heard the knocking signal on the door. Hailey entered and handed a bottle of water to Meredith, who quickly opened it and guzzled down its contents, while Jill and Hailey gawked in amazement.

"Thanks," said Meredith, now holding an empty bottle. "It's important to stay hydrated."

With the enthusiasm of someone setting up for a slumber party, Hailey returned to the hallway to retrieve an assortment of supplies, itemizing and explaining as she brought them into the room. First, three fluffy pillows given to Jill to prop up Meredith more comfortably. Second, a pizza box with the leftovers from dinner in the event they got hungry. Third, the remaining two bottles of water for her and Jill to drink with the pizza, having not expected Meredith to finish hers so quickly. Fourth, her laptop for doing research online. And finally, a stack of books of fairy tales, legends, and folklore about mermaids, through which they could search.

"So, Hailey, I suppose you're the island's top mermaid aficionado?" asked Meredith.

Hailey squinted her eyes and crinkled her forehead. "Uh,

well, I-D-K what that word means. I just think mermaids are really cool, and I know a lot about them."

Meredith shook her head and groaned. "Someone hand me my glasses, please. They're on the dresser." She pointed across the room.

Under closer inspection, Meredith could see that adjacent scales weren't necessarily the same; the tail was comprised of scales of many hues, the differences between them subtle. Orange was the most prominent color, but there were different shades, some deeper and darker towards red, and she even noticed lighter and paler ones that were yellow. As she leaned back, those subtle differences became less noticeable, harmoniously blending together to form a pattern, orange with some faint red and yellow streaks. Forgetting for a moment that she had unwillingly become this mythical creature, she couldn't deny that she found the tail stunningly beautiful, no matter how scientifically impossible her current form was.

The seamless transition from her skin to scales intrigued her. There weren't any around her navel, but about an inch further down, there they were as if they had sprouted out of her skin. She touched the scales right above where her knees would be, and then leaned and stretched forward to run her hands slowly down her former legs. The scales were smooth and slippery, perfectly designed to reduce drag when gliding through ocean waters—not that she was planning on swimming with that tail anytime soon. Without realizing it, she had reached all the way down to her single tapered "ankle" where the darkest scales ended.

She wished she could stretch a little further but then leaned back when she remembered she didn't have to. As Meredith imagined herself bending her knees opposite how they should, the bottom half of her tail curled towards her until she could hold her fluke in her hands. It was wider than her shoulders, and again, the colors and details amazed her; there were ridges that radiated from her bottommost scales out to the edge of her fin. She grasped its sides, noting that it felt like a thick but floppy rubber swim flipper, but it was clearly so much stronger, forceful enough for underwater propulsion. This tail was part of her anatomy now, and as bizarre and frightening as it was, there was a small part of her—the scientifically inclined part of her—that found it fascinating. She just wished she could have been observing it happening to somebody else.

"It must be awesome," said Hailey, enthralled by how flexible Meredith's tail was.

Realizing she had been caught not helping research her own cure, Meredith let go of her tailfin, which smacked the mattress. Jill shushed her and whispered, "We don't want to wake Aunt Susan."

With the laptop in front of her at the foot of the other bed, Jill was lying on her stomach with her knees bent and her feet kicking the air. She had searched dozens of internet sites for any information about mermaid tails being disguised as pieces of clothing, but without having seen the mysterious skirt, she wasn't having much luck. The most similar legend she discovered was from the Scottish folklore surrounding selkies—seal-creatures that could shed their pelts to become human on land.

"There's no way we could have gotten a big seal up here." Hailey turned to Jill, who gave her a cross look. "Oh, J-K, Merri. Your tail is so much prettier than seal skin."

To avoid saying anything else that could offend anyone, Hailey grabbed a slice of pizza. Before she started eating, Meredith asked her for a slice. Without realizing it, Hailey had taken two slices with anchovies on them. After one bite, the salty and fishy taste made Hailey gag, but Meredith ate her entire slice quickly.

Throughout the night, Hailey read pertinent excerpts from fairy tales and other stories. She started with the classic— Hans Christian Andersen's *The Little Mermaid*—but since Meredith hadn't traded away her voice to an evil sea witch, there was no reason to fear that she'd suffer the same fate as that mermaid: being turned to sea foam. Most of the other stories employed the standard legs-when-dry-tails-when-wet transformation, which they ruled out because of their earlier unsuccessful attempts.

Jill changed her online search to plot synopses of movies. She sat up upon finding an interesting detail from one movie.

"Oh yeah, I saw that one," said Hailey. "The mermaid comes on land, but if she gets wet—"

"Yeah, we get it. The tail appears." Jill reached over and touched Hailey on the shoulder to calm her down. "But in the movie, she can only stay on land until the full moon or she won't be able to go back."

The three girls all turned to the window by Meredith's bed, which overlooked the beach, but the shade was still down. Meredith reached over and raised the shade while the other girls approached. Together, they looked out the window—Meredith on one side, then Jill in the middle, and then Hailey. The ocean waves twinkled with light reflected from the bright yellow moon. The full moon.

"O-M-G." Hailey leaned closer to the window.

Jill also inched forward. "Do we think that a full moon on the same day this happened means something, or is it some weird coincidence?"

"I'm not sure." Meredith winced in discomfort. "But can the two of you please get off my tail?"

Hailey and Jill apologized and returned to their research, this time looking for other stories, movies, or television shows that connected mermaids to full moons. They found a few, but nothing exceptionally helpful. Meredith, however, was transfixed by the moon, which reflected the sun's light more brightly than it usually appeared to at home where there was more light pollution from nearby cities.

Even after midnight when the others finally fell asleep in their shorts and tank tops, Meredith stayed awake, lying diagonally across the mattress with her tail contorted not too uncomfortably to keep it all on the bed. They had tucked in the sheets as tightly as possible to hold her in place all night, and they had covered her with some extra blankets to keep her shape hidden. Fortunately, she didn't feel too warm, probably because of the nighttime sea breeze.

Lights in the room had been switched off, but Meredith was illuminated by the moonlight shining through the window. She stared at the moon, wondering if its full phase had any significance to what had happened to her, and wondering if she'd ever get her legs and feet back.

Meanwhile, sitting on a large rock further down the beach away from the houses, Marina was cooled by the same sea breeze and illuminated by the same bright moonlight. She also stared at the same moon, wondering what would happen to her now that it was full, and wondering if she'd ever get her tail back.

~ Chapter Eight ~

There was faint light from the sky, but the sun had not yet made its entrance. Marina had been watching the eastern horizon for what felt to her like an eternity.

During the long night, she had explored equal stretches of beach on either side of the red cottage with the footbridge. She searched atop the rocks, behind the rocks, and in the cracks and crevices between the rocks. Her eyes seemed to work differently on land; everything was more difficult to see. The glow of the full moon would have provided enough light to shimmer her tail, which was nowhere to be found.

Whenever she stayed in one place for too long, her body would quiver uncontrollably. Wrapping her arms around her body or rubbing exposed skin with her hands alleviated the strange sensation, but not for very long. Moving around helped to some extent, so she spent intermittent stretches of the night simply walking back and forth along the beach, before ultimately settling at the footbridge near the spot where Lorelei promised she'd return.

Marina's bare feet had grown sore and weary from walking all night—an inefficient method of getting from one place to another, she thought. Two steps required much more coordination than a single undulation of her tail. The air flowed by her as she walked, sometimes similarly to the way water flowed, but otherwise the breeze was an unfamiliar, uncomfortable entity. Though not at all difficult to move through, the air was empty around her, and she yearned for the way water surrounded her like it was always protecting her.

This is your fault. The words replayed in her head throughout the night, over and over like waves crashing on the beach. *This is your fault.* If she hadn't said them, it wouldn't change whatever had happened to her tail, but sadly, she had meant it when she said those words to her best friend. *This is your fault.*

The sky got brighter and brought some life to the colors of the water, the sand, and everything else in view. She hung her head in shame, and instead of her long blonde hair floating around it, it hung over her face and blocked her view of her ugly feet. It wouldn't be much longer until the sun rose and fully illuminated the beach, just as the night spent alone had illuminated the terrible guilt she felt for blaming her missing tail on Lorelei.

All her friend had wanted to do was spend a day with her and share new experiences. She couldn't find a reason to be angry about that. Lorelei was guilty of nothing other than being herself, and Marina had admired her friend's confident, carefree spirit. Lorelei was like the older sister Marina never had. Ever since they had been young, Lorelei had always included Marina in her adventures, and most of the time, Marina followed along. Except when it came to leaving the ocean. Lorelei had enthusiastically invited Marina to join her on land every cycle, and except for the one instance where Marina had dove back into the water immediately after the pair of legs had appeared, she refused. Yet Lorelei would ask anew at each new cycle.

Until this cycle—the first time Marina had explored land without her tail. It would be the final time she could accept Lorelei's invitation since, without her tail, there couldn't be a next time for Lorelei to ask.

But it wasn't Lorelei's fault, and Marina knew that. In school, all mers were taught the rules and risks about leaving the water. From sunrise to sunset, no longer; only once a cycle. Walk amongst them as if one of them; for if they suspect otherwise, they may pursue. Do not allow humans to view you in your true form; transformation must be treated as sacred and never witnessed. And find a safe hiding place for your tail near the water; only there will it retain its power.

The final rule was considered the most important, but Marina hadn't learned the whole truth about it until recently. Hiding the cloaked tail was to protect the existence of all merkind in the event she was captured; unable to transform without the tail in her possession, her true identity wouldn't be revealed. Also, it allowed for a quick escape if needed. If activated by heavy rain or any other unexpected soaking, it was a short ways to the ocean. Because once worn and wet, it would return to its true form.

And it was this rule—the final rule—that Marina had broken by hiding her tail in the wrong place, an unsafe place. If anything was to blame, it was her ignorance of the human world. How was she supposed to know where the best place to hide her tail was? Lorelei always insisted that many of the humans didn't pay enough attention to the experiences around them, and Marina had observed as much walking amongst them on the other side of the island. But that didn't explain how her tail had vanished from the crevice between the rocks.

Just as the sun poked above the horizon, the sparkling silhouette of a tail poked above the water's surface in the distance. Slowly rising from her perch on the footbridge stairs, Marina squinted to see the tail's true color, though there was too much glare. Her best friend was true to her word—always true to her word—and Marina's anxious heartbeat relaxed as she murmured, "Lorelei?"

As if the tail had responded to Marina's voice, it splashed on the surface of the water before going under. Seconds later, Lorelei's head and shoulders appeared about half the distance away. Bobbing as she treaded water, Lorelei waved at Marina. After Marina waved back and started jogging towards the shoreline, Lorelei dove forward, her green fluke rising above the water and then slapping down as it went back under.

They met in the water, at a depth shallow enough that Marina's knees only got sprayed by the incoming tide, but deep enough that Lorelei could sit with her tail submerged and periodically covered by the foam of the breaking waves.

"Lore, I said some things to you yesterday that I wish I could take back." Marina was trembling as she spoke, the sea breeze blowing her blonde hair across her face. "I want to tell you that I am sorry. This was not your fault."

"Oh, you silly minnow. You think I am angry at you?" said Lorelei, the hint of a smile appearing on her face. "It is I who should apologize. I should have waited for you before putting on my tail. When you could not find yours, I could have let you take mine."

Marina gasped and shook her head. "But that is forbidden!"

"If I had waited, I could have helped you look for it. Or I could have stayed with you to keep you calm. You were not yourself yesterday."

Marina glanced down at the two legs stemming from under her wrinkled sundress. "I am still not myself."

Lorelei outstretched her arms, and Marina took the opportunity to bend down and hug her friend. "You just let it float," Lorelei whispered melodically into Marina's ear. "It took a whale of courage to take your first steps on land. I am proud of you."

"You are?" Marina kept hold of Lorelei's arms, but stepped back and straightened herself out, only to see Lorelei's wide smile shining up at her.

"Of course I am. And you did something I have longed to do; you spent a night as a human. That makes you one of the bravest mers I know." Lorelei pulled her arms away and folded her hands on her lap. "Will you sit with me, please? My neck hurts looking up at you like this."

Marina tentatively crouched down in the water, and the soaked parts of her sundress clung to her thighs. She closed her eyes and recalled the one other time she transformed— her aborted previous attempt to join Lorelei for a day on land a few cycles back during their south season. Terrified as soon as she saw that the legs had appeared, she sat back down in the water with her eyes clenched shut until she could feel her cloaked tail binding itself around the thighs. She continually kicked the feet in and out of the shallow water until she could hear the familiar sound of water being smacked by a mermaid's tail—her tail, back to its full orange glory.

As the memory faded away, Marina opened her eyes to see the two pale legs in place of her tail. Their odd contours appeared foreign and distorted as the shallow water rippled over them. She glanced over at Lorelei's tail, its V-shaped streaks of slightly different shades of green scales running from her waist down to her fluke. Lorelei had one of the most beautiful tails Marina had ever seen, much more dazzling than any pair of legs.

"Why would you prefer these to a tail like yours?" Marina kicked her feet and gently splashed the water. "These have got to be the ugliest things ever."

"Are you sure about that, Marina?" Lorelei carefully examined her friend's smooth, shapely legs. "Because I think yours flow."

"I think your head is in a whirlpool."

"I have been on land enough times to know that some human-men enjoy looking at the legs of a maid." Lorelei smirked. "And some human-maids take extra care to have a pair that looks like yours."

Marina shook her head. The only reason the legs were remotely bearable at that moment was because they were submerged in the comfort of the waters of home, but like the nighttime air, even the water was giving her the chills. "They do not like staying wet, and I do not like keeping myself dry."

"True, but those legs, even at their driest, will still be much smoother than when our scales get too dry."

"I searched the beach all night, Lore. I could not find it." Marina stared again at the legs and feet that were in the place her tail should be. "And even if I could find it, the full moon has passed. What good will it do me now?"

"That may not be entirely true," said Lorelei. "When I swam away yesterday, I went directly to my father. I caught him before he had to scout ahead, but he told me something that might make you happier. He said that if you found your tail soon—today, or perhaps even by moonrise tomorrow—then you may be able to put it back on and return home."

Leaning forward, Marina's eyes widened. "Are you sure? What about the first rule? It says one daylight only."

"My father says that is more of a guideline than a rule."

Marina had only recently learned that the most important final rule had more to it than she originally believed, so she wasn't pleased upon discovering that the first rule also wasn't fully truthful. The rules seemed nothing more than lies, designed for mer-elders to keep their youth in line. Were the other two rules also used deceptively, and would her parents have misled her the same way other mer-parents had done to their children? Sadly, Marina knew she would never be able to answer that question.

"The biggest catch is that the longer it takes to find it, the less likely a transformation will happen. He said it is risky because the power of a tail slowly wanes until it is no more."

"Until it is no more?" whimpered Marina. "What if I cannot find it, Lore? What happens to me then?"

"You are going to find it, Marina. If you have not by the time he returns, he will wash himself ashore to help us." Lorelei floated herself forward to face Marina, their hips resting almost side to side. She caressed Marina's cheek to wipe away the salty tear trickling down. "Can you sense your tail? It is not far away."

"I sense nothing like that. I am not a mer right now."

Lorelei scanned the panorama, her gaze ultimately settling on the red house beyond the footbridge. "Wherever it is, it is safe."

Marina shook her head, thinking back to Lorelei's lengthy explanation why she always surfaced at that particular location during their north season, especially since it was so unlike her to settle on one place instead of exploring new ones. First, she gave practical reasons: the private beach was regularly free of humans, and it was at a point on the island's southern shore where both the sunrise in the east and the sunset in the west could be easily viewed. But Marina smirked, remembering the way Lorelei's eyes glinted, and her tail shimmered when she provided the mystical reason: she sensed some quality about the house, an aura of protection to merkind.

"But what if it is not safe?" Marina's voice trailed off. "It is hard enough being alone in the water, but to be alone out here…"

"You are not alone, Marina." Lorelei enveloped Marina and drew her closer until Lorelei could feel droplets from Marina's eyes land on her bare shoulder.

"Do you think something like this happened to my—?"

"Do not dwell on them," Lorelei gently hushed Marina and stroked her hair as she continued crying. "I will always be here for you, sink or swim."

~ Chapter Nine ~

When Meredith awoke the next morning, her entire body from her neck down to her fluke ached. She had never slept with her body so twisted, but she never before could twist her body the way the flexibility of her tail allowed her to. The sheets and blankets had remained tucked in, restraining her in the bed and adding to her discomfort. Yawning, she stretched her neck and arms. As her brain sent nerve impulses to stretch her misplaced legs, feet, and toes, her tail started straightening to its full length, and her tailfin curled upward, prying the sheets from under the mattress. *Mermaids aren't supposed to be confined,* she thought, *they're supposed to swim freely.*

She bolted into an upright seated position, questioning where on Earth her thought had come from. Fearing that the transformation had altered her mind as well, she worried about what changes were still to come.

Even her throat was sore. Parched. She grabbed her eyeglasses from the window sill and put them on to look for the previous night's water bottles. Four empty bottles rested on the floor by her bed. The first one she had chugged, the next two she had emptied what Jill and Hailey didn't finish, and the fourth was from the second round of drinks Hailey had gotten them.

There were two more bottles on the blue oval area rug between the two beds, but they were a little too far out of her reach. She looked over to the other bed to ask for assistance, but a quick glance at the clock, partially obscured by the covered sleeping body, changed her mind. The first digit was a seven, and they had stayed up late, so she didn't want to wake them up for something she could hopefully do herself.

She rolled onto her side, her tailfin easily able to do so since it extended past the foot of the mattress. While stretching her arms as much as possible, her fingers crawled on the rug until they got to the bottle. But as she went to grab it, the condensation on it made it slip out of her grasp. Without thinking, she dove and caught it, but then immediately felt herself falling off the side of the bed.

The reflexive actions of her arms and hands sufficiently braced her upper body, but not her lower half. Her fluke flopped loudly upon the hardwood floor.

"I'm up! I'm up!" Hailey burst out from the other bed, sheets and pillows exploding in all directions. The pink streaks at the ends her hair frizzed in all directions as well.

"Sorry, Hailey." Meredith struggled to turn over and sit up against the bed. Then she unscrewed the bottle cap and started downing the refreshing water.

Four knocks on the door later, Jill stood in the doorway with her arms crossed in front of her. "What's going on in here?" Seeing Meredith on the floor, she swiftly closed the door and barricaded it with her tallness. "And what are you doing out of bed?"

Meredith took her final swallow and waved the empty bottle in the air. "I was thirsty."

"You are so lucky I was out there keeping watch and that Aunt Susan went to take a shower."

Hailey still couldn't believe a mermaid was in her house, and she couldn't help fixating on Meredith's gorgeous tail. But it didn't look quite right; something about it was different in the morning. When she realized what it was, she hopped to her feet and emphatically pointed at the pale orange scales. "Nine-one-one! Nine-one-one!"

Jill and Meredith followed Hailey's emergency alert to its destination and saw that the tail didn't shimmer the way it had the day before. Its colors were significantly duller.

Meredith reached forward and touched her scales. No longer smooth, they were coarse and jagged when stroked in either direction. "I'm drying out," she said hollowly, and then looked up at her friends. "I need to be in water. Quickly."

Opening the door, Jill peeked into the hallway to make sure the coast was still clear. Running water could faintly be heard coming from the master bedroom at the other end of the hall. Aunt Susan and Uncle Greg had their own private bathroom.

Jill and Hailey lifted Meredith off of the floor and carried her into the main bathroom, which was the door after Hailey's bedroom. Gently, they lowered her into the vintage-looking freestanding bathtub. Meredith's fluke hung over one short end of the tub, and she leaned back against the opposite end, grasping the sides of the longer ends. "I'm going to go get some salt," said Hailey. "B-R-B."

Hailey was gone before Meredith could explain the chemical differences between table salt and ocean salt.

Reaching for the controls across the center of the tub, Jill closed the drain and turned the faucet valves. She held her hand in the stream of falling water, then jerked it back. "Oh, that's cold."

As the water splashed upon her tail, Meredith recalled lessons about heat transfer from her physics class. Jill had felt the water as cold because heat energy flowed from a warmer object—Jill's hand near normal body temperature—to the cooler room-temperature water that had been sitting in the pipes all night. But Meredith didn't sense the water as cold, which would only be possible if there was no flow of heat energy between the water and her tail because they were at the same temperature. For people, that wouldn't have happened. But it would for fish.

"Jill, it's gotten worse." Meredith's voice trembled, along with her fluke. Whatever that skirt was had altered so much more than her appearance. Her anatomy, physiology, and even her mentality were becoming less and less human as time progressed. "I think I'm cold-blooded now."

Jill knelt down and put an arm around Meredith's shoulders, drawing her friend closer to her and letting her cry into her collarbone. She wished there was something she could say to assure Meredith it would be all right—that there was a way to change her back—but Jill didn't know what those words were. She hoped her presence would be enough.

Hailey reached the top of the stairs with the box of salt, but before she opened the bathroom door, something on the floor caught her attention. She reached down and picked up a small, translucent disc; it was about the diameter of a nickel, but much thinner, and it wasn't perfectly circular. There were others, maybe a dozen or two, scattered on the floor and leaving a path like Hansel and Gretel's breadcrumbs from the bathroom door to the guest room. Or heading in the opposite direction, she realized. In their dryness, some of Meredith's scales had flaked off.

Suddenly, the sound of rushing shower water from her mother's bathroom stopped. There was no way Hailey could let her see the scales on the floor—and not only because her mother was a neat-freak. Now that she knew they were real, Hailey would protect any mermaid, not just the best friend of her close cousin. She collected the scales, meticulously making sure she got each and every one of them before rushing into her bedroom. She let the scales fall out of her hands into a heart-shaped glass dish on her desk, after dumping out the pink paperclips in it first.

Hailey slipped into the bathroom, barely avoiding being seen by her mother, who had emerged from her bedroom fully dressed. Susan heard the water running in the bathtub and noticed the doors to Hailey's room and the bedroom closed. One in the bath, two still asleep, she figured, knowing that a group of teenage girls on a sleepover would have stayed up late the night before. Smirking nostalgically, she headed down the stairs to the kitchen.

"We've got to go cover for you," said Jill, after hearing from Hailey that Aunt Susan had finished her shower. "Will you be all right in here, Merri?"

"Where else am I going to go?" sobbed Meredith.

Reluctant to leave her friend in such a fragile state, Jill led

Hailey out of the room, closed the door behind them, and headed downstairs.

Alone, Meredith soaked in the bathtub, now with salt sprinkled in the water. For the first time since her transformation, her tail didn't feel as heavy because the water made the submerged part of her practically weightless. Keeping one hand clutching the rim of the bathtub, she reached the other underneath her shoulder-length hair and rubbed the back of her neck.

With nothing else to do, she decided that conducting a quick scientific experiment could calm her down. Releasing her hold of the bathtub, she watched as buoyancy took over supporting her. But while her mermaid hips floated upward, the human parts of her started sinking.

Downstairs in the kitchen, Hailey's mother was preparing her lunch to take to work. "So let me guess," she said, placing the top slice of bread on her sandwich. "Meredith's taking a bath."

Jill and Hailey simply nodded.

"It would be nice to finally meet your best friend, Jillybean." Aunt Susan stuffed the sandwich into a plastic baggie and zipped it shut. "I haven't seen her since she was a toddler, and her mother and I were close friends in high school."

Before either Jill or Hailey could say anything, a car horn honked outside.

"That's my ride to the library. Now I'm going to insist that all three of you, especially Meredith, be at the table for dinner tonight." She placed her tuna salad sandwich into her lunch bag. "Or I'm going to suspect that something fishy is going on with her."

As Hailey started giggling, Jill yanked her into the dining room where they had a clear view of the living room windows and the car outside. From there, they heard the front door close and watched Aunt Susan get into the passenger seat of the waiting car, which then took off down the street and out of view.

After closing all the shades and curtains on the first floor of the cottage, Jill and Hailey darted back upstairs to the bathroom. "She's gone," said Jill.

Meredith sighed in relief. "Good. Now can you please get me out of here?"

Her hands grappled with the sides of the bathtub in a losing battle to keep her shoulders above the water as her tail was keeping itself afloat.

"Right now, it's the safest place for you," insisted Jill.

"Yeah." Hailey pointed at Meredith's tail. "See how much prettier it looks?"

All submerged scales had returned to their full orange iridescence while the parts of the tail above the water's surface, especially the fluke, though slightly improved, were still paler in comparison to the rest of her.

"Hailey's got a point," said Jill. "You look much healthier in there."

"But this thing attached to my waist has got a mind of its own. All it wants to do is float, and there's barely enough room in here for me to fit." Meredith flapped her faded fluke to call their attention to her full length. "Can we at least drain the tub? Because I think I...well, let's just say that I've been drinking a lot of water lately, and I think...no, I *know* that...that, well I...relieved myself in the bath water."

"First thought, eww, T-M-I!" Hailey crinkled her face and shuddered. "Second thought, how exactly do mermaids go to the bathroom?"

"I don't precisely know *how* it happened, but I felt the human sensations, so I know it *did* happen."

"Did the water get warm?" asked Hailey. "Like when a kid pees in a pool?"

Jill rolled her eyes and reached to open the drain while Meredith pondered Hailey's question. If the water's temperature had changed, she hadn't sensed it.

As the water level lowered, the tail seemed to get heavier, but Meredith regained her ability to sit up. "I can't stay here in this bathtub until this tail goes away, *if* it goes away."

Meredith glared up at Hailey. "Please don't tell me how cool that would be."

Hailey frowned. It wouldn't just have been cool, she thought, it would have been a childhood dream come true.

Meredith turned to Jill. "And you can't keep hiding me from your Aunt Susan. If she hasn't gotten suspicious yet, she's going to be soon."

Ever perceptive and logical and correct Meredith, thought Jill as she folded her arms in front of her. "Then what do you propose we do with you?"

"As much as I loathe the idea, you're going to have to bring me to the ocean."

~ Chapter Ten ~

The back door of Hailey's house was a sliding door, so Jill bumped the handle with her hip to open it. She backed out of the doorway, hunched over but keeping a hold on where Meredith's shins would be. Meredith was swaddled waist-down by beach towels, and though the actual tail was concealed, its shape wasn't, for the fluke flared outward too far. Crouching down, Hailey was holding Meredith under her arms and barely keeping her hovering above the floor.

Once onto the deck, they struggled to lay her down on an open lounging beach chair. As Jill released her grip, the final towel loosened from the one before it and blew off in the breeze, revealing the pale fluke. With quick reflexes, Jill's long arm shot out to grab the stray towel, and she rewrapped Meredith as best she could.

For the remainder of the trip, Jill and Hailey tried what they hoped would be a more efficient method to transport a mermaid. Facing each other and flanking Meredith's two sides, they each placed one of their arms across Meredith's back at her waist, and they slid their other arms under approximately where the bend in Meredith's knee would be, forming what they hoped would act as a bucket seat. Meredith placed her right arm around Jill's shoulder and her left arm around Hailey's. On the count of three, Jill and Hailey lifted while Meredith held on tightly.

After a brief wobble, everyone steadied themselves, and the girls were pleased by their success. Jill and Hailey side-stepped slowly down the deck stairs until they reached the lawn where their pace could quicken. However, the lower half of Meredith's tail, not being supported, started to droop. Sensing a towel slightly out of place, Meredith quickly straightened herself to prevent it from sliding off while there weren't any free arms to catch it.

"There's got to be another way, Merri," said Jill as they stepped onto the footbridge. "We can call your parents and tell them you're really sick or something. I know your mom. She'd leave the safari to come here and see you. For Pete's sake, she's a doctor. She might be able to do something."

"I didn't know your mom was a veterinarian!" Hailey was looking straight at her cousin and knew by the look on her face she had said something wrong. "S-B-T. Er, sorry 'bout that."

"Hailey, she's a surgeon," said Meredith. "And, Jill, the last thing I want while I'm the only known mermaid in existence is to be examined by someone who cuts into people for a living, even if she is my mother."

Carefully, Jill and Hailey descended the stairs one at a time, ensuring their steps were in sync. The slight change of angle from straight to downward, accompanied by the straining of Meredith's tail muscles, caused some of the lowest towels to dislodge from the others. A sudden gust of wind carried two towels away. All three of the girls saw it happen, and in a panic, Hailey blurted, "R-U-K-M?"

Before Hailey's shout, she and Jill had been intently concentrating on getting Meredith to the ocean, and Meredith had been too busy trying to prevent her tail from being exposed, so none of them noticed Marina and Lorelei sitting in the shallow water. And Marina and Lorelei had been too preoccupied with their discussion, which had now lasted for a few hours. Marina was still mourning her misplaced tail, and Lorelei was comforting her, so neither of them noticed Jill, Hailey, and Meredith approaching.

Until Hailey's shout.

With an instinct to flee from humans, Lorelei leaned to her side and dove toward the open seas, and her tail briefly popped up out of the water before splashing down on the surface and disappearing.

Marina's head jerked toward the sound. Slowly rising, she stared at the three human-maids, two of them holding up the other in a seated position in their arms. The sunlight reflected brightly off of where the third maid's feet would be, so Marina was unable to see why this one wasn't able to walk for herself.

"Forget the towel, Hailey," said the taller one with the dark, wavy hair to the one with the straight, pink-tipped hair. "Just get her to the water before anyone can see her."

As they approached, Marina squinted and saw they were carrying a mer instead of a human-maid. The mer's tail hung down in front of her and glowed brightly in the sunlight, making it difficult to identify her. Marina felt pity for the unfortunate mer because she had clearly broken the walk-amongst-them rule and perhaps the transformation rule as well, though Marina had some doubt that those rules mattered anymore.

The two human-maids didn't seem to be harming the mer; instead, they seemed to be doing the opposite by helping her return to the water. Marina had heard legends about humans luring mers above the surface, capturing them, and putting them on display. Maybe Lorelei's intuition about the red house was somewhat correct, as the human-maids running from it were protecting the mer. *Could the legends about humans be wrong as well,* wondered Marina.

Finally, Meredith noticed the girl in the yellow sundress. Standing knee-deep in the water, she wasn't moving, but it was clear she was staring at them. "Guys," said Meredith as she looked down at her tail, which was clearly visible and unmistakably identifiable. "We've been spotted."

Jill and Hailey froze in their tracks, quickly looked at each other, and then slowly turned their heads to see the girl, probably about their age, looking back at them. A girl who had seen a mermaid. Already, Jill's brain was trying to improvise a story about testing out the swimming capabilities of an elaborate costume, but the girl was stepping closer.

Marina wondered how the mer had been found and rescued by the two human-maids, who were now staring apprehensively back at her. She took a few steps forward, trying to recognize the mer in their arms. The face wasn't familiar, so Marina focused on the mer's unique tail. Her orange tail.

Her orange tail.

~ Chapter Eleven ~

Marina trembled as she pointed at the tail—*her* tail—extending from some other mer's body. Mers were usually identified by the colors and patterns of a tail's scales, and Marina knew hers was one of the easiest to recognize. She knew that purposely exchanging tails was explicitly forbidden, but she was unsure if there was any punishment for it happening accidentally. She needed to know the other mer's intentions. "What are you doing with *that?*" Marina finally asked.

Keeping her eyes locked on the stranger on her private beach, Hailey whispered, "What do we do?"

"Still thinking," said Jill, standing firmly in place on the sand.

"I'm going to end up on display in an aquarium," muttered Meredith. "Or on a dissecting table."

"We could make a run for it." Jill looked around, trying to decide which direction would be the safest one for Meredith not to be seen by others.

Somewhat relieved that her tail wasn't completely lost, Marina marched out of the water and towards the mer who had taken it. Maybe this other mer had also been exploring land and had hidden her tail nearby. If the unknown mer had taken the wrong tail, then why hadn't Marina found hers during her night? Closing her fists against her hips, Marina yelled, "Where did you find it?"

"She's already seen *this*." Meredith kicked her tail slightly. "And it seems like she knows what it is."

"If she tells someone, who'd believe her?" asked Jill.

"Mermaids don't exist."

Hailey said, "Four-one-one, Jill. We're holding one."

"*We* all know that." Jill rolled her eyes, and then cocked her head to the side to indicate the girl. "But that doesn't mean *she* knows that for sure."

"It will dry out if you stay there," called the girl. Then she gestured at the water.

"She's right," said Meredith, who could feel her scales, especially the ones in direct sunlight, losing their moisture.

"How does she know that?" asked Jill.

Hailey shrugged. "I-D-K."

"It happens to all fish out of water," said Meredith, who suddenly realized the scientific explanation wasn't necessary. The girl wasn't referring to Meredith as a mermaid, she was referring to the tail as if she were the owner of the mysterious skirt. "Bring me closer to her."

Hailey didn't hesitate taking small side-steps toward the girl, but Jill reluctantly kept pace. "I don't trust her, Merri," Jill spoke softly through clenched teeth.

"We might have to trust her." Meredith kicked her tail until another towel fell off. "I think she knows what happened to me."

As they got closer, the wind blew the girl's blonde hair away from her face. She didn't wear an expression of anger; instead, her forehead was creased with a look of confusion. "Can you please tell me why you would take something that does not belong to you?" she asked.

"She doesn't belong to anybody," said Hailey. "She's our friend."

"I was not talking about *her*." The girl raised her arm and pointed at Meredith, not at her face but at the tail. "I was talking about…"

Finally close enough to see beyond the mer's tail, Marina noticed that everything else about the mer wasn't right. Instead of seashells, she wore a blue human top. Dark outlines circled the mer's eyes, which sometimes reflected the sunlight at Marina's face. Unlike every maid Marina had ever known, this one had short hair.

Marina's face froze with her mouth wide open, and her arm fell limply by her side. The unknown mer wasn't careless or reckless enough to be spotted by human-maids, albeit human-maids who appeared helpful. And she hadn't accidentally put on the wrong tail. This was far worse than that, potentially breaking all sorts of rules of merkind—rules probably so treacherous that no mer-parents dreamed they'd even have to teach them to their youth. She was a human-maid with a mer's tail. *Her* tail.

Turning her head toward the ocean, Marina called, "Lorelei!"

Out in the water, Lorelei was treading a distance away, far enough not to be spotted by the humans, especially since only from her eyes to the top of her head were above the water's surface. It was allowed for her to interact with humans while her tail was off, but not while it was on. The existence of merkind had to remain a secret, and even though the occasional mer had been spotted in full tail, she did not intend to be one of those mers.

She had watched the humans approach Marina and was surprised to see that they were carrying a mer with an orange tail. She deduced that the tail was Marina's at about the same time Marina had figured it out, and she was relieved that it hadn't been lost. But a human-maid wearing it presented complications that she wasn't sure how to solve, and if certain powerful mers discovered what had happened, there would be severe consequences.

Her father would know what to do, but she couldn't leave Marina alone. She wanted to maintain a safe distance, but she also wanted to be by her friend's side. She knew Marina didn't know how to handle the situation or the humans.

"Lorelei!" called Marina one more time, louder than before. "I need your help!"

By barely flicking her tail back and forth, the rest of Lorelei's head and her shoulders emerged from below the water. Lorelei saw Marina standing in the shallow water, looking out to the ocean, probably trying to find her. The human-maids had probably figured out that Marina was calling for another mer, so Lorelei was getting reeled into the situation whether she liked it or not. It was only fair, since she had dragged Marina ashore the previous day whether her friend had liked it or not.

She kicked her tail as she brought her head back under the water, and her tailfin flipped briefly above the surface before she quickly swam back to the beach.

"Quiet down," said Jill to Marina. "You don't want to alert the neighbors."

At the shore, Jill and Hailey reached the chilly water and removed the final few towels before gently lowering Meredith into the shallow surf. As an approaching wave caressed Meredith's tail, she sighed in relief and said, "That feels so much more comfortable."

Marina ran toward Meredith and splashed water with each semi-coordinated footstep. "Thank merness it is not lost." Marina knelt down beside the middle of the tail, and she gently stroked the familiar smooth orange and red scales.

The analogous human sensation Meredith felt was discomforting, and chills flowed up her spine. She shuddered, and the ends of her fluke curled and folded inward. "Please don't do that," she said.

Pulling back her arm, Marina kept her gaze on the tail and didn't turn toward the human thief's face when she said, "But it is *my* tail."

"You can gladly have it back." Meredith thrust her arms toward the tail in a sweeping there-it-is gesture. "Just tell me how to get it off, and it's yours."

"I am sorry I left you alone, Marina," said a new voice. "I did not mean to."

Meredith, Jill, and Hailey turned toward the voice. Riding a wave toward them was a female with long, darkish hair, wet and matted. As she got closer, her full shape was revealed, all the way to the flare of her sea green fluke.

Upon seeing there was a mermaid, Hailey's eyes widened.

She squealed but quickly covered her mouth with one hand while pointing with the other. She backed away and jumped erratically as if the warm sand was far too hot for her bare feet.

Jill put a hand on Hailey's twitching shoulder blade. "Calm down."

Taking in many short breaths quickly, Hailey started waving her hands in front of her face. "O-M-G. O-M-G! An actual, real, live mermaid."

The girl in the yellow sundress withdrew from Meredith and moved closer to the mermaid, who had flipped herself over to a seated position beside the girl and reached up to take her hand.

"I think I'm gonna faint." Hailey was still hyperventilating.

"Snap out of it, Hailey."

Before Jill could stop her, Hailey had already skipped over to the mermaid. "Long red hair. Pretty green tail. Sparkly scales." Hailey gasped with each new feature she could see in much more detail, itemizing each with emphatic finger points. Then she noticed the mermaid's white seashells. "Seashell bra! I always imagined that's what they'd wear!"

Jill tried to pull Hailey away, but she continued to bounce around like a little kid on her best birthday ever.

"I'm sure you probably get asked this a lot," said Hailey. "But by any chance, is your name Ari—?"

"Hailey, don't be so rude." Jill quickly faced Hailey away from the mermaid, holding her by the sides of her head to prevent her from turning around, and looking straight into her eyes. "You've got to calm down."

"Excuse me," said Meredith, smacking her tailfin against the water to get everyone's attention. "I think we have more pressing problems to solve here."

Marina clutched Lorelei's hand more tightly and pointed down at her orange tail. "Look, Lorelei, she has my tail. What do we do?"

"Your name is Lorelei?" asked Hailey. "That's such a prettier name than—"

"Hailey, shush." Then Jill stepped into the shallow water and stood at a point about halfway between Meredith and the mermaid Lorelei, but a few steps back so she wasn't blocking their views of each other. She took a quick but deep breath, hoping that calmness would lead to some cooperation.

"Lorelei, you said? Well, it appears there's been a little mix-up. My friend Meredith here..." Jill gestured to Meredith, who waved her fingers at Lorelei while giving her a half-smile and shrug. "She found, well she found a *something* that turned into a mermaid tail, which I guess belongs to your friend. What did you say her name was?" She beckoned the girl in the yellow sundress to state her name.

Lorelei looked up and nodded, as if to say it was okay to her friend, who meekly said, "Marina."

"Thanks, Marina." Jill smiled at her. "It's a pleasure to meet you. My name's Jill. Now that we know each other's names—"

"And I'm Hailey!" She was waving and still bouncing giddily on the sand.

"Yes, that's my cousin." Jill gestured back toward the house. "She lives here. My friend Meredith and I are on vacation. We don't want any trouble, and we promise we won't tell another human about your existence. It will be our little secret. Meredith wants to give Marina her tail back, more than anything else in the world."

Meredith nodded her head, trying to concentrate on not moving her tail in any way whatsoever.

"I am afraid it is not that simple," said Lorelei.

"We know. We've tried." Jill hoped that pointing out their human ignorance would appease the mermaids so they would help. "Drying it off didn't work like it does in stories or movies, but that's all we knew to try. Clearly, you know how it really works. We're hoping you would tell us." A little patronizing, Jill thought, but hopefully persuasive enough.

"There is nothing I want more than for Marina to have her tail once again." Lorelei looked up at Marina, who was already crying. "Even though it is against the rules of our

71

kind, I can teach your friend how to transform back."

Meredith leaned forward, eager to learn.

"But she is going to have to wait," said Lorelei, gently squeezing her sobbing friend's hand. "Until the next cycle."

"The next cycle?" asked Jill, looking down at Meredith, both of them dreading the impending answer.

A full day wouldn't be that bad, thought Meredith, having already made it through the night. A few more hours soaking in the bathtub behind a locked door was worth the wait to get her legs back.

"Um…how long is a cycle?" asked Hailey, scratching her head.

Knowing the answer, Marina started bawling. "Until the next full moon."

After quickly processing the information, Meredith spoke factually, her shock rendering her devoid of any emotion. "The lunar cycle is approximately twenty-nine and a half days." She collapsed backwards and lay there on the wet sand with her tailfin trembling as she covered her teary eyes.

Then a wave washed right over her.

~ Chapter Twelve ~

"One month?" shouted Jill, standing over Lorelei and hoping that her six-foot height made her appear imposing. "My best friend is going to be a mermaid for a whole month?"

"And my best friend?" asked Lorelei. "Yesterday was her first day out of the water. She is not prepared to walk among your kind for a full cycle."

"Are you saying *you* would be?"

"Yes." Lorelei carefully considered whether revealing further information was a wise strategy. She needed to gain the trust of the two human-maids because someone needed to care for Marina on land. "I have visited this island many times. I actually enjoy walking among your kind. This would be somewhat easier if I was the one with legs."

"So you've been on my beach before?" asked Hailey, whose face beamed when she saw Lorelei nod affirmatively. "O-M-G, mermaids have walked on my beach! I think I need to sit down."

"Chill out, Hailey." Jill turned around to further chastise her cousin for geeking out about mermaids instead of taking the dire situation seriously, but her eyes focused on the houses on either side of Hailey's. People lived there, and she didn't want them to catch a glimpse of the mermaids. "Make yourself useful and stand guard."

Happy to oblige, Hailey jumped to her feet and looked out for her neighbors, even though she was certain neither of them—especially nosey Mr. Dobbins—was home at that time of day on a Friday.

"Where am I supposed to stay for that long?" asked

Meredith, still lying on her back as the water passed over her and then uncovered her again. "I have to stay somewhere wet, or else my tail will dry out."

"*My* tail," blubbered Marina as her head sharply turned toward Meredith. Then she sank to her knees so Lorelei could console her more closely.

"I'm sorry." Meredith sat up to apologize to Marina's face. "I didn't mean to refer to it that way. If I wasn't completely and utterly terrified about what happened, I would have to say that this tail—I mean, *your* tail—has been like a unique scientific experiment. Trying to figure out how to control it without feeling a pair of legs—*my* legs, wherever they went—has been bizarre, but intriguing."

"Thank you," said Marina, sniffling. "I wish I could say the same about these legs."

"Okay, people." Jill clapped her hands once. "Love fest over. We need to figure out where and how to keep both of you hidden for the next month."

"The next month?" Meredith's thoughts had been so clouded by the news of the transformation schedule that she had neglected her own vacation schedule. "Oh, Jill, this is bad. This is very bad. We're only staying on the island for three weeks."

Hailey, keeping watch with her back to everyone, added, "And my mom expects Meredith to join us for dinner tonight. Just sayin'."

Meredith groaned and fell back onto the damp sand, splashing water as she anxiously flipped her fluke up and down. "My parents are coming out here to visit with your aunt and uncle that last weekend." Nervous pressure built up inside her head, so she ran her hands through her short, wet hair to massage her scalp. "What are they supposed to do? Take me back home on the ferry like this?"

"My tail cannot go to your home," said Marina. "It belongs in the ocean."

Lorelei said, "Your parents cannot see you like this. No other humans can see you. You will be captured, and then

Marina will never get her tail back. You will both be forever stuck this way."

Jill clapped her hands again. "But we're not going to let that happen. Focus, people, focus."

Lorelei looked up at Jill and said, "We prefer to be called *mers.*"

"Fine. Focus, people and mers. One month. How do we hide Meredith, and where do we keep Marina?"

Meredith rolled over onto her stomach and tried to crawl towards Lorelei. Reaching ahead with her hands, she was able to pull herself forward, but her tail dragged in the shallow water. "I can't make it a month like this." A slightly larger wave broke and gave her the necessary additional push toward Lorelei. When the wave subsided, Meredith propped up her head with her clasped and pleading hands. "There's got to be a way to change us back sooner."

"I wish I could help you," said Lorelei. "Because helping you helps Marina too. But I know no way to transform other than at sunrise on the morn of the full moon."

"You're saying that the worst case scenario is that they switch back at the end of the month." Jill crossed her arms. "Are you sure?"

"The morn of the full moon." Lorelei turned away and looked at her tail that skimmed the surface of the water.

Jill circled around Lorelei and crouched down to look her in the eyes. "I asked if you were sure. Are you completely sure they can change back?"

"I cannot be completely sure," answered Lorelei, turning toward Meredith. "A human has never before taken the tail of a mer. You may not have the power to transform."

Meredith buried her face into her hands. "No, no, don't say that. Senior year, college applications. I can't miss all that."

"How will I live like this?" asked Marina. "Do you think your father will know what we can do?"

"Or if there's some way we can transform before the next full moon?" added Meredith.

75

"I will ask him when we return."

"We?" Marina pulled away from Lorelei. "How can I come without my tail?"

"I am sorry, Marina, but I do not mean you." Lorelei gestured at Meredith. "I mean her."

"Me? I don't swim." Meredith thrust one shoulder over the other and let the momentum flip her onto her back. Winded, she sat up in the shallow water. "See? I move like a beached whale in this thing."

"Then you will have to learn how to swim with it," said Lorelei.

Meredith pointed to the southern horizon, at the miles and miles of ocean rippling with waves and sparkling in the late-morning sun. "Out there? Do you know how much water is out there, and how deep it gets? Oceans make up over seventy percent of Earth's surface, and the deepest point is deeper than Mount Everest is tall!"

"We do not live that far away." A smile appeared on Lorelei's face. "Those sound like fantastic adventures, but not for a beginner mer such as yourself."

"Gee, thanks." Meredith folded her arms in front of her and loudly smacked her tail on the water. "But you're forgetting that I don't swim."

Lorelei opened her arms. "I will teach you."

"This could work," said Jill, pointing at the mers as she named them. "Lorelei will always be with you, not only to help you, Merri, but also to keep Marina's tail safe."

"But where do *I* go for a month?" asked Marina.

Meredith glared at Jill. "And how do you explain my continued absence to your Aunt Susan?"

Without breaking her concentration on her neighbors' houses, Hailey said, "Mom insists that Meredith be at the table for dinner tonight."

"Well, she's not going to be there, Hailey." Jill started pacing in the sand, improvising a scene in her head, muttering to herself. "Objective: cover for Merri's disappearance. Tactics: locked doors, pillows under the covers to look like…"

"It would be nice for Mom to finally meet your best friend, Jillybean," said Hailey. "Mom hasn't seen her since she was a toddler."

Jill stopped pacing and stood frozen in the path she had kicked through the sand. "Hailey, that's brilliant."

"Yay, me!" Hailey applauded and then crinkled her forehead. "What did I do?"

Jill strutted over to Marina. "My aunt hasn't seen Meredith yet, so it's simple. You pretend to be her."

Marina furrowed her brow. "How do I act like a human-maid I know nothing about?"

"Human-maid?" repeated Hailey. "O-M-G, that is too cute."

Jill rolled her eyes and then touched a hand to her chest. "I take acting classes. I can teach you to pretend to be someone else."

"Won't her family miss her while she's gone?" asked Meredith, indicating Marina.

Lorelei could tell Marina was saddened by the question, so she took Marina's hand and said, "True, my father and I will miss her," replied Lorelei. "He will be told what has happened, but no other mer can learn the truth."

Clapping her hands one last time, Jill said, "We've got a plan. We should decide a time to meet again. Maybe by then one of us will have found a way to switch things back to normal sooner."

"This could be an exciting adventure," said Lorelei, swaying her tail back and forth in the water. "We shall meet at the next half moon."

Last quarter, Meredith thought but decided there were more pressing matters than to correct the mermaid. "One week from today, then," she said. A scowl appeared on her face as she beckoned for Jill. "A word with you please, Jill? In private."

Lorelei nodded and then turned to her friend. "Marina, join me for a swim. I apologize; join me for a walk."

While Marina walked across the oncoming waves, Lorelei jumped forward into the water and swam parallel to Marina's route. They soon met a little further down the beach.

"Should I trust them?" asked Marina.

"I get a good feeling from them." Lorelei looked over her shoulder at the human-maids. "The longer one has a good head on her shoulders, and she will look after you for the sake of her friend. The one with pink in her hair is clearly a friend to all mers. They should keep you safe."

"I guess this is a sink-or-swim experience?"

"No." Seeing a concerned look appear on her friend's face, Lorelei reached up and took hold of Marina's hands. "Sink or stand. Choose *stand.*"

Marina smiled down at Lorelei and saw that her green tail was shimmering.

Meanwhile, like a child throwing a temper tantrum, Meredith was flapping her tailfin repeatedly, splashing water and thwapping the packed wet sand. "Jill, how many times do I have to tell you that I don't swim? And that's with legs, not with one of these."

"I'm sure it's easier with that, Merri. It's adapted for swimming."

"But that girl—mermaid, mer, whatever you call her—has already mastered walking. If I don't master swimming, this whole ruse is sunk."

"Who better to teach you how to be a mermaid than an actual mermaid?"

"A month, Jill. I can't last a month. What about my parents? What about all the summer reading I have to do?"

"Okay, now you're just spouting."

Hailey ran over to them. "Forget schoolwork. You gotta do this! YOLO!"

After turning Hailey back towards her lookout position and pushing her away, Jill knelt in the water beside Meredith and said, "You're probably the smartest person I know, so think about it. Really think about it, Merri. There's no other solution. You're going to have to go with this Lorelei

mermaid, and she'll have to take care of you because if
something bad happens to you, something bad happens to
her friend also. And I know you well enough to know that
once you get down there, wherever you're going, you're not
going to rest until you know everything there is to know
about changing a tail to legs and back again."

"You're right," said Meredith. "It's the best plan. The only
plan. With so many variables to consider, let's hope it works."

Hailey heard a car rolling onto the gravel driveway to the
right of her house. "Nine-one-one!" She was pointing and
jumping. "Mr. Dobbins must be home for lunch or
something."

Meredith and Jill hugged while Marina did the same with
Lorelei. Hailey called for Marina and Jill to join her, but Jill
turned back and took Meredith's eyeglasses from her.
"Sorry," Jill said when Meredith contended she needed them
to see. "Don't want them to make you look like a fish out of
water. Or whatever."

Jill caught up with Hailey and Marina at the stairs to the
footbridge. As the human cousins jogged up the stairs,
Marina lagged behind. Keeping her hand on the railing to
steady herself, she turned toward the ocean. She saw Lorelei
disappear under the surface and then swiftly emerge beside
Meredith, who had been sitting with her back to the land.
Meredith looked over her shoulder at the house, took
Lorelei's offered hand, and then dove with her into the ocean.

Marina couldn't hold back the tears as she watched her tail
swim away without her.

~ Chapter Thirteen ~

Unsure what to do next, Meredith had waited alone in the shallow water, which had risen past her navel while the tide had been slowly coming in.

Lorelei's silhouette approached in the slightly deeper water a little further out than Meredith. There was just enough depth to keep her fully submerged until her upper body surfaced. Her tail twisted around underneath her until she was floating in a seated position. Then she rode the next wave to shore until the friction of the upwardly sloped sand brought her to a stop beside Meredith.

"Wow," said Meredith. "That was very graceful."

"Thank you. I have practiced." Lorelei flicked her tailfin while she lowered her head in a slight bow to her audience of one. Then she reached for Meredith's hand. "Sink or swim."

"For me, they might be one and the same." Meredith looked over her shoulder to say one last goodbye to her friends, but they were running into the house. Only Marina stood watching at the bottom of the stairs. Her heart frantically beating inside her chest, Meredith turned back toward the ocean and took Lorelei's hand with much trepidation.

"Hold tightly," said Lorelei, and Meredith could detect what looked like a mischievous smirk on the mer's face.

Then Lorelei's upper body lunged forward, and her tail automatically flipped up behind her. When she finally broke through the surface of the water, she was several feet further ahead.

Suddenly jerked forward, Meredith felt as if she were

riding a jet ski. Or that she *was* the jet ski. While Meredith clutched onto Lorelei's hand, the left side of her body skimmed along the surface like a water ski, with her tail slicing a white-capped rippled path behind her.

Meredith's right arm flailed wildly in the air, and she could feel her left hand slipping out of Lorelei's grasp. Letting go meant being left alone in deep waters, and Meredith had no idea how far from shore they were. With all her strength, she rolled onto her stomach and reached into the water until her free hand had found and taken secure hold of Lorelei's wrist. Though her speed hadn't decreased by much, Meredith's feelings of terror had.

Sighing calmly, Meredith finally opened her eyes. She had difficulty seeing, not because she wasn't wearing her eyeglasses, but because water sprayed into her eyes as she was skimming the surface so quickly. There wasn't much to see other than endless ocean water all the way to the horizon. She glanced behind her, but there was practically nothing but ocean water in that direction also; the beach reduced to a thin crescent sliver in the distance, and the houses small boxes.

Such great distance in such short time equaled a high velocity, and Meredith tried to estimate how fast Lorelei was tugging her. She looked into the water and saw Lorelei's lithe figure under the surface, her iridescent scales sparkling and her fluke fluttering rapidly. Meredith had no idea where Lorelei found the strength and stamina, but more disconcerting to her was the notion that she'd soon have to do the same.

Their motion slowed until they came to a stop. Without the speed zipping her above the surface tension of the water, Meredith's heavy lower half sunk, and she found herself in an upright position submerged from her shoulders down. Remembering how much she didn't like even being in the deep end of a swimming pool, Meredith panicked upon feeling that the only thing below the tip of her tail was more water.

"I can't feel the bottom!" Meredith thrashed her arms. Her

hips wiggled like she was spinning a hula-hoop while her tail hung limply below her in the water.

"The bottom is far below us," said Lorelei. "You will not feel it."

"I'm going to die." Meredith bobbed up and down with the waves, still splashing around. "Don't let me drown here."

"I do not understand *drown*." Lorelei floated over to Meredith and took her hands, pulling them together in front of her. "You are safe in the water. You are a mer now."

Lorelei's voice was soothing, almost like a lullaby. A wave of calmness spread throughout Meredith's body, all the way down her tail, and she stopped moving and found herself naturally treading water. "Why are we way out here in open water?" she asked.

"No one from land can see us this far out," replied Lorelei, releasing Meredith's hands. "Now show me how you swim."

Meredith gulped as she remembered swimming lessons at the Y when she was much younger. During the first lesson that had involved more than getting accustomed to the water itself, she floundered head first underwater, swallowing some and clogging up her ears. Terrified, she refused to go again, but her parents insisted she learn. After that, it had taken her many separate series of classes before she could cross the pool, and it frustrated her that so many of the other children were better at it than she was. But once the instructors and lifeguards had given her a certificate of completion, she avoided all further opportunities to swim. There was printed proof she could do it, and that was good enough for her. So at pool parties over the years, she would attend if invited, enjoy the company of her friends, and occasionally play games in the shallow end that didn't require dunking her head underwater. But never in the deep end, and never too far from the shore at the beach.

She did know how to swim, or at least she remembered the fundamentals. Leaning forward onto her stomach, she floated horizontally and then closed her eyes. Simple application of Newton's Third Law, she thought, reciting the lesson from physics class to herself in her mind. Mr. Peterson was quite insistent that they memorize those laws verbatim. Whenever one object exerted a force on a second object, the second object simultaneously exerted a force of equal strength in the opposite direction on the first object. She pushed the water backwards with her arm, so the water could push her forward.

One stroke with one arm, followed by a stroke with her other arm, and before long there was forward motion. Meredith was swimming, barely. She tried concentrating on the kicking movements that her legs—if they had been there—would make to swim further with each stroke, hoping her brain would send the correct signals to her tail. However, her tail slightly twisted one way, and then it twisted back the other way, accomplishing nothing as it drifted along.

Lorelei chuckled. "You swim like a human."

"No kidding," said Meredith, groaning.

"A real mer swims under the surface." With that, Lorelei grabbed Meredith's wrist and pulled her underwater, head first.

Meredith was flipped completely upside-down, and her head was dizzy as her equilibrium had become so abruptly unbalanced. If she had known Lorelei was going to drag her under, she would have taken a deep breath first. Instead, she had to settle for keeping her mouth shut. The deeper they went, the faster Meredith's heart started beating. Pressure pushing her on all sides, she imagined walls made of thick liquid closing in on her. Her view darkened as claustrophobia took over. She wanted to escape. She wanted to breathe. But there was nowhere for her to go, and there was no air for her to inhale.

Lorelei gradually changed directions from straight down to horizontal to straight up, having made a wide U-turn in the ocean depths. Slowing down, she released her hold on Meredith.

Suspended there, Meredith looked up. Though noticeably

dimmer, the sun still shined and appearing near its usual size at its usual location and distance in the sky. Its round shape was randomly distorted by the ripples of the ocean surface, which appeared more like a transparent funhouse mirror. There were fish of all shapes, colors, sizes, and species, many of which she couldn't identify; they were swimming about, oblivious to her presence as if she were just another undersea dweller. But she wasn't a fish. She reminded herself that she was a mammal, and thus, she needed to breathe. When she looked up and realized how deep in the water she was, she thrashed about, terrified that there was no way she could get to the surface in time to catch some air.

"We can swim here," said a voice that Meredith was sure sounded like Lorelei. "Calm yourself down."

Humans weren't adapted to understand many sounds they heard underwater, as noise was usually distorted by the fluidity of the water. Not only had Meredith heard sounds but clearly-spoken words, and she wondered how she had been able to comprehend them.

"How are you talking down here?" Meredith quickly covered her open mouth with her hands to avoid swallowing more water, but then she realized she had spoken as well. "And how am I able to talk down here?"

"You are mer now." Lorelei rotated rapidly like a figure skater on ice, but she also sunk slightly such that her long, red hair swirled fluidly above her. "We can all talk down here."

"But how do you do it? And how do you breathe?" Meredith felt around her neck, curious to see if she had sprouted gills.

"We just do." Lorelei swam around Meredith. "Why ask why?"

"Because the ability to breathe underwater could be one of the greatest scientific discoveries of all time."

Lorelei rushed through the water until she was face to face with Meredith. "We are not *your* discovery." Lorelei flipped her tail a little to propel her slightly upward such that she was looking down at Meredith. "For all you know, we have existed long before you."

"I'm sorry." Meredith held her hands in front of her as she slowly backed her shoulders away from Lorelei. "Let's not get started on the wrong foot—er, tail?"

"We avoid letting humans see us in our true form or even know about our kind. The only reason I revealed myself to you and your friends was to help Marina. The only way to help her now is to make my kind believe you are one of us. Start swimming."

Meredith repeated the swimming motions she had performed at the surface. Her hips shimmied, and her fluke barely wiggled. She moved forward but marginally more successfully than above water. The only difference was that dragging her tail along wasn't as difficult now that it was underwater and buoyant. It annoyed her that she had been able to operate the tail when she was lying on a bed, but in its natural habitat, it was uncooperative. If swimming was what the tail was specifically adapted for, then why wasn't it letting her do it?

"You do not need to use your arms." Lorelei swam away, her arms held by her sides.

As Lorelei passed by, Meredith watched her sleek form, perfectly streamlined with the only source of propulsion being her tailfin flapping up and down. Logically, Meredith knew what she needed to do; she simply couldn't do it yet, just like at the Y.

Meredith shrieked when she felt something grip the end of her fluke, which kicked up with a startled reflex and propelled her forward.

Lorelei let go of Meredith's tailfin and then patted it. "You use this to swim."

"I *was* using that." Meredith tried to prove her point, but again, she went nowhere. "Why isn't it working when I concentrate on it?"

Lorelei glided alongside her and said, "Do not concentrate. Just swim. Flip your tail." Lorelei gently wiggled hers and drifted away.

"I didn't have a tail until yesterday." Meredith tried again, and when the same result occurred, she groaned in frustration.

"I do not expect you to master it right away." Lorelei swam around her. "You cannot be good at everything on the first attempt."

Knowing she was excellent at subjects in school, Meredith wondered if there was something she had already learned to help Lorelei's lesson make more sense to her. Maybe some reverse psychology? "You've been human before. You've had legs. You know how to use them. Explain to me how you think you would swim with legs."

Further ahead of Meredith, Lorelei stopped and looked back. "I have never swum with legs. When I go on land, I go to explore new places. I can swim any other day."

"You're not being helpful."

"You are not being patient."

Meredith groaned, furious that she was being treated like a petulant child. "You've had a tail your entire life. I've had it for one day, and I don't intend to keep it."

"You think too much like a human." Lorelei was circling Meredith. "Pretend you have always had that tail."

Meredith sighed and closed her eyes, thinking back to the night before on the bed in the guest room. She remembered herself explaining her sensations and observations to Jill and Hailey. Bending her knees, she pictured, but at the same time, like they were bound together.

Water rushed by her, and she opened her eyes. She was swimming. "Hands at your side!" called Lorelei.

Following the instruction, Meredith withdrew her arms, and the decreased resistance upon her made her glide faster. Lorelei caught up with her, and they swam side by side. Meredith was astonished by how instinctual swimming was, like walking is eventually learned by a human child. Though she didn't understand how, it stood to reason that if the mermaid tail had altered her anatomy and physiology, it could also alter her instincts, making her into a swimmer. If only she had grown a mermaid tail in the pool at the Y, then she would have swum circles around the other kids—and the lifeguards.

Occasionally, Lorelei would swim faster and dare Meredith to catch up. Before long, Meredith could, though she suspected Lorelei was purposely slowing down to make her believe she could swim faster. Meredith didn't care. Instead, she relished in her latest accomplishment, especially since success at swimming eluded her for much of her childhood. It was one more item she could place on her college resume. She knew how to swim.

She practiced how to navigate wide turns simply by leaning to the side. Slowing down and stopping was achieved by slowing the rate of fin-flapping, sometimes accompanied with swinging her arms outward. They swam up to the surface and dove back under, curving their bodies around so their flukes flipped above the water.

By the time the sun had completely passed over the sky, Lorelei believed that Meredith's slightly below average ability would suffice to convince others she was a mer.

"Now we must do something about *that*," said Lorelei, pointing at Meredith's blue tankini top.

Meredith glanced down at the top half of the swimsuit, and then she stared at Lorelei's seashells and how little of her upper body they covered. "There's no way you're getting me to wear two of those things in front of my—"

"Wearing your human clothes will draw attention." Lorelei flipped her tail and started swimming away. "You may not want that when I bring you to school."

Following Lorelei and smiling, Meredith was confident in the knowledge that school was one place where she truly excelled.

~ Chapter Fourteen ~

"We're going to start calling you Meredith right away," said Jill, standing between the two beds in the guest room. "It will get you used to it sooner."

Sitting alone at the foot of one of the beds, Marina looked at her smooth legs and wigged her toes, unsure what their purpose was. She could tell that the bed and the floor were supporting her, but when she lifted a foot and held it in place, it started to tremble until she felt discomfort and pain. Once released, the foot dropped to the floor and landed with a thud. Being on land made her feel confined, unlike the freedom of floating in the glorious ocean.

"Did you hear what I said, Meredith?" asked Jill, awaiting an answer.

"Pssst, Marina," whispered Hailey, sitting cross-legged on the other bed. "That's you."

Marina looked up at Jill. "What did you say?"

"You have to respond to the name *Meredith*." Jill looked at the alarm clock. "My aunt's going to be home in a few hours. I know that's not enough time to learn a full backstory, but you at least need to know your name."

"I am sorry." Marina turned away and glanced out the window at the ocean. She was higher up than she ever had been before.

"Cut her some slack, Jill. Can't you see she's scared?" Hailey stood and crossed the room to sit beside Marina. Gently touching her shoulder to console her, Hailey frowned when Marina pulled away from her. "I know this is strange for you, Marina, but we're trying to help you."

"I know," said Marina, turning to look into Hailey's green eyes. "I am thankful to have the help."

"Good, now let's move on." Jill clapped her hands once. "Your name is Meredith, and that's what we have to call you. It's like in my drama club; when we're doing a show, Mr. Shapiro won't let us call each other by our real names—only our character names. Your character is Meredith."

"G-M-A-B, Jill. She's not an actress. Can't we at least call her Marina when we're alone with her? It is her name." Hailey turned to Marina. "And B-T-dubs, Marina is, like, a totally perfect name for a mermaid. You rock."

Marina stared blankly at Hailey. "I do not sit on rocks. Why do you think that? I would be seen."

Hailey giggled. "No, no, no. *You rock* means that you're cool." Marina's lack of expression didn't change, so Hailey continued, "That you're awesome?" Another pause. "Very, very special?"

Marina smiled. "Thank you. Why not say that first?"

Jill groaned. "Can we get back to business? Marina, your name is Meredith around Hailey's mom, got it?"

They started with vital statistics: Meredith's age, grade in school, and names of her parents. Then they moved on to Meredith's favorite color, foods, music, books, and subjects in school—many of the names and concepts didn't make much sense to Marina, and the explanations seemed to confuse her more. Jill glossed over Meredith's dislike of swimming and moved on to her career goals. Feeling some pressure from both her parents to enter their respective fields, Meredith was considering biomechanical engineering. When Marina asked for more details, however, both Jill and Hailey were unable to explain.

Because she was Meredith's best friend, Jill included some of her own information. She revealed how they met, how long they had been friends, that she had a brother who had just graduated high school, and that her mother and Aunt Susan were twin sisters.

Somewhere along the way, they had taken a break to eat

the leftover pizza from the night before. Marina devoured the remaining slices with anchovies, and her comment on pizza was, "It flows."

"Awesome mermaid saying," said Hailey, upon learning it was the equivalent of saying something rocked or was cool. "That's what I was trying to say earlier!"

When they learned that Marina didn't have the word cool for describing temperature in her vocabulary, they tried to explain by showing her ice cubes, which fascinated her when she learned they were water that had been frozen. Jill wished Meredith had been there to better explain the physical change of something freezing, and then Jill realized that if Meredith had been there, the explanation would have been unnecessary.

As Marina was told more about Meredith's life, Jill stopped for some pop quizzes along the way. Had they been in school, Marina would have received low grades. They took several breaks throughout the day because of the sheer amount of bottled water Marina believed she needed to consume. Teaching her to use the bathroom was an adventure, and the idea of water coming from a faucet astounded her, but at least she learned. Trying to explain any toilet problems would definitely make Aunt Susan more suspicious than she already was.

As the afternoon drew to a close, Marina's head was throbbing. "This is much information to memorize," said Marina as she massaged her temples. "Can we rest again?"

Jill glanced at the time. "One more quick quiz. How old are you?"

Too weary, Marina automatically answered, "Two hundred nineteen."

"O-M-G!" Hailey's eyes bulged as she checked out Marina. "You look super hot for your age. Mermaids really must be immortal. That flows!"

Marina smirked at Hailey's usage of the phrase and her misunderstanding of how mers measured time. "That is two hundred nineteen moon cycles."

Hailey stared blankly into the air, trying to figure out how to do the math in her head. Meanwhile, Jill had already taken out her smartphone and found its calculator setting. She vaguely remembered Meredith saying there were about thirty days in a lunar cycle, so she calculated with that number, figuring it would be a good enough approximation. "That's about eighteen years old," said Jill, double-checking her calculations.

"Hey, she's like our age!" Hailey turned to Marina. "Me and Jill are both seventeen, but Meredith is—"

Covering Hailey's mouth before she could answer, Jill said, "Don't say it! Let *Meredith* answer." Jill had put air-quotes around the name.

"Sixteen?" Marina concentrated on the information. "I am younger than Jill because my parents put me in kindergarten a year early. Is that correct?"

Jill nodded while Hailey bounced on the mattress and applauded.

Marina shrugged. "I do not know what it all means, but I think I understand—how did you say it, Jill?—the motivation of my character."

Jill smirked but then groaned when she glanced at the clock. "I wish we had the time for some dialect coaching to make you speak more like you're from New England."

"I do not understand." Marina's forehead crinkled. "What is wrong with my speech?"

"Ooh, ooh! I know!" Hailey raised her hand and wiggled her fingers like an eager student waiting for the teacher to call on her. "You gotta say things like *don't* instead of *do not*. We humans sometimes smush words together."

They tried teaching Marina some contractions, but the words that came out of her mouth sounded like a blend of a person phonetically speaking a randomly arranged set of letters and a sea lion wailing in excruciating pain. The lesson ended abruptly when Aunt Susan called them downstairs for dinner. Hailey rubbed Marina's back to calm any anxiety while Jill opened the door and said, "Showtime."

The dining room table was already set with four plates, glasses of lemonade, napkins, and the appropriate silverware. Susan came into the room, carrying a large serving bowl of spaghetti and meatballs covered in marinara sauce. After setting it on the table, she walked over to Marina and said, "So glad to finally meet you, Meredith. I'm Hailey's mom, Jill's Aunt Susan."

"Hello, Aunt Susan," said Marina, thrusting her arm forward. "I am Meredith."

Jill's crossed her fingers behind her back and hoped that Marina's robotic delivery of the rehearsed lines wasn't a dead giveaway that something wasn't quite right.

"Sure, you can call me Aunt Susan." She took Marina's hand and politely shook it. "After all, Jillybean here sometimes calls me mom. I'm sorry you were sick yesterday, Meredith. How do you feel today?"

"Dry."

Susan nodded at the odd reply. "Well, outside is the beach. You three girls can go swimming later and get as wet as you'd like."

"I do not swim."

Finally hearing Marina say something that Meredith would have said, Jill sighed in relief.

They sat at the table, Jill next to Marina on one side, Hailey facing Jill on the other side, and Susan in the remaining chair.

"I got home a little later than I wanted to tonight." Susan gathered the four plates and started scooping dinner onto them. "Someone rearranged an entire shelf of books, and Hailey can tell you I get a little miffed when library books aren't in the right place. So I went for something quick and easy tonight. Hope you don't mind spaghetti and meatballs, Meredith."

Marina was staring at her plate, which was piled with long strands like thin, yellow eels with four small spongy orbs strewn about, all drenched in a red sludge.

"Meredith, is something wrong?" asked Susan, curiously

watching how intensely the girl was observing her dinner.

Jill gave Marina a nudge and said, "Meredith, my aunt asked you a question."

"Oh!" Marina looked diagonally across the table. "I am sorry, Aunt Susan."

Finally serving herself, Susan repeated, "I said I hope you don't mind spaghetti and meatballs."

"Spaghetti and meatballs?" Marina knew the words were familiar, and her face brightened when she remembered them. "Spaghetti and meatballs! That is one of my favorite foods."

She turned to Jill and Hailey and was pleased to see they were smiling back at her, and then Marina returned her gaze to the bizarre concoction that was in front of her. Jill quietly cleared her throat, trying to get Marina's attention but not Aunt Susan's. When Marina turned to her, Jill demonstrated how to eat the meal by curling spaghetti around her fork, putting the fork in her mouth, closing her mouth, and pulling the empty fork out of her mouth.

Mimicking Jill's actions, Marina swallowed her food and proclaimed, "This tastes wonderful." Then she proceeded to stuff two more clumps of spaghetti into her mouth.

After only a few more forkfuls, Marina's face was smeared with marinara sauce. Jill dabbed her own mouth with a napkin as a subtle hint for Marina to do the same, but Marina continued to eat heartily. Hailey could sense her mother staring across the table, so she started eating just as messily as Marina to make it seem like it was normal behavior.

"What's going on here?" Susan put her fork down on the table loudly enough to get everyone's attention. "Are you two in a rush to get somewhere? Why are you eating so fast?"

Seizing the opportunity to improvise, Jill said, "It's a new craze they saw on the internet—eat fast, and you won't feel hungry later."

"Make sure to come up for air every now and then."

Hailey squealed out a giggle. "Up for air? That's so funny, because she's a—"

Jill kicked Hailey in the shin under the table before she could blow Marina's cover. "Because she's a big fan of your spaghetti and meatballs, Aunt Susan. Right Meredith?" When Marina didn't give an immediate answer, Jill repeated, "Right, *Meredith?*"

Marina mumbled a positive response and then swallowed. "Thank you, Aunt Susan. This is nothing like the food I have at home."

"Then how can it be your favorite?" asked Susan.

Jill immediately answered, "She must mean that you make it the best."

Susan shook her head as she looked down at her plate, and Jill showed Marina how to wipe her mouth.

"School ends for the summer, and you girls get all wacky." Susan sighed. "How many weeks until you all go back?"

Jill laughed, nodding her head up and down to get Hailey and Marina to laugh along with her, which they eventually did.

The rest of the dinnertime conversation went without incident. Marina started speaking in less of a monotone as she settled more into her Meredith persona. Jill breathed more easily, knowing that this first encounter with Aunt Susan would be the most difficult. Everything afterwards would hopefully be smooth sailing. Then she hoped that Meredith was having at least as easy a time. Meanwhile, Hailey kept her attention on Marina and was overjoyed with the fact that a mermaid was sitting at her dinner table without her mother's knowledge.

By nightfall, Marina's brain and body were exhausted from the long and challenging day, but her usual resting position—on her stomach—was not comfortable in the bed. The mattress and blanket were soft, but they didn't envelop her the same way water did when she rested at home. So she lay there until Jill in the bed beside her fell asleep.

There was enough light in the room from outside for her to see Jill lying on her back. Figuring the human-maid had mastered the correct way to sleep on an uncomfortable bed, she turned herself over to try the new position.

She closed her eyes and listened to the calming sounds of the ocean waves through the open window. Though she tried to imagine herself back at home, the awkward sleeping arrangement reminded her how far from home she was. Her eyes popped back open, and she looked outside at the moonlight beautifully reflecting off the water's surface. *A new adventure.* She could hear Lorelei's voice saying it in her head, and she wished that Lorelei were with her to get her through the experience.

The experience would last an entire cycle. The moon was no longer a perfect circle, and a sliver was missing on one side. Wondering how many more nights she would spend resting in such uncomfortable positions, she squirmed and then winced when something on the bed jabbed her in the back.

She reached underneath her and found a small, thin, translucent disk, not quite a perfect circle. As she held it up to the light from outside, she noticed its faint orange tint and instantly recognized it as one of her scales—a dried scale, presumably shed off of Meredith the previous night. She sighed in the knowledge that the rest of her scales on her tail were wet and someplace safe.

This scale, approximately the same shape as the waning moon in the night sky, twinkled faintly as Marina closed her eyes.

~ Chapter Fifteen ~

"When you said *school*, I should've known this was what you meant," said Meredith as she watched the long parade of mers in the distance.

There were hundreds of them swimming in formation. They all had their arms by their sides and using only their tails to move, exactly as Lorelei had taught her. Approximately half had long hair—the females, she figured—flowing behind them to their waists as they swam. Meredith knew all that hair would increase fluid resistance and make it require more propulsion from their tailfins, but the mermaids didn't seem to care, and they seemed to be swimming fine. The mermen had short hair, and even without her glasses, Meredith could tell they were shirtless. There were children, too, families even, and older mers with gray hair. As amazing as their existence was, what amazed Meredith more was that such a population evaded human scientific observation, even with all the advances in technology. But, then again, she realized she had no idea exactly how deep in the ocean they were.

"Does *school* mean something else to humans?" asked Lorelei.

"We use the word like you do," said Meredith. "But it also means a place we go to learn."

"Mers learn all they need from their parents. My father, Marina, and I scouted ahead, and now we are joining the school."

"But where are they all going?"

"To the place where we settle during the north season," said Lorelei as she started swimming forward.

As Meredith approached the school, she saw the tails of the merpeople glistening in a variety of colors, predominantly different shades of blue and green, like Lorelei's tail. There were also purples, reds, and even silvers, but she didn't see any orange. Glancing over her shoulder at Marina's tail attached to her waist, she wondered if the color of the scales had any significance. Could it mean that she was a different class of merfolk? Maybe a unique breed of the species, specially adapted for something that the others weren't?

Or was she an outsider?

As she considered her appearance further—orange tail, a human tankini top, and short hair—she couldn't deny that she would stand out. "Is it safe?" she asked, painfully aware that she was indeed an outsider, different from them in more ways than just the color of her scales.

Looking over to Meredith, Lorelei said, "We shall see, but it would be wise for me to speak to them first."

Lorelei flipped her fin and slowly swam ahead. Following, Meredith asked, "What if they find out what I really am? What will happen to me?"

"If they learn, there are strict punishments, both for you and me. We cannot dwell on it. Sink or swim."

Meredith froze, her heart racing like it did in those last moments of anxiety before an exam. In her school back home, Meredith always studied so she could have all the answers. But in this school, she felt ill-prepared for the upcoming barrage of questions.

Lorelei called for her, so Meredith flapped her tailfin vigorously and swished herself through the water to catch up. Meredith didn't want to drift too far away from Lorelei, her one study guide for the big test up ahead.

"We will swim on the outside," said Lorelei. "Then it will not matter as much if you cannot keep up."

As they approached the others, Lorelei knew that Meredith wouldn't know how to merge into the school. At the last moment, Lorelei grabbed Meredith's arm and wove her way into the crowd. Any mer whose immediate path was blocked adjusted almost instantaneously without incident, and Meredith found herself swimming among the outskirts of the school, with Lorelei by her side on the right.

Mermaids and mermen swam past them—not only beside them, but also above and below them. Meredith was slower than most of them, as she wasn't accustomed to the amount of energy and concentration it took to keep her tail flapping at that rate for so long. Lorelei's suggestion to stay on the outside was good advice, because had she been swimming at that speed in the middle of the school, she would have caused a severe traffic jam.

The other benefit of swimming on the outside was that fewer of the merfolk spoke directly to them. Many passed by, oblivious to Meredith's presence, as if they were driven by a collective instinct to continue forward. Either that or they simply didn't know who Lorelei was; there were hundreds of them swimming together, after all.

Occasionally, a passing mer would address them. "Hello, Lorelei. Hello, Marina," was the typical greeting. At home, Meredith would have most likely corrected someone calling her the wrong name, but amongst the school, she didn't dare. If they were calling her Marina, it meant that they were assuming that's who she was by either the color of her tail or her association with Lorelei. Then they continued on before noticing obvious details such as her having the wrong color and length of hair. Meredith preferred not to be noticed; she desperately needed to blend in unobtrusively until she could change back.

"Marina, Lorelei," said a squeaky male voice. "Wait up."

With all her attention focused on moving forward, Meredith barely registered the voice as she grew more and more fatigued.

Looking over her right shoulder to the school, Lorelei saw the approaching mer who belonged to the voice. She flipped her fin a little faster, speeding forward to avoid him. Then she looked over her left shoulder at Meredith, more than a full tail length behind her and clearly struggling to catch up.

Groaning as she slowed herself down, Lorelei knew she couldn't abandon Meredith in the school, so she'd have to spend some time with Barney.

"Hi, Lorelei." He caught up to them and was swimming next to Lorelei. "Yesterday was full moon. Did you go up on land? Of course you did. You go there almost every full moon. Off on your adventures. You are just like your father. How is he?"

"He is doing well, Barney." Lorelei avoided making eye contact while she spoke to him, instead focusing on swimming with the school. "He has gone ahead to scout further."

"You said you were taking Marina up on land with you. Did you?" Barney lowered his voice. "Or did she guppy out like last time?"

Barney didn't wait for Lorelei to answer. Instead, he sank lower in the water, keeping the same pace as Lorelei, and then he swam sideways underneath her and Meredith, only to rise again on the outside of Meredith. "Hi, Marina," he said. "Did you go on land with Lorelei? How was it? Did you…"

He finally caught a glimpse of Meredith's face, and in his confusion, his fin abruptly stopped flipping, and he floated there as they continued forward.

"That is Barney," said Lorelei. "It is short for Barnacle. He gets himself attached to certain mers, and he is sometimes difficult to get rid of."

Meredith chuckled and looked back at him. He was swimming to catch up with them. Due to her inexperience with the tail, Meredith started to slow down and veer off in the direction she was looking. Once she realized, she looked ahead and performed a slight course correction to swim beside Lorelei. However, she wasn't aware that Barney was swimming into the space between her and Lorelei so he could talk to both of them. Their flukes flapped one another, knocking them each off course. Their tails twisted around each other, and they found themselves face to face, just outside of the flow of the school.

His eyes were gray, and he had a thin face and overall scrawny build. Most of the mermen Meredith had seen passing by her in the school were buff and muscular, so she wondered if Barney was still a merboy—if that was even an acceptable term. His tail, as shimmery as any other mer's tail, was a silvery gray.

"I'm so sorry. I didn't mean to…" said Meredith, unsure of how to uncoil her tail from his, and even more unsure what else to say to him. "Well, it's that I don't really…"

"You speak strangely," said Barney, swimming out of their tangled situation. "Are you new to the school? And where is Marina? Does she know about you? Do you know about her? She is the only other one with—"

"An orange tail?" asked Meredith, trying not to smirk at Barney's unending list of questions and the speed at which he asked them.

Meredith saw Lorelei waiting up ahead, so she swam to join her. Barney followed and continued speaking. "You must be new. I would remember another orange tail. That is something you do not forget."

When they reached Lorelei, they reentered the school. Barney swam between the two mermaids, with Meredith still on the outside. Lorelei handled the introductions: "Barney, meet Meredith."

"Murr-ih-dith?" Barney repeated her name slowly, mispronouncing it slightly. "You have *mer* in your name. That flows. Lorelei, did you hear that? We are mers, and *mer* is in her name. Murr-ih-dith."

"It's actually Meredith, with an *eh* sound. Mare-eh-dith." When Meredith said it, she had done so slowly and over-exaggerated each syllable. Mispronunciations, especially of her name, irked her.

"Meredith?" He had said it correctly but seemed confused when Meredith gave him a thumbs-up gesture. "Where is Marina? You have yet to tell me."

"Marina is ahead with my father," answered Lorelei, hoping that Barney wouldn't stick to his line of questioning.

"I did not join them because I wanted to go up on land at the full moon."

"What is land like? I have never been on land. My parents tell me I am too young." Barney gasped. "Is that where you met Meredith? Was she also visiting land?"

Her heart skipping a beat, and Meredith feared that she had been found out by the naive, immature, talkative, and otherwise innocent mer. She felt her fin flipping less often as she drifted behind, only to snap out of it and swim to catch up to the other two.

"I found her in the water on my way back to school," replied Lorelei. "She was alone, so I invited her to come with me."

In a sigh of relief, Meredith breathed out—or whatever her mermaid physiology did to release air. She was pleased with Lorelei's answer, which wasn't technically a lie. Her quick thinking reminded Meredith of Jill's improvisational skills and then of how much she missed her best friend.

"That is just like your family to take in urchins," said a female voice from above them.

Upon hearing the voice, Barney launched himself forward like a torpedo. Meredith couldn't see the owner of the new voice hovering over her, and she wasn't entirely sure she wanted to look.

Lorelei swam closer to Meredith and whispered to her, "Try not to make waves."

"In what polluted waters did you find this mer, Lorelei?" asked the voice, followed by the laughter of two other mers.

"*She* found *us*, Calliope," replied Lorelei, not looking up at the mermaid to which she was speaking. "I am surprised you are swimming this far back. Why are you not ahead with your father, leading the school?"

"Some mer has to see what chum is back here." Calliope's comment was followed by snide giggles from two nearby mers.

Wonderful, thought Meredith, *this mermaid brought a fawning entourage.*

Calliope looked down and examined Meredith's tail. "Another orange tail, just like Marina's. Where is your friend, anyway, Lorelei?"

"We do not have to answer you."

Keeping her attention on the orange tail, Calliope brought herself down to Meredith and Lorelei's level. "You have a strange appearance. Why would you not have long hair like every other maid? And that human cover you wear, the color does not mesh with your tail."

Without answering, Meredith sneaked a glance at Calliope. She had long dark hair flowing all the way down to the start of her purple tail. Her white seashells with dark purple streaks were held in place by pieces of black fishing nets that had been cut and arranged into the shape of a halter-top, tied around the back of her neck. Meredith could tell that Calliope considered herself a high-fashion mermaid.

"Did you give her that human cover?" Calliope turned her head towards Lorelei. "Gathering human items is something you would do. I do not understand the appeal of removing your tail for those unattractive legs. A true mer stays in the water and never interacts with filthy humans."

"You should not judge something that you have never experienced," said Lorelei.

Impressed with Lorelei's tact, Meredith allowed a slight grin on her face but hoped that Calliope wouldn't see it. She let the grin fade when Calliope articulated a condescending humph and asked, "What should we call you?"

Meredith glanced at Lorelei, who nodded her head. Taking the nod as a signal to answer the question, but also to be brief, Meredith introduced herself.

"Well, Meredith, I wonder how Marina—Lorelei's dearest friend—will react when she sees a tail almost exactly like hers." Calliope slowly rose back up to her friends. "She may be pleased to learn she is no longer so alone."

Once above Meredith and Lorelei, Calliope swam ahead with her two cohorts.

As Meredith watched their purple tails flapping away into

the distance, her head filled with questions about Calliope's comments.

"I will explain later. For now, let it float," said Lorelei, as if she sensed Meredith's curiosity. "I will say, however, that Calliope is nothing more than a crabby blowfish."

Dorky boys, mean and petty girls, and outsiders, all trying to establish their places within a community. Meredith realized that this was exactly like the type of school she first had in mind.

~ Chapter Sixteen ~

When Jill woke up on Monday morning, she noticed that Marina wasn't in the other bed. She stood and stretched, and then dragged herself out of the guest room.

The door to Hailey's bedroom was closed, as usual. Jill chuckled, wondering why Hailey was so secretive about her room, especially since everyone in the family knew how childishly it was decorated.

Before knocking on Hailey's door, Jill glanced towards her aunt's bedroom. The open door signified that she was downstairs or had already left for work. Jill couldn't be sure because being more concerned with locating Marina, she had neglected to check the time. With no one around, she gave the four-knock signal and waited for Hailey to respond.

"Just a minute," called Hailey from her room. Then the door opened enough for Hailey's face to be seen. "What's up?"

Jill stood on her toes, trying to glimpse into the room over Hailey's head. "Is Marina in there with you?"

Hailey squeezed through the narrow opening and then closed the door behind her. "R-U-K-M? She would totally flip out." She started laughing. "O-M-G, flip out. Get it? Because mermaids flip their tails."

Jill rolled her eyes. "Yeah, I get it. Now do you have any idea where Marina is?"

"I know she wakes up before sunrise. Don't know why. She just does."

They returned to the guest room, and Jill looked at the alarm clock. It was shortly after eight-thirty, so they were safely alone in the house. Hailey glanced out the window and noticed Marina sitting alone on the beach, about halfway between the footbridge and the water.

Jill and Hailey changed out of their sleepwear and into jeans and tees. The sky outside was overcast, and the weather report indicated it would be a little cooler than the previous week of warm, sunny days.

They walked slowly on the footbridge, so Marina wouldn't be startled or disrupted by their approach. Bending her knees while she leaned forward, Marina sat there gazing at the ocean, wearing one of Meredith's gray hoodies with a pleated white skirt to her knees. Marina had been reluctant at first to wear anything other than the yellow sundress, but Jill and Hailey convinced her that humans typically changed their clothes at least daily, and her not doing so could draw attention to herself.

And Marina didn't seem interested in drawing attention to herself, preferring to keep to the background, so she agreed to try Meredith's clothes. Fortunately, they were close enough to the same size that most of what Meredith had packed would fit Marina fine. Marina had wanted to wear the one dress Meredith had brought with her, but Jill discouraged her since it was packed in the event they went out somewhere fancy for dinner. Instead, they urged her to try shorts and pants, but Marina said they made her legs feel even more separated from each other.

When Marina noticed a shadow passing over her from the east, she looked over her left shoulder and saw Hailey standing there, swaying and smiling. "Good morning. Mind if we join you?" she asked.

"You may," replied Marina, keeping her attention on the water. "It is your beach."

Hailey and Jill sat on opposite sides of her and looked out at the waves, which were a little rougher than the previous days. None of them said anything for a few minutes, until Jill tied up her hair into a ponytail to keep the gusts of wind from blowing it into her face and said, "Marina, I know all this is difficult for you."

"You do *not* know how difficult this is," said Marina, still watching the ocean waves.

"You're right." Jill shrugged. "You called me out; I don't know anything about this. But you can't change what happened. You're here on land whether you like it or not. Like I told Meredith on the ferry ride over, live outside your comfort zone and enjoy the vacation while you can."

"I appreciate what you are trying to do, and I am grateful to have seen parts of your island." Marina thought back to the previous two days when Hailey and Jill had taken her all over the island in what Hailey called her convertible. The vehicle moved quickly, and the sights she saw were different, many of them interesting and even beautiful, but they reminded her that she didn't belong. "Hailey, your island home is impressive, but it is not my home. I have never been away from Lorelei for this long."

"I got nothing left." Jill groaned, stood, and turned towards the house. "I'm gonna get some breakfast. Come find me if you decide to go anywhere."

"We should go somewhere." Hailey jumped up and reached out an arm to help Marina to her feet. "Somewhere that might have answers we haven't found yet."

Susan had already put up the roof to the convertible in anticipation of rain and Hailey's flightiness. They climbed inside, and Hailey pulled out of the driveway towards the library. She figured that they had searched through all of her books at home, while Jill had declared the internet full of contradictory information, most of which was untrue according to Marina.

When they arrived at the library, shortly after it had opened, Hailey led them directly to the mythology and folklore bookshelves. They skipped over about two-thirds of the titles because Hailey owned them, and they had spent the previous few nights looking through them.

They stayed in the folklore aisle to research so they could easily return the books and try new ones. Jill leaned against the set of shelves opposite the books they were using while Hailey sat cross-legged on the floor. Marina lay on her stomach, as the position reminded her the most of swimming in the ocean.

Aunt Susan was carrying a small stack of books when she appeared in the aisle. "I thought I saw the three of you. The weather must have driven you indoors, but why here?" Adjusting her librarian glasses, she realized in which section of the library they had gathered. "Mermaids. Should've known."

"Doing some research for Hailey," said Jill. "You know how she is."

"Does Meredith?" Susan looked down and was dumbstruck to see the odd girl lying on the floor on her stomach.

"W-T-H, Mom," whined Hailey, holding the book open against her face to hide her embarrassment. "Please don't tell her."

In an effort to cause less confusion for Marina, Hailey and Jill had adopted the use of pronouns instead of Meredith's name to refer to Marina when around Susan. That way, only Aunt Susan called her Meredith, and Marina could get used to responding to the name. Jill had told her that the decision was mainly so Hailey wouldn't use the wrong name and potentially reveal their deception.

Aunt Susan giggled. "When she was six years old, Hailey decided she wanted to be a mermaid when she grew up."

"Stop it, Mom!" squealed Hailey from behind the book, mortified that her mother had unknowingly revealed her biggest childhood fantasy—one that she hadn't fully abandoned—to an actual mermaid. "Big time T-M-I!"

Marina sat up and gently touched Hailey's arm, and together they slowly lowered the book. Hailey's cheeks were bright pink, and Marina couldn't help but smile, waiting for a crescent of a smile to appear on Hailey's face.

"Considering how much time Hailey spends sitting around fixing her hair, she'd make an excellent mermaid." Aunt

Susan placed one of the books in its proper place on the shelves and then turned to leave the aisle. "Have fun, girls. Be home for dinner."

Marina's smile transformed into a frown. "Why does your kind insist that all we do is comb our hair? The images in these books and the statues in that place Lorelei and I saw continue this myth—"

"What statues?" asked Hailey. "What place?"

Marina described a building among other buildings near a beach. Lorelei had persuaded other humans to drive them to the opposite side of the island, where there were many people and a large white boat near the shore. She and Lorelei had stayed outside the building and looked through the window at all of the aquatic artwork, including images of the merfolk.

"A shop that sells mermaid stuff?" Hailey leapt up from the floor. "We need to go there A-S-A-P."

They arrived at the beach near the ferry terminal, which wasn't crowded because it was a cold and damp Monday. The rain was merely drizzle, so the girls didn't bother with the large umbrella in the convertible's trunk. Trying to avoid getting her hair too wet, Hailey ran across the street to the row of shops. Unfazed by the rain, Jill didn't rush, and Marina took the time to enjoy the feel of the misty droplets on her hair, face, arms, and even her legs.

"How have I never seen this place?" asked Hailey when the others joined her. "We bought swimsuits just down the street the other day. It must be new."

They looked up at the sign hanging above the door. The ornate golden letters carved into the wood spelled out *The Mermaid's Lagoon.*

The door creaked open and rang a bell hanging from the door frame. Though there were some lights on inside, the cloudy sky outside made the store interior seem eerily dim. The square shopping area wasn't large. Posters, prints, and paintings were displayed on one side of the store; shelves filled with books and cases displaying figurines and statuettes lined the opposite side. In the middle of the space were a few rotating racks for postcards, keychains, nameplates, and other small collectibles. Every item in the store was of a nautical or aquatic theme, including the largest collection of mermaid paraphernalia that any of them had seen.

Hailey slowly spun in the center of the room, her mouth wide open in unbridled awe. "O-M-G, isn't this the coolest place you've ever been?"

Jill simply shrugged, but as Marina looked around, she replied, "Absolutely none of this is right."

"What, pray tell, is wrong with it, dearie?" asked a short woman with long but matted gray hair. She was draped in a floor-length black dress, its sleeves flaring out at the end such that she gave the appearance of being some kind of witch.

"What my friend means to say..." Jill stepped forward. "What she means to say is that most of these mermaids are sitting on rocks, or they're poking their heads out of the water. Not much variety."

The woman grinned. "That's how the sailors of long ago first saw them, or thought they saw them. Those long, hot days at sea made them see the most fantastical things."

"They should be in the ocean, away from the surface." Marina's attention was caught by one figurine of a blonde-haired mermaid lounging on a rock. She picked it up and examined it closely. Of all the mermaids she saw in the shop, it was the only one with an orange tail. Just like she was the only one. "She should be swimming."

"I understand what you're saying, dearies, and you can rest assured. This isn't my entire inventory. I'm still settling in. Been open a few weeks now. Not many customers yet, but tourist season is soon to come." The woman tottered over to Hailey, who was fingering the books on the shelves. "And how may I help you?"

Pulling a book off the shelf that she didn't recognize, Hailey said, "Your shop is really cool. Why'd you name it *The Mermaid's Lagoon?*"

"I've always adored them, dearie. I like to think of my establishment as a safe and secluded place where mermaids can relax."

Jill rolled her eyes as Hailey started chatting with the woman. Hoping they wouldn't drone on for too long, Jill kept herself occupied by flipping through a bin of matted drawings and prints. A blue-tailed mermaid sitting on the rocks, a green-tailed mermaid combing her hair, another green-tailed mermaid combing her hair while sitting on a rock, and several other similar pictures. Yawning, she considered that maybe Marina had a valid point about the lack of originality in mermaid art until she found one of a woman standing amidst stormy waters.

"So what would a mermaid do if she lost her tail?" asked Hailey.

Letting the prints drop back into place in the bin, Jill dashed across the shop. "That's a silly question." She started escorting Hailey towards the door. "Everyone knows all she'd have to do is get her legs wet, and then her tail would show."

"Lost her tail, you say, dearie?" The old woman followed Hailey. "I would suppose that as long as it wasn't found, she'd be perfectly fine."

Jill and Hailey stopped in their tracks and turned to Marina. The figurine still in her hand, she was examining a painting of a blonde-haired mer with her pale green tail partially immersed in the water. As she reached for a human-man sitting in a boat, he leaned over with his face close to hers. The picture confused her, but the old woman's comment demanded her attention. "What do you mean by that?" asked Marina, walking past the cashier's counter toward the woman.

"Oh, dearie, there are stories about sailors capturing mermaids, or mermaids washing ashore." The woman made her way to her cash register. "Some legends say that if you were to help a mermaid back into the sea, she'd grant you a wish. Others say that even a mermaid's tear can cure illnesses. Imagine the restorative powers of an entire tail."

Marina placed the orange-tailed figurine on the counter and said, "I cannot listen to these lies."

"Wait!" The woman raised her arms, and then beckoned for Marina. "Come closer, dearie."

Marina didn't obey the command, instead remaining still and watching the shopkeeper hunch over as she leaned forward. The woman squinted as she stared at Marina's face. Across the room, Jill kept a wary eye on the situation and was ready to pounce if Marina needed rescuing.

"Your eyes, dearie, they are blue." The woman backed away and bowed her head. "Blue like the ocean, and blue with sadness. You have lost something quite dear to you."

"We'd better leave." Jill reached over and took Marina's arm to guide her toward the door. "This is all a bunch of mumbo-jumbo."

Marina was poised to leave with Jill until the woman added, "I see pain and loneliness in your eyes. I'm so sorry. But it's not a something that you've lost; it's a someone, isn't it, dearie?"

Trembling, Marina backed away, wondering how in all the waters could this land-dwelling old maid know that. Marina had been very young when her parents disappeared, so she didn't even have full recollections of them. All she remembered from her early childhood was joy and happiness and love, feelings she desperately wanted again. Though she was grateful to Lorelei and her father for taking her in, and though she knew that they cared for her and loved her in their own way, she knew it wasn't the same as the memory of being in her mother's arms.

"I need to leave," she said, running out the door and into the rain outside.

"Not too smart, Hailey." Jill went out after Marina.

Hailey brought the book of mermaid artwork to the cash register, took her debit card from her purse, and handed it and the book to the old woman. Putting on her bifocals that had been hanging on a chain around her neck, the woman searched the book cover for the price. While Hailey waited, she quickly filled out a mailing-list information card, leaving her address and phone number.

"Did you find everything you need, dearie?" asked the woman.

On the counter was the orange-tailed mermaid figurine that Marina had been holding. Hailey pushed it towards the woman and said, "This too, please."

~ Chapter Seventeen ~

"Meredith?" Lorelei had watched Meredith floating horizontally in place for some time before nudging her shoulder. "Wake up."

Meredith's tailfin twitched, and she shot forward. The sudden motion jolted her out of her daydream, and her arms flailed about, flipping her into a more vertical position until she steadied herself. "That was one of the strangest dreams I've ever had," she announced to no one in particular. "I was swimming with mermaids."

Then Lorelei swam past her, and Meredith recognized the green tail.

Looking down, Meredith saw her orange tail dangling in the water below her waist. "That's right; I keep forgetting. I am a mermaid." She yawned, stretching her arms and curling her fluke. "How long was I...?"

Meredith wasn't sure what term to use. The sensation was similar to sleeping in that she seemed to have been lying down, letting buoyancy keep her from sinking, but she wasn't sure how she had done it. She had vivid dreamlike recollections, but she also had a vague feeling that for at least some stretch of time, her eyes had remained open, and she had been able to see things going on around her. She also had heard sounds, though she couldn't respond to anything, as if her brain was somehow turned off for the time. Until Lorelei had woken her up, or had broken her trance, or ended her dormant period, or whatever it was called.

"You were resting," said Lorelei. "Much different than how I have seen humans do it. What is the word you use?"

"Sleep," replied Meredith. "How long was I...resting?"

Lorelei turned herself upright and looked toward the ocean's surface far above them. "The sun has passed twice."

"Two days? How could I have been sleeping, or resting, for two days?" As Meredith shouted, her tail flung itself back and forth. She didn't realize she was rising in the water because Lorelei was following alongside her. "Does that mean you just left me floating here? Why didn't you wake me?"

Lorelei reached out and put her hands on Meredith's shoulders, slowing and ultimately stopping their ascent. "The school dispersed upon reaching its destination. When we came here, you appeared quite weary. You needed to rest. You swam very far."

Meredith remembered swimming with the school—and she concluded they had been migrating somewhere—but she had no idea how far they had traveled, or how far they were from the island, or how deep they were in the water. For all she knew, she was somewhere in the middle of the Atlantic Ocean. There hadn't been any particular frame of reference to determine where they had been swimming, for she had been completely surrounded by the color blue. Darker blue was below her, and brighter blue above her, but there was nothing but blue ocean wherever she looked. And despite the significant pressure she knew from physics class should be exerted upon her, she barely felt the water around her, just like when standing on land, she only felt the air if it was windy or if she was moving. She wondered if growing accustomed to her environment was another effect of putting on the tail.

However, Meredith could clearly remember overexerting herself, so her muscular system wasn't fully accustomed to having to swim. She had felt somewhat confident after her swimming lesson with Lorelei, but all that confidence was shattered when she was with the school. The mermaids and mermen were so quick compared to her. She had tried to keep up but failed miserably. At least for the time being, she was alone with Lorelei, where she wouldn't feel inadequate much longer. She told herself to be thankful for the long rest, as her body clearly needed it, and it brought her two days closer to returning to her normal self.

"So where are we?" Meredith asked, noticing her current location for the first time.

"Home," answered Lorelei. "At least where my father, Marina, and I stay during the north season."

They were in an underwater cavern or grotto, jagged rock walls in all directions except at the cavern's mouth leading out into the open ocean. Meredith was surprised by the amount of light in the cavern, so she looked up. There were openings in the rock formation, but she believed they were too deep for much sunlight to reach them.

Then she realized the rocks were faintly glowing. As she swam to them, their glow became greener. She dragged a finger along the cavern wall but discovered it was coated with a slimy film. Some came off, so she squished it around in her hand. Some species of bioluminescent algae, she figured. "Fascinating," she muttered.

Lorelei swam up next to her. "It definitely flows."

"Where is my little maid?" asked a deep voice from the cavern's opening.

"Father!" Lorelei whisked off towards her father and embraced him.

Meredith stayed where she was and observed. Lorelei's father had spiky dark hair, a square jawline, broad shoulders, and a muscular chest. Like the majority of the other mermen Meredith had seen, with the exception of Barney, Lorelei's father was strikingly handsome. His tail was green, a darker shade than Lorelei's, and approximately a foot longer with a slightly less curvy fluke.

"I wish you had been able to scout ahead with me, Lorelei." He placed a fisherman's net full of items in a corner of the cavern while casually glancing towards Meredith. "But it is good to see that Marina has found her tail."

Lorelei said, "Father, the situation is more difficult than I first thought."

Her father didn't react to her comment. He swam about the cavern as if he hadn't heard what his daughter had said. "You would have enjoyed the adventure. There is a sunken vessel with all kinds of human items. If the school chooses to continue north, I will take you there."

"Father." Lorelei tried to keep up with her father's motion. "Marina did not find—"

"Continue north?" shouted Meredith as she swam over to Lorelei and her father. "As in, migrate further? I can't go too far away from the island."

Meredith's unfamiliar voice and speech patterns caught Lorelei's father's attention. He floated motionlessly as the unknown maid awkwardly swam toward him with her arms folded across her chest.

"I take it that *she* found Marina's tail instead," said the merman.

"Yes, Father." Lorelei took his hands in hers. "Please do not be angry, but Meredith here needs our help as much as Marina does. I brought her here because I did not know what else to do. She possesses Marina's tail."

"And I'd like to take it off as soon as possible," pleaded Meredith.

"So you are human?" He flicked his tail and started circling her.

Meredith gulped, terrified by the imposing figure looming around her, and then words started spilling out of her mouth. "I didn't know what it was. I'm not even sure why I put it on, except that I was curious. I'd never seen anything like before. Then I walked to the water, and I don't even know why I did because I don't particularly like the ocean." She gasped, afraid that she had just insulted them. "I'm sorry. I've always been a bad swimmer, so I haven't appreciated swimming until I had one of these, but I'd prefer my legs back."

Lorelei's father stopped circling but kept his watchful eye on Meredith.

During the silence that followed, Meredith could feel the

pressure of being underwater. Too deeply.

"Father?" asked Lorelei, her voice quavering.

His silence continued.

Then, he smiled broadly. "I have met many humans on land, but never in my years did I expect to meet one in the ocean. With a mer's tail, as well. You may call me Finn." He extended a hand towards Meredith. "This is the way humans greet each other, correct?"

Nodding, Meredith hesitantly reached forward until Finn squeezed her hand tightly and shook it briskly. She winced from the discomfort in her hand, but her pulse rate returned to normal.

"Welcome, Meredith," he said. "You may stay with us until the cycle is over."

"You are not angry, Father?" asked Lorelei.

"Why would I be? You are protecting a friend."

"Exchanging tails among mers is strictly forbidden. If we are caught harboring a human, the punishment must be severe."

"Then we must not get caught." Reaching for Lorelei, he pulled her closer to him and nestled her head under his arm. "This will have to be our greatest adventure yet."

Meredith and Lorelei explained the ruse they had created, including how Jill and Hailey were passing Marina off as Meredith back on land. They detailed Meredith's tight schedule: one lunar cycle stuck as a mermaid, but only a three-week vacation on the island. "You see?" Meredith said. "It's crucial that I leave as soon as possible, both for my own sake and for your family's safety."

"I am sorry, Meredith. There is no other way. You must wait until the next full moon." He swam away from them to the far side of the cavern.

Before Meredith could follow, Barney zipped through the cavern's entrance. "Can I help? Please? Can I?"

"Barney, you should not have come back." Lorelei swam to the mouth of the cavern and checked to see if other mers were outside. With the coast clear, she returned to the others.

"Why are you here?"

"I wanted to see your friend Meredith." He over-exaggerated his pronunciation of the name, and Meredith nodded to indicate he had said it correctly. "You said yesterday she was resting. She is awake now." Barney spun around to face Meredith. "Are you feeling better? Are you going to stay here until you can change back?"

Meredith didn't reply as she swam towards Finn. Still asking questions, Barney tried to follow, but Lorelei took him aside. Knowing he talked a lot to any mer that he came across, Lorelei carefully explained to him how important it was to keep Meredith's true identity a secret.

Sensing Meredith approaching, Finn rotated around and said, "I wish I could tell you something more hopeful."

"Could you at least tell me how the transformation works?" Meredith could tell from the puzzled look on his face that he didn't quite understand what she was asking. "What will I have to do that day to turn back? And if it's Marina's tail, then why did it work on me?"

"At sunrise on the morn of the full moon, you must be on land with as dry a tail as possible. Your legs will reappear. But you cannot try at any other time, for it will not work." His voice had grown much louder as if he was giving her a command. Then, he composed himself and continued, "You transformed because you touched the tail. Its power is overwhelming, especially at full moon. You were drawn to the water, to where the tail belonged."

"Are you telling me that I was compelled to put on the shimmery tail-skirt-thing and walk into the water because of the full moon?" asked Meredith.

"Yes," replied Finn. "The pull of the ocean is strongest then. That is why—"

"The tides!" Blinking rapidly, Meredith brought her hands to the sides of her head as she recalled simple astronomy lessons. "The moon affects the oceans, the tides. The highest tides occur when the sun and the moon are in line with Earth, as in a full moon. But not just at the full moon; also at the new moon."

"The new moon?" asked Barney. "What is that? The moon looks the same each cycle. How can it be new?"

"During a moon cycle, there are different phases." Meredith wished she had some paper or a chalkboard to draw diagrams. "We—humans—call the first phase the new moon. It occurs when the moon is on the side of Earth facing the sun."

"You are smart," said Barney. "Are all humans as smart as you?"

Lorelei whacked Barney in his backside with her fluke to stop him from talking.

Meredith continued her explanation, using her closed fists to represent the Sun, Earth, and Moon as she taught her lesson. "On those nights, because the moon is on the other side of Earth, it can't be seen in the night sky. But like the full moon, the tides are also at their highest at the new moon."

Finn nodded as if he understood. "You mean the night of no moon."

"New moon," repeated Meredith, correcting him.

"*No moon.*" This time, he spoke sternly. "You cannot transform at no moon. Only at sunrise on the morn of full moon. That is the rule."

"Forgive me, Sir." Meredith paused a moment to calm herself down, closing and reopening her eyes as she swallowed the lump that had formed in her throat. "I don't know your customs, but the new moon is approximately two weeks before the full moon. I'll be able to return to land before my parents can wonder what's happened to me, and Marina can return here where she belongs."

"No, she cannot. Not at no moon. I forbid it." He started swimming toward the cavern entrance.

"Father!" Lorelei swam quickly to catch up, waving Meredith and Barney to follow. "If what Meredith says is true, then I do not understand why she cannot try—"

"You must not try." He didn't turn back to look at her. "I have forbidden it."

"Excuse me." Meredith flapped her tail as forcefully as she could until she was beside Finn. "Human science says that there's little difference in the height of tides at full and new moon. I don't see why I can't at least test this hypothesis."

"It has been tried." He slowed down and turned himself vertically so he could address all three of the young mers, but specifically turning to his daughter. "Lorelei, when you first informed me that Marina had misplaced her tail, did I not tell you that the transformative power of a tail in its concealed form will wane?"

Lorelei nodded. "You did, father."

Wane, wondered Meredith, like the waning phases of the moon, where less and less of the moon is visible in the night sky until it isn't anymore. And after that, the new moon, when it isn't visible at all.

A somber look appeared on his face as Finn bowed his head. "Mers that transform on the morn of no moon cannot transform back. This is no guideline. Marina would lose her tail. Forever."

~ Chapter Eighteen ~

"She's been sulking all day, even more than usual," whispered Jill in the upstairs hallway after dinner that night. "No thanks to you, Hailey."

"Hey, that's not fair." Hailey was pouting. "That nice old woman knew stuff. I was just trying to help."

On the ride home from the shop, Hailey had asked Marina some questions about the old woman's comments about seeing pain and loss in Marina's eyes. The remarks sounded like a psychic reading into Marina's past, but Marina evaded answering. Hailey prodded until Jill convinced her to stop, but when they got back to the house, Marina closed herself in the guest room. She came downstairs only for dinner and then returned upstairs to her perch by the window that overlooked the beach.

"It's going to be a long month if she stays like this," said Jill. "Not how I wanted to spend my vacation. And what if she's so upset that at the end of the month, she and her friend do something bad to Meredith?"

"They won't, silly. Mermaids are nice, or at least all the mermaids we've met are."

"We've only met two. Don't you want to cheer her up?" Jill watched Hailey nod. "Good, because you're the one who's got to do it."

"Me? How?"

Jill cocked her head towards the closed door beside her—the door to Hailey's bedroom. It took Jill repeating the gesture a few more times before Hailey's puzzled expression turned into one of dread.

"Oh, no!" Hailey shook her head and stepped in front of the door, her hands clutching the door frame to block possible entry. "No, no, no, Jill. Don't ask me to show her!"

"I can't think of any other way."

Her head whirring back and forth, Hailey looked down and held one hand in front of her cousin's face. "T-T-T-H, Jill!"

Jill raised an eyebrow. "Talk to the hand? Seriously?"

"She can't see my room. It's fine that our family knows, and I'd be okay if Meredith saw it because she's your B-F-F, but what would a real mermaid think? You saw how she reacted to all the stuff in the shop."

"But did you see how she reacted when your mom brought it up?"

Hailey remembered back to that one moment, specifically the gleam in Marina's eye when she smiled. Maybe she had found someone who could understand. "Gimme five minutes to clean up in there, K?"

Hailey disappeared behind the door and gathered up a few small piles of dirty laundry scattered on the floor. Then she quickly made her bed, knowing that her mother would reprimand her for the household neatness violations. Once as satisfied as she could be, Hailey scanned the room for anything that could potentially offend Marina. The walls were fine, the bed was fine, the shelves were fine, the closed closet was fine, but the desk wasn't fine.

She gently lifted the heart-shaped glass dish from the desktop. Since first collecting the dry scales that Meredith had shed onto the hallway floor, Hailey had soaked them in salt water. As the bath water had returned the entire tail on Meredith to its original color, the submerged scales were glistening vibrant orange. She couldn't let Marina see them. Hailey already knew how Marina had reacted to posters and such, but there was no telling how she'd feel about seeing her own scales on display.

Wanting both to hide and preserve them, Hailey opened a desk drawer and carefully placed the dish inside, just in time to hear the four-knock signal from Jill out in the hallway.

"Coming," she called, slowly closing the desk drawer.

After one final look around the room, she took a deep breath and opened the door.

Standing on the other side was Marina, wearing a melancholy expression on her face. Jill stood behind her. "Here we are, Marina. Welcome to Hailey's mermaid shrine."

Hailey stepped aside so Marina could enter, and then there was silence while Marina studied the room. The walls, at least the parts that weren't covered with posters or picture frames, were painted bright pink. Like the shop, there were mermaid images and sculptures, but unlike the shop, some of them depicted mermaids in situations familiar to Marina. Her eyes focused on one of the larger statues, maybe a foot or so in length, showing a blue-tailed mermaid swimming alongside a pair of dolphins. She smiled, reminiscing about the times Lorelei had taken her on such an adventure. Pointing at it, she turned to the cousins, grinned, and said, "This is more like home."

"I'll leave you two alone," said Jill as she closed the door behind her. As she trudged back to the guest room, she decided to start her summer reading because Hailey and Marina were probably going to be occupied for a long time.

In Hailey's bedroom, Marina sat on the bed, its coverings adorned with mermaids. She tried to absorb everything Hailey was so enthusiastically telling her. Every mermaid in the room—whether she be an image, a figurine, a doll, or something else—had special significance to Hailey.

She recalled her first mermaid, a fashion doll fitted with a fabric tail. There was the porcelain mermaid Hailey received from her parents on her sixteenth birthday. Hanging on the wall was a caricature of Hailey, her over-exaggerated head giving way to a slender body with a lithe bright pink tail, drawn per her request by a street vendor among the touristy locations on the other side of the island. A clipping from the local newspaper, matted and framed and hanging on the wall, proclaimed that "Mermaid Hailey" led her swim team to an important victory.

"O-M-G! There's something I totally have to show you." Hailey pranced to the closet door and opened it a tiny crack, only to shut it back tightly. She turned to Marina and said, "Promise you won't laugh or freak out on me?"

After receiving an explanation from Hailey on what it meant to freak out, Marina made the requested promise. Then Hailey made Marina sit on the bed with her back to the closet so Hailey could surprise her with the mystery item. It was taking longer than it should merely to retrieve a single something when Marina asked, "May I look now?"

"Just a sec," replied Hailey, followed by a loud, strained breath. "Now you can look."

When Marina turned, Hailey was standing there wearing a mermaid costume. The top half was a nude-colored dancer's leotard, accessorized with seashells made of purple felt and detailed with glitter. The bottom half was a long skirt made of green sparkling sequined fabric, somewhat form-fitting down to Hailey's shins, where ruffles of stiff, crinkly taffeta flared out to look like a tailfin. Completing the look, Hailey wore a long red-haired wig with a starfish-shaped hair clip over her right ear.

She looked almost like Lorelei.

"It is exquisite," said Marina. "But what is it for?"

"Last Halloween," answered Hailey, who then had to explain the tradition of dressing up and trick-or-treating. "I sewed it myself."

Marina laughed. "I am surprised you chose green over pink."

"I made a pink tail the year before." Hailey took a second costume from the closet and showed it to Marina. It was only the bottom skirt, similarly constructed to the green one Hailey was wearing, but made from a much more elastic fabric. "It's a little too tight down at my ankles. I could barely walk in it, and my friends at the Halloween party were R-O-T-F-L at me."

"Would you mind if I tried it on?"

"O-M-G, really?!" Trying to control her giddiness, Hailey eagerly handed Marina the pink costume.

Marina ran her fingers over the smooth, stretchy fabric, noting that it did not feel much different than her own tail when in its concealed form. Although the costume was opaque, it was almost as shimmery as her translucent tail-skirt.

She pulled open the waistband and slid her legs inside the costume. Just as Hailey had stated, the tail end brought her ankles close together. As Marina snapped the waistband in place, she giggled, imagining Hailey wearing it and waddling like a penguin. She swung her legs as one onto the bed and stared down. Except for the color and the flimsy fluke, she almost looked like her usual self.

"I do not understand why you would make something like this."

"Because it's cool." Hailey sat on the other side of the bed, stretching out her costumed legs beside Marina's. "There are mermaid costumes out there that you can actually swim in. They've got, like, one-piece scuba flippers sewn into the fin. They're super expensive, and I've been saving up, but Mom said that if I got one, I could only use it in a pool and not the ocean, because of the waves and undertow and stuff. O-M G, Mom, I know how to swim."

"So your mother spoke truthfully at the library?"

"Yeah. I'd love to maybe work someday in an aquarium or water park and perform as a mermaid. How many little kids do you think would smile at me every day? Now *that* would be cool."

Remembering Hailey's first reaction to seeing Lorelei, Marina imagined Hailey as such a young child. A big part of that little child was still living inside Hailey, and Marina couldn't help but smile at Hailey's unconditional love for all merkind. "That is sweet," said Marina. "But why would you want to be something you are not?"

"Think about your friend Lorelei. Why does she take off her tail and try out legs every now and then?"

"She says it is all about the adventure, to experience something new, instead of simply dreaming it."

"Well, it's kinda the same for me, I guess. Out in the ocean, under the stars, and free." Hailey clicked off the light on her nightstand to reveal glow-in-the-dark star-shaped stickers shining on the ceiling. She lay back and rested her head on her pillow to stare up at the substitute nighttime sky. "Swimming like a mermaid would be, like, the best dream come true."

Noticing one sticker in the shape of a crescent moon, Marina lay back beside Hailey and sighed. "I have had the same dream these past few nights."

~ Chapter Nineteen ~

Meredith was drifting in the water in the cavern, her tail not flipping and her arms not moving. She hovered there, reeling from the unexpected news. There was a solution to her problem, but it wasn't a fair solution. Though she respected Finn's reason to forbid her from trying, she wanted to know more information. Maybe between her understanding of basic astronomy and Finn's understanding of mermaid culture, they could use the next two weeks to figure something out.

"Maybe there's a way that hasn't been discovered by your people." After Meredith had said it, she wondered if it was correct or appropriate to call them *people.*

"It is not possible," said Finn, slowly swimming away.

Meredith flicked her fluke and glided towards him. "We can do research. There must be somewhere you have the rules written down."

Finn turned around to face Meredith. "You do not understand. I made a vow when Marina was young to watch over her. Her tail must stay safe."

"Her tail is on me, in case you haven't noticed." Meredith swung herself around to emphasize her statement by showing the tail. "Am I really safe down here?"

"We will keep you safe." He looked over to his daughter and encouraged Meredith to do the same. They watched her nod her head in agreement, and then Finn continued, "I have seen a concealed tail not revert on the morn of no moon. With no scales to form, it vanishes into the air." Finn looked downward as if he were in mourning. "I have lost dear friends because of no moon."

"Really, Finn?" asked Barney, flitting around. "You know mers who have lost their tails? That is unfortunate. And that is also frightening."

Finn glanced at Lorelei and cocked his head toward the cavern's entrance. Understanding the cue, Lorelei took Barney's hand and swam outside with him to remind him about keeping the secret he had just learned.

Once he was sure Barney was out of the cavern and out of earshot, Finn whispered, "You have already experienced more about our kind than any other human. I suppose it is only fair since we have the ability to walk amongst your kind unnoticed. There are some mers, like myself, who believe we can learn tremendous things from one another."

"With all due respect, Finn, I agree, and learning is something I do well." Meredith clasped her hands together. "Please let me learn about this."

"I understand your desire to return home quickly, but I am asking you not to pursue this possibility any further."

Meredith looked into his sincere brown eyes and assured him she wouldn't ask him any longer out of respect for his lost friends, even though she still had several questions. She assumed there would be another mer she could ask, but she was afraid that her line of questioning would blow her cover. No one could know she was a human, so she'd have to play the part of an obedient mermaid for the time being.

She still couldn't fully accept that the skirt she had found and touched and put on would cease to exist simply because of a certain phase of the moon. The object was tangible matter, and she reminded herself that matter couldn't be created or destroyed. That was a law of physics, so it had to apply to the realm of mermaids also.

Finn had left the cavern, and Meredith started swimming after him to make that point, but he was much faster than she was and already too far ahead. It didn't matter, she told herself, for he'd tell her that she didn't understand the rules of the mer world. After a few days, she still didn't understand how the skirt had turned her into a mermaid in the first place.

She refused to accept magic or folklore as an answer, and none of it made any scientific sense to her. Yet there she was, stuck that way for almost a month, even though there was a way for her to change back earlier.

"Are you going to change back at no moon?" Barney swam over to Meredith now that she was outside of the cavern. "That would not be fair to Marina. You would not do that. Right, Meredith? You are too smart and kind to do something like that."

"Barney, she will not betray Marina," said Lorelei, who then turned to Meredith. "You will not betray her, correct?"

Meredith quickly answered no, and then swam past them. She couldn't quite remember how they had gotten to the cavern the other day, so she wasn't sure where the other mermaids and mermen in the school were located, but she figured she'd eventually find someone. She wasn't sure what she'd say if she found someone, but she hoped to figure it out along the way.

Lorelei caught up to her and swam beside her. "Meredith, do you even know where you are going?"

Barney flitted along Meredith's other side. "You just got here. Where would you go? We are all the mers you know, right? We will help you. What do you need? Where are you going?"

Meredith groaned, "I want someone who'll teach me all the rules about transforming back and forth."

"What do you want to know?" asked Barney. "I know all the mers in the school. I can take you to one who might know. I want to help you. Can I help you?"

Lorelei swam ahead of Meredith to cut in front of her. "If my father says there is no way, then there is no way. Let it float, Meredith, because I will not let you experiment with Marina's tail."

Tilting her head downward to swim underneath Lorelei, Meredith said, "I wouldn't do something like that. I just want to know about the new moon."

"You mean *no moon*." Barney followed after Meredith.

"You want to know about no moon."

They continued forward, and Barney led the way until Meredith started swimming beside him. He was telling Meredith what little he knew about the rules of mer transformations, which wasn't anything she hadn't already learned from Lorelei and Finn. Barney admitted that he had heard stories from his grandparents about mers that lost their tails, but he never knew what could cause it. Even thinking about Finn's lost friends made him shudder in fear.

Even though she couldn't get a word in edgewise, Meredith enjoyed listening to him. He reminded her of a few boys from her advanced courses at school, so there was something familiar and comfortable about his behavior. While Meredith got the impression that Lorelei felt obligated to look after her, it was Barney's choice to get to know her and to help her. She figured that made him her first friend under the sea.

Listening but not adding anything to the conversation, Lorelei was grateful she had never dared to disobey her father when it came to transforming. She always believed the stories were told to keep mers from taking on legs at times other than the full moon, and she was shocked to learn that her father had friends who had lost their tails. He had never mentioned them before, so she wondered who they were. Mers left the school occasionally, either to join new schools or to start their own. Mers passed away, either from old age or by falling ill, like Lorelei's mother had. There were also tragic stories of mers being left behind when the school moved on, or being lost in storms, or disappearing without explanation like Marina's parents. But Lorelei had never heard of mers who were trapped as humans forever.

They passed by an undersea rock formation, unable to see a small ledge high up on its opposite side where Calliope and her two friends were sitting with their purple tails dangling below them. Calliope was sticking a starfish to her dark hair above her right ear when one of her friends pointed out Barney, Meredith, and Lorelei swimming by below them.

Then the three of them snickered.

"I do not understand why she has short hair," said the red-haired maid. "It is not beautiful at all."

Calliope's blonde-haired friend pointed at Meredith's blue tankini top. "And she is still wearing that human covering. Lorelei also has a fascination with human stuff. How strange."

"Would you look at that?" Calliope leaned forward, studying the order in which they were swimming. "Lorelei is following the new mer instead of leading. Come on, maids, let us go say hello to them."

The three mermaids dove off the ledge and silently swam towards the others. As they approached from above and behind, they overheard Barney talking about mers transforming on the day of no moon and losing their tails.

"Are you thinking of leaving us so soon?" asked Calliope, zipping forward and then snaking around in front of Meredith.

Upon hearing Calliope's voice, Barney instantly darted away but called back, "I'll catch up with you later, Meredith."

"You have just joined our school." Calliope slowly sank down in front of Meredith, who had stopped and curled her tail behind her into a U-shape. "Why would you want to leave at no moon? Unless you want to be one of those filthy humans." She pulled on one of the shoulder straps to Meredith's tankini. "Looks like you are prepared to be one."

Before Lorelei could insist that Meredith would not be leaving the school at no moon, Meredith spoke up. "I'm only asking questions. Is there something wrong with that?"

"Would you listen to that, maids?" Calliope turned to her friends, who had lined up behind her. "This orange-tail has some shark bite." After the girls behind her snickered, Calliope glanced at Lorelei. "She may have a tail like Marina's, but unlike your usual silent shadow, this one speaks up for herself."

"Do not insult Marina," said Lorelei as she swished forward, but she was stopped by Meredith extending an arm to her side.

Feigning fear, Calliope put her hand to her mouth. "This is new, maids. Lorelei is the shadow now."

Calliope and her cohorts turned to each other and laughed. Meredith twisted around to calm Lorelei, whose face had turned red.

"The only reason a mer would transform at no moon would be if they were being banished for openly breaking our rules." Calliope swam around to Meredith's side in order to look her in the eyes. "As leader of the school, my father issues those kinds of punishment. I could speak with him if you feel you do not belong."

Nervous from Calliope's insinuation, Meredith could feel her palms getting all clammy. "No, we're fine here, Calliope," she said. "I was only curious."

"You speak strangely, not like a true mer." Calliope flicked her tail and started swimming away, her two friends slightly ahead of her, but then she turned around. "And remember what they say, Meredith. Curiosity killed the catfish."

With a strong flip of her tail, Calliope shot forward and ahead of her friends. The thrust of her tail sent bubbles backwards into Meredith's face, distracting her from noticing Lorelei heading off in the opposite direction back to the cavern. As Meredith watched Calliope and her entourage disappearing into the distance, she said, "You were right, Lorelei. She *can* be a blowfish."

When no answer came, Meredith turned and realized that Lorelei had also left her. She lunged forward and started flapping her fluke, but she couldn't catch up to the speedy Lorelei, so Meredith called to get her attention.

Though she heard Meredith's call, Lorelei didn't reply. Maintaining a constant distance between herself and Meredith, she continued forward until they arrived at the cavern.

"I advised you not to make waves," said Lorelei. "But you could not let it float."

Meredith swam over to her and said, "I'm sorry, but she

was being mean to us. Back on land, I would never stand up to someone like that. I don't know what came over me."

"Now Calliope will be watching you, and that is not a good thing. I would recommend no further standing. Down here, it is sink or swim."

~ Chapter Twenty ~

Jill was instantly jolted out of bed when the alarm clock blared. Barely conscious enough to know that she didn't want to wake Aunt Susan, she swatted at the clock and switched it off. She swung her long legs over the edge of the bed and sat hunched over with her mane of dark hair hanging over her face. Yawning, she reached under her hair to rub the sleep out of her eyes, but she knew it would do no use. It was five o'clock in the morning, which was far too early to be awake during her summer vacation.

She peered through her hair and over to the other bed. As had been the case all week long when Jill awoke, Marina wasn't there, and the bed had already been made. She assumed Marina was already down on the beach and waiting for sunrise. Jill pushed back her hair and lifted her heavy eyelids as widely as she could, but when she looked out the window at the beach, Marina wasn't to be found. And Marina's bed wasn't just already made; it appeared as if it hadn't been slept in at all.

Jill wasn't surprised. Marina and Hailey had spent the past few nights together talking in Hailey's room long after Jill had fallen asleep. That was how Jill expected her vacation with Meredith would have been—two best friends staying up late every night chatting and gossiping—but Meredith had been somewhere else.

But this was the morning she'd see Meredith again. The plan was to meet at sunrise on the morning of the last quarter phase of the moon. Why the mermaids were so obsessed with sunrise and moon phases, she didn't understand, but the reason didn't matter simply because she would get to spend a little time with Meredith.

Expecting to have to spend that time with Meredith in the water to hide her tail, Jill changed into a swimsuit worn under her beach robe. Then she went to find the others.

Shortly after Jill lightly tapped Hailey's door four times, it opened its usual small force-of-habit amount. Hailey's eyes struggled to stay open as well, and her hair was somewhat flattened, but her smile indicated that she was ready to spend time with mermaids.

"Did Marina sleep in your room again last night?" asked Jill, groggily.

"Again?" Hailey yawned and stretched her arms behind her. "She's never slept in here. We talk, and then she goes off to bed."

"Well, if she's not sleeping in your room, and I don't think she sleeps in the guest room with me anymore, then where does she—?"

The bathroom door opened. Out walked Marina, wrapped in a large beach towel, but her exposed legs, shoulders, arms, face, and hair were all still dripping wet. "Good morn," she said, avoiding looking up to make eye contact with Jill and Hailey before scampering into the guest room.

After watching the guest room door close, Jill turned toward the bathroom and then towards Hailey. "You don't think she…? In there…?"

Hailey peered through the open door. "I-D-K. Maybe it makes her think of home, right?"

"But shouldn't we tell her that it's not safe to—?"

Jill's concerns were interrupted by the last gurgle of water emptying down the bathtub drain.

Moments before the sun rose, the three of them were sitting on the beach watching the eastern horizon. Since the rainy day at the start of the week, the days had progressively gotten sunnier, warmer, and more humid, with that day predicted to be the hottest of the week. The morning temperature was already at a sticky seventy-five degrees, and

Jill could feel her hair frizzing out, so she looked forward to dunking it in the cold water when Meredith arrived.

As soon as the first burst of sunlight appeared, the girls turned their attention southward to the ocean. On cue, two heads appeared in the distant water followed by two pairs of shoulders and two waving arms. Hailey, Jill, and Marina waved back and then watched as the two heads dove forward and disappeared under the water's surface.

Lorelei reappeared in the shallow water first, and Marina ran out to embrace her friend. "Lore, I have missed you so much," she said, waist-deep in water and not caring that the plaid skirt she had borrowed from Hailey was getting drenched.

"Have they been treating you well?" asked Lorelei.

As Marina happily started to explain Jill's expertise at hiding her true identity and Hailey's adoration for all things mer, Meredith surfaced.

Expecting that Meredith and Lorelei would have arrived together, Jill had already been waiting in the water. The delay had frustrated her, but once Meredith was floating before her, she was too happy to dwell upon it.

"Sorry," said Meredith, taking a big gasp of fresh air, her first above the surface in a week. "My swimming is improving, but I'm nowhere near as fast as she is."

"Yeah, not a surprise." Jill smirked. "After all, she's been a fish longer than you have."

"Jill, it's more than being a fish." Meredith entered into scientific lecture mode. "Fish are further down the food chain. We're an undiscovered new species. If I were naming us, using the standard binomial nomenclature, I'd replace the *sapiens* with *aquaticus*. What do you think?"

Jill had smiled upon seeing the passion in Meredith's eyes for her favorite subject. But her smile turned into a straight-mouthed stare when Meredith included herself among the mermaids. "I think you know best," Jill finally replied.

"Four-one-one, all peeps and mer-peeps," said Hailey from the shore, glancing over at her neighbor's house. "We don't want Mr. Dobbins spotting us, so let's go someplace else."

Farther up the shoreline in the direction away from Mr. Dobbins's house, the beach narrowed until only the wall of rocks remained. There were no houses in the immediate vicinity there, and the water's edge curved inward, closer to the main road. It was still early in the morning, so there were scattered sounds of occasional passing cars, whizzing too fast for anyone to see them through the trees and bushes that lined the roadway.

Having no other option but swimming there, Lorelei arrived first, followed closely behind by Meredith. Taking long strides from one rock to the next rock, Jill made her way over to the secluded area and looked back at the others. Hailey was assisting Marina, who, though adept at walking with her legs, had never had to navigate such jagged terrain, and was taking each step cautiously.

Hailey glanced at Lorelei and Meredith floating in the approximate center of the area of calm water. "Cool, it's like our own little private mermaid lagoon."

Lorelei rolled her tailfin and swam towards the low rock where Marina sat down. Keeping her tail afloat just under the surface, she rested her elbows on the rock and looked up at Hailey, who was crouched down behind Marina. "Hailey," said Lorelei, "Marina tells me that you dream of swimming like a mer."

Hailey nodded sheepishly. "Well, yeah. Since I was, like, little."

"She also tells me you are a champion swimmer. Do you think you could keep up with me?" Lorelei smiled invitingly.

"Like a race? You're on." Hailey tossed her beach robe and towel onto the rocks behind her and then shrieked to herself, "O-M-G, I'm gonna go swimming with a mermaid!"

"I have never swum alongside a human before," said Lorelei, who then glanced toward Meredith and decided to correct herself. "Alongside one with legs. It will be a new experience for both of us, sink or swim."

"Oh, I'm gonna swim!" Hailey carefully made her way to a different rock, one still at the water's edge, but slightly higher than the one she was on with Marina. She turned to Jill, who was already standing shoulder-deep in the water with Meredith. "Hey, me and Lorelei are gonna have a race!"

Jill watched Meredith calmly bobbing up and down with the gentle waves. Baffled by the lack of an immediate response from Meredith, Jill called back, "Lorelei *and I.*"

Waving an arm in a *whatever* gesture at Jill, Hailey looked down into the water. There weren't any rocks directly below, and it appeared deep enough to use the rock as a diver's block. She wished she had brought her swim goggles and had worn her team swimsuit instead of the hot pink bikini, but she told herself that she didn't wake up that morning expecting to race a mermaid.

Once they decided how far out to swim, Marina provided the signal for them to go, and Hailey dove in. She had an early lead until Lorelei started vigorously flipping her fluke.

"Is she going to be all right out there?" Jill asked Meredith.

"The tides are calm, and Hailey's a strong swimmer, right?" Meredith waited for Jill to nod. "If we see any sign of trouble, then I'll swim out there and help Lorelei bring her back. Let it float."

"Let it float? Are you listening to yourself, Merri? You don't sound like yourself."

"I'm not completely myself right now, Jill. I've got one of these." Meredith swam around Jill, jokingly whacking Jill's hip with her tailfin.

"And I guess you know how to use it." Jill laughed and splashed Meredith. "How are you holding up?"

"Just fine." Meredith flipped onto her back and entered into a slow backstroke.

Jill knew that when Meredith looked away while answering a question, she was trying to evade the question. And Jill knew Meredith was evading the obvious truth that she wasn't *fine*. Barely recognizing her best friend, Jill watched the elegance of the mermaid's motion as the light from the sun well above the horizon gave the scales of her tail a golden glow. But it definitely wasn't Meredith.

Jill looked over at Marina, smiling and laughing as she watched Hailey frolic with a mermaid. Suddenly she seemed accustomed to having legs. Why wasn't she pining away for her tail, Jill wondered, now that it was floating there right in front of her.

When Jill looked back at Meredith, it was obvious that the tail had not only improved Meredith's swimming abilities but also her overall confidence in the water. Jill could count the previous times she had seen Meredith swim on one hand— much less than one hand.

And then there was Meredith's false calmness; even before tests where Jill was certain Meredith knew all the answers, she had seen Meredith's irrational anxiety, fearing she'd bomb some of the questions. Instead, Meredith was being aloof and carefree like the other mermaids—Marina, Lorelei, and swim-team-champ Hailey—were.

This wasn't Meredith, thought Jill, but a shell with parts of the real Meredith floating somewhere inside.

Before Meredith could drift further away, Jill reached forward and grabbed Meredith at the tapered end of her tail, right where her ankles should have been.

"Hey!" Meredith bent at her waist, which sunk. Raising her fluke above the water's surface, she flapped it against Jill's arms to get her to let go. "What gives?"

"I know you better than anyone, so I know when you're lying." After letting go of the slimy scales, Jill pulled her arms back quickly as Meredith's fluke hit the surface and splashed water in her face.

"You want the truth?" Meredith swam forward and turned her tail until it curled behind her. Her upper body had settled into a vertical floating position such that she was face-to-face with Jill. "Down there, I feel like I'm losing myself. Certain things I do, I have no idea how I'm doing them. I'm acting on aquatic instincts that I shouldn't have. I've been underwater for a week, and do you know why my skin's not wrinkled like a prune? Do you know how I breathe and eat down there?" Meredith paused, pretending to wait for Jill to answer. "Good, because I don't know either. Apparently, I breathe in and swallow water, and my lungs know how to take in the dissolved oxygen, and my stomach digests plankton and who knows what else."

"At least you're breathing and eating," said Jill in her best attempt to sound optimistic. "I was worried about that."

"But I don't know *how* I'm doing it. Up here, I can describe specific bodily functions and chemical reactions, but down there, I can't. I keep looking for scientific explanations because *that's who I am*, and I don't want to forget that part of me. But what if it starts sinking away?" Meredith wiped salty droplets away from her eyes. Whether they were tears or ocean water, she didn't care. "I'm terrified that after spending a month down there, I won't be the same person I was up here."

Jill pushed herself through the water until she was close enough to wrap her arms around Meredith. "I won't forget who you are up here." She let Meredith's head rest against her shoulder.

Suddenly, Jill felt something strange and slimy brush against the backs of her knees. Meredith's tail was hugging her in return, and she wondered if the action was involuntary or not. "We've been researching up here," said Jill. "If there's a way to turn you back sooner, we'll find it, Merri."

Meredith bit her bottom lip, internally debating whether to reveal the new moon information she had. She glanced at the rock where Marina was standing and joyfully applauding for Lorelei and Hailey further out in the water.

Keeping her gaze away from Jill, Meredith whispered, "What if I've already learned a way?" Then she wiped away the tears that started dripping down her cheeks.

~ Chapter Twenty-One ~

"What do you mean you've already found a way?" Jill pulled out of the hug, letting Meredith's tail slide away from her legs.

"Forget it." Meredith started to swim away. "Forget I even mentioned it."

Jill lunged forward and grabbed onto Meredith's tail once again.

Unable to escape, Meredith twisted around and splashed water towards Jill. "Will you please stop doing that?"

"You can't drop a bombshell like that and think you can swim away."

Meredith groaned, knowing Jill wasn't going to let go—both of the subject and her tail—until she explained. Left with no other option, Meredith revealed everything she knew about transforming at sunrise on the day of the new moon. Overjoyed that Meredith could return on time, Jill loosened her grip on her friend's tail, but then Meredith made it clear that the process was irreversible and that Marina wouldn't be able to return to the ocean.

"What right do I have to change Marina's life forever?" asked Meredith as she slithered away.

"You believe all that?" Jill folded her arms in front of her. "Because for all you know, it's just some old fish tale."

"Whether or not I believe it, Lorelei's father seemed pretty adamant about not trying it."

"This doesn't sound like the straight-A science-brain Meredith I know." Jill crossed her arms in front of her, still visible below the water's surface. "*That* Meredith would immediately start gathering data to test her theory—"

"Hypothesis," corrected Meredith.

"Whatever. Point is that we have a week to figure this out. We have a lead, something to go on." Jill turned to the others in time to see the race still going on, with Marina standing on the rock, cheering and smiling. "You never know, someone may change her mind about things by then."

On the outward leg of their race, Lorelei had stayed a tail's length ahead of Hailey, knowing full well that Hailey's legs were no match for her tail. Though Hailey had appreciated the gesture, she requested that Lorelei swim as fast as she could on the return trip. As soon as they turned around, Lorelei took off, her tailfin flipping up and down mightily. After a few strokes, Hailey realized she wouldn't catch up and conceded the race, stopping to admire the strength and gracefulness of Lorelei's swimming. Watching the green fluke go, Hailey wished she had her camera or phone with her to preserve the wonderful memory forever. If swimming like a mermaid had been Hailey's dream, swimming with one would substitute for that unrealized dream well enough.

"You kicked the pants off me," said Hailey when she had finally reached the rock. "That was totally awesome!"

"You swim fairly well," said Lorelei, sitting on a submerged rock such that her full tail remained underwater. She smirked at Hailey. "For a maid with legs, that is."

Hailey reached up for Marina's hand and climbed onto the lower rock, and then sat at the edge, dangling her feet into the water. "Seriously, I could never kick the pants off you." Hailey burst into giggles. "Not that you could ever really wear pants, L-O-L." She glanced to her side, where Marina was standing beside her on the rock. "Been trying to get Marina here to try pants, but she ain't going for it. I think she likes showing off those shapely legs of hers."

"That is embarrassing, Hailey." Marina blushed.

Lorelei smiled up at Hailey sitting on the adjacent rock. "It is reassuring to see that Marina has found someone like you to look over her during this cycle."

"And you can count on me till the full moon." Hailey

stood and gave Lorelei a military salute. "F-Y-I, we don't have it all figured out yet, but we will."

"What if you could switch back sooner?" Jill was up on the rocks, climbing over to Hailey and Marina.

Meredith was swimming towards them. "Jill, don't."

But Meredith was too late, and Jill was already explaining. "There's a way for Meredith to take off the tail at the new moon."

Lorelei's head immediately turned towards Meredith, who could feel the anger in Lorelei's stare piercing through her like shark's teeth.

The new moon, wondered Marina. The concept sounded strangely familiar to her, yet she was unable to place what she had remembered about it. She looked down at the orange tail in the water and smiled, imagining herself down there with it.

"Marina, there will be no transformation at no moon," said Lorelei, still looking at Meredith. "Your tail would disappear."

The expression of hope on Marina's face was suddenly drowned with sorrow. She looked from Lorelei to Meredith and then to Jill. Squinting at Jill and shaking her head, Marina then turned and climbed haphazardly to the beach after the rocks.

"Marina," called Lorelei. Upon hearing a response that consisted of nothing but sobbing, she turned to Hailey. "You will take care of her?"

After Hailey nodded to Lorelei, she turned to her cousin. "W-T-H, Jill? Why'd you have to be so catty?" Then Hailey followed after Marina.

Lorelei swam to Meredith and said, "I am disappointed in you." Then she ducked under the surface and swam out to sea.

"I've got to go, Jill," said Meredith, staring out at the ocean in the direction Lorelei had swum. "I need to follow her back."

"Promise me something, Merri." Jill stood on the rock and pointed down at her friend. "Promise me you'll come back here—right here at these rocks—the night before the new moon. Just in case it's the only way."

Hoping that by then it wouldn't be the only way, and hoping that Lorelei hadn't gotten too far ahead, Meredith looked over her shoulder at Jill and nodded. "I promise."

Then they parted company. Jill quickly but carefully climbed over the rocks to the start of the sandy beach beyond, and Meredith plunged under the water and swiftly swam to find Lorelei.

Vaguely recalling how she had gotten to Hailey's beach, Meredith swam in what she thought was the general direction back to Lorelei and her father's cavern. As she got deeper and passed by a variety of different species of fish and other aquatic life, she couldn't see Lorelei anywhere. She knew Lorelei had every reason to be angry and storm off, but she couldn't be held accountable for Jill's actions. And she had confided in Jill because they were best friends, and it was all an effort to discover some way to get her back on legs and Marina back in the tail as soon as possible.

Being alone in the ocean didn't frighten her as much as she expected it would. The tail was Marina's, so Meredith believed she wouldn't be abandoned in the middle of the ocean. Lorelei would have to be somewhere nearby keeping an eye on her best friend's tail. Meredith still swam as quickly as possible, hoping to find Lorelei, but she allowed her visual memory and whatever mermaid instincts she had to guide her journey.

She could tell she was swimming faster than she had been a week ago. Practice makes perfect, she reminded herself, and at least she still had that human part of her that desired to be the best at things she did. Flapping her tail more briskly, she could feel herself accelerate, the water flowing by her much faster than before. Maybe by the end of her time as a mer, she would be swimming as quickly as others in the school.

From a far distance away, Meredith instantly identified Lorelei from the long red hair trailing behind her and the V-shaped pattern of her green scales. Had her new instincts allowed her to recognize other mers by their tails? When she first arrived at the school, mers simply swam by her and assumed she was Marina. Though Meredith was grateful many others hadn't looked closely enough to discover the truth, she wondered if Marina had always been ignored because of the unique color of her tail.

Meredith realized Lorelei had gotten further away. Thinking too much about other things slowed down her swimming, so she called, "I'm sorry. I didn't think Jill was going to say anything."

Lorelei slowed down to let Meredith catch up, but she didn't turn back to look at Meredith while she said, "If your friend is any indication, maybe the legends about humans being unkind are true. I am grateful Marina is with someone as kind and caring as Hailey."

"Hey, you don't know Jill, so don't judge her. She was looking out for me the same way you're looking out for Marina."

"But to suggest that Marina give up her—"

"It wasn't meant like that." Meredith was furiously flapping to keep up. "We may be able to find a way to reverse this if everyone knows all the information."

Lorelei accelerated, but then swerved around to block Meredith's path. She floated vertically in place and looked down into Meredith's eyes. "Why do you believe you must know it all? Can you not merely accept my father's wisdom without question?"

Meredith hovered, stunned such that she seemed unable to answer.

Feeling like she had made her point, Lorelei swam into a backflip and then twisted herself stomach-down to head back for the cavern. She swam considerably slower than her full speed so Meredith, in Marina's orange tail that Lorelei had vowed to protect, wouldn't get lost in the ocean. But neither of them spoke for the rest of the journey.

On land, Hailey had managed to console Marina. They sat on the beach for a few hours while Jill kept her distance on the deck, knowing they were upset with her. She knew it would blow over with Hailey as most little tiffs between them over the years typically did. Hopefully, Marina would realize that she was throwing it out there as a springboard to start brainstorming new ideas and not to suggest Marina live on land for the rest of her life.

A car pulled into the gravel driveway, so Jill stood and peered around the corner of the house. The navy blue SUV belonged to her Uncle Greg, finally home from his business trip. She could greet him later, instead choosing to sprint to the beach to tell Hailey her father was home and to warn Marina that it was time for an encore performance of her introduction as Meredith.

They all went back to the house and into the kitchen. Uncle Greg was already unloading bags of groceries into the fridge, freezer, and cabinets. Aunt Susan was helping him, and when she noticed the girls enter, she introduced him to "Meredith."

He was a tall man with a well-groomed beard and mustache. After firmly shaking Marina's hand, he said, "So, Meredith, how do like the island so far?"

Marina replied, "It is very different than home."

Hailey and Marina giggled while Jill tried to roll her eyes without anyone catching her.

"They've been like this for the past few days," said Susan. "Teenage girls and their private jokes that I simply don't get."

"Oh, honey, I'm sure you were like that when you were their age." He strolled over to his wife and kissed her on the forehead. "Now, girls, after the ferry, I stopped off to get barbecue supplies. And because Fourth of July wouldn't be the same without him, I brought a surprise guest along from the mainland."

Jill and Hailey turned to each other, their eyes bulging out in fear. Then they heard a familiar voice. "Hi Hailey, Hi Sis."

Standing in the doorway between the kitchen and the dining room was Jill's brother Jeff, all six-foot-two of him. His short brown hair was slightly unkempt from the windy ferry ride, and his blue tee shirt hinted at a muscular frame.

Across the room from him stood his aunt and uncle, his cousin Hailey, and his sister, but he didn't recognize the other girl. Happy to soon be meeting her, he smiled at her until he had gotten her to smile back at him.

"How silly of me not to introduce you, Jeff," said Aunt Susan, slyly and curiously noticing the eye contact and smiles between the two teens. "But I would have thought you already knew Meredith."

"Yeah, I know Meredith," said Jeff, in a slow, confused tone of voice. His sister Jill had been friends with Meredith for years, and he was positive without a doubt that the pretty blonde standing between Jill and Hailey was *not* Meredith.

~ Chapter Twenty-Two ~

"Uh, Hailey, why don't you and *Meredith* go upstairs?" said Jill, putting extra emphasis on her friend's name. "And I'll take Jeff outside to find out what he's doing here."

It took a moment for Hailey to process Jill's request, but she ushered Marina out of the room and toward the stairway while Jill grabbed her brother's arm and pulled him through the sliding door to the back deck. As Jeff and Marina passed each other, they were still smiling. "Catch you later, *Meredith*," he said, echoing Jill's way of saying the name.

Outside, after making sure that Aunt Susan and Uncle Greg weren't watching, Jill punched her brother in the arm. "What are you doing here?"

Jeff winced and started rubbing the pain out of his arm. "Sis, what the heck was that for?"

"You're not supposed to be here," muttered Jill, pacing around the deck and running her hands through her frizzed-out hair.

"I took the weekend off. Mom said you'd be here with Meredith." Jeff glanced upward at the open window to the guest room, figuring that was where Jill and her mystery friend were staying. "And that babe is not your smarty-pants friend Meredith."

"You don't call girls that!" Jill punched him again, harder, in the same spot she had the first time.

The already bruised arm stung, and Jeff jumped back. "If you keep doing that, I'll go tell Aunt Susan something's up."

To prevent her potential defeat, Jill ran ahead of him and blocked the sliding door. "You're right. I'm sorry. She's not

Meredith."

Jeff tilted his head to one side and gave Jill a *no-kidding* kind of look.

"Jeff, swear to me you won't tell anyone." While Jill waited for him to respond, her brain was already in overdrive trying to create an explanation. The cover story for Aunt Susan was significantly easier since she didn't know Meredith, but Jeff did. The whole truth about Marina was unfathomable, and Jeff probably wouldn't believe her anyway. The less he knew about the existence of mermaids, the better for everyone involved.

"Consider me intrigued," said Jeff. "Who is she?"

After a long, deep breath, Jill started improvising without a net. "She's this girl that I met on the ferry. She's traveling alone for the summer before she goes off to college, always wanted to come out to the island but doesn't have the money to afford a hotel room. Her name's not really Meredith. The real Meredith is back home. Mom dropped us off at the ferry and then left, and Merri had another friend come get her." She paused a moment, both for air and to devise a plausible reason Meredith would stay at home. "Yeah, she doesn't swim, you know that, right? She wanted peace and quiet to do her summer reading and other summer homework project things." She looked at Jeff, who nodded his head as if he believed that part of the explanation—the part that contained the most truth. "Merri's parents are away, and they didn't want her staying home alone, but she knew she'd be fine, so she's there. You can't tell anyone because Merri would get in deep trouble. And Aunt Susan and Uncle Greg would never let us take in a perfect stranger, so Hailey and I could get in trouble, too."

"So, you're passing this girl off as Meredith? Pretty clever of you, Sis. You always were good at making stuff up."

She wondered if he was convinced or commending her for making up most of the explanation, but then she decided she didn't care either way. The story was out there, and she hoped he'd play along.

"Secret's safe with me, Sis." Jeff patted Jill's arm in the same place she had hit his. "I'll even call her Meredith."

Only when Jill sighed in relief did she realize that all her muscles had tensed, her hands had clenched into fists, her shoulders had risen, and she had been standing on tiptoes. As she finally sank back down to a relaxed position, Jeff appeared to grow before her.

Jeff smirked. "But you'll have to get me her digits."

Trying not to burst into laughter, Jill contemplated how long distance that phone call would be.

Upstairs, Hailey had brought Marina to the guest room and closed the door behind them. "I do not understand," said Marina. "All I want to do is smile and look at him again."

Hailey squealed with glee. "Sounds like you're crushing on him."

"Why would I want to crush him? That would hurt him."

"L-O-L, you are too cute." Hailey took Marina's hands. "Let me give you some pointers on how to talk to guys. Smile at him a lot. Compliment him a lot. And definitely laugh at his jokes, a lot, even if you don't get them."

While Hailey gave examples for all her flirting tips, voices were occasionally heard from the deck below the guest room's window. Whenever she heard Jeff's voice, Marina's attention was immediately drawn to the window, and Hailey had to stop her from looking outside. "Don't make it *that* obvious," said Hailey, then continuing with her lessons.

Eventually, they all joined each other in the kitchen, and Uncle Greg described all the food he was going to barbecue that afternoon: steak, marinated chicken wings, corn on the cob, burgers, and hot dogs. Jeff asked if the volleyball net was still in the shed, to which Uncle Greg nodded, so he went outside to get it and set it up. Jill suggested the girls go change, especially since she and Hailey were still wearing swimsuits under their beach robes, but Jill used the time upstairs primarily as an opportunity to tell them the cover story she had told Jeff.

Jill and Hailey changed into tees and shorts, and they tried to convince Marina to do the same, but she refused and insisted on staying in the plaid skirt. After rummaging through her wardrobe, Hailey found a pale blue button-down that coordinated well enough with the skirt. Despite Jill's protests, Hailey tied the shirt at Marina's waist, showing off her bellybutton.

When they finally came out onto the beach, Jeff had the volleyball net almost assembled. His shirt had been removed and was hanging on the deck's railing, and beads of perspiration glistened on his bare chest in the humid sunlight.

"O-M-G," said Hailey, lowering her sunglasses as she noticed Jeff's muscles. "Where did Jeff get that six pack?"

Jill rolled her eyes. "Hailey, you do realize he's your cousin."

"Yeah, I know that." Hailey shuddered, her full body shaking as if she had stepped upon hot coals. "Eww! Don't be gross."

Marina leaned forward with her forearms crossed and resting on the railing, and she smiled, her head slightly tilted to one side. When Jeff turned to them, he saw her, smiled back, and waved.

Jill noticed that their attraction to each other was undeniable, but she wasn't sure if she should discourage them or allow things to play out in the summer-loving way she had described to Meredith on the ferry ride over. Still, Jill wondered if Jeff would have reacted the same way if he knew the girl he was smiling at was half fish. Maybe telling him the truth would be the ultimate prank to play on her big brother.

"Usually Hailey and Uncle Greg take on you and me, Sis," said Jeff, strolling up the footbridge. "But since he's busy with the food, how 'bout two-on-two: you and Hailey against me and Meredith?" He had timed it perfectly so that he had reached the yard and was gazing at Marina at the same moment he playfully uttered her alias.

After putting on sunscreen, they made their way to the volleyball net on the beach. "I have never played before," said Marina.

"Just follow my lead." Jeff winked at her. "I could take them both by myself. They may both be tall, but Jill's kinda clumsy at sports. You should see how bad she is at basketball."

Not understanding what Jeff meant by basketball, but remembering Hailey's advice, Marina giggled at the supposed joke.

Jill, accustomed to the ribbing from her brother, shouted back, "Yeah, well you're going down, Jefferson."

Jeff cringed at her usage of his full first name. "No, you're going down, Jillybean!"

First serve was won by Jill in a game of rock-paper-scissors against Jeff. In an effort to be nice to the mermaid rookie, Hailey served the ball away from Marina, but barely over the net and directly in front of Jeff. He charged the net and jumped, spiking the ball to the sand on the other side of the net.

Marina's eyes widened as she watched the fluidity of Jeff's motion. For her whole life, she had been so easily and passively supported by water all around her. Even for the week or so on land, she had felt stuck, pulled down by forces she didn't understand. But then she watched Jeff take off from the ground, his feet in the air, and she felt uplifted. Tension left her shoulders, and she could feel her spirits, along with her heart, rising.

"W-T-H, Jill?" said Hailey. "You *so* should've had that."

Jill groaned, and the game resumed. Jeff served next, and Marina intently watched, partially to learn what he was doing but mostly to look at him. After each serve, Jeff would run forward in time to return the volley from either his sister or cousin. He knew he was showing off, but his teammate didn't seem to mind. She applauded him every time he got the ball over the net.

Their score rose to five points versus Jill and Hailey's zero when Jill grew frustrated with Jeff's antics. She returned his serve towards Marina's side furthest from Jeff. Seeing the ball coming at her, she shrieked and backed away. Jeff lunged but landed in front of her, and the ball touched down on the sand just out of his reach.

"Sorry," said Marina.

"No problem." Jeff stood and brushed off some sand. "We're still winning."

"You play very well," said Marina, remembering another piece of Hailey's advice.

"Thanks," he said, jogging to his start position backwards so he could still see her.

On Jill's turn to serve, she seized the opportunity to target Marina for another point because she refused to let her brother beat her so easily and act so cocky about it. Instead of fleeing, Marina shielded her face with her arms. The ball bounced up off her palms, and Jeff used the assist to spike the ball over the net before Hailey could reach it.

"Nice set," said Jeff, holding his hand up expecting a high-five.

Sensing she was safe from the volleyball, Marina uncovered her face and saw Jeff smiling at her and standing there with his hand raised. Not understanding the gesture, she mirrored it, complete with a smile.

Jeff chuckled and gently took hold of her wrist with his other hand, bringing her palm up to slap his. As soon as he touched her, Marina felt a pulse surge down her arm and throughout her entire body, as if she had been shocked by an electric eel. But the sensation was pleasing and fulfilling instead of painful. She wondered if Lorelei had ever experienced such enjoyable feelings from playing a game on the beach, laughing with humans, or having her hand held by a boy—Marina reminded herself that Jeff was to be called a boy and not a human-man. *A boy*, she thought as she closed her eyes and slowly breathed in the salty air, *a boy that I want to know more about.*

"Hey, if we're gonna be a good team, can I at least know your real name?" whispered Jeff. "I promise I won't use it around Aunt Susan and Uncle Greg."

Her eyes fluttered open, and they made instant contact

with his brown eyes. "Marina," she replied without hesitation or worry.

When it was Marina's first turn to serve, he stood behind her and guided her arms through the action. On her first attempt, the ball didn't reach the net, but on her second try, it did. However, both Jeff and Marina were too busy celebrating to return Hailey's volley, and so Marina had to wait for another lesson from him. Even though she had figured out what to do, she liked having Jeff that close to her, so she pretended she didn't remember how to serve the next time it was her turn.

As the game continued, Marina grew less afraid of the oncoming ball, and Jeff took less of an interest in winning singlehandedly. Before the game ended, Marina managed to jump up high, feeling as if she were flying, and spike the ball to Jill's feet. When she eventually landed, she shook the stinging pain from slapping the ball out of her hand while she happily initiated a high-five with Jeff.

They stopped the game when the rising tide reached the edge of their playing area. Marina and Jeff were leading nineteen to sixteen at the time he started breaking down the net. "Technically, not a win yet, Jefferson," called Jill as she and Hailey headed toward the footbridge while Marina stayed back to help Jeff.

"Look at how cute they are!" squealed Hailey, bouncing up and down like a jackhammer. "If they keep hitting it off like this, then maybe someday I'll be related to a—"

Covering Hailey's mouth before she could utter the M-word in earshot of Jeff, Jill wasn't sure how she felt about the growing connection between Marina and her brother.

They sat on the deck and drank Aunt Susan's homemade lemonade while they inhaled the mouth-watering aromas that emanated from Uncle Greg's barbecue grill. There was much laughter as they recalled silly family stories, each trying to embarrass one another.

"Mom couldn't find Jeff anywhere," said Jill, dramatically reenacting the events. "I was still a baby, barely walking Mom says, so she put me in the playpen. Jeff was like three years old. She found him wearing his brand new shoes, standing in the toilet, and stomping his feet."

Rocking back and forth laughing, Hailey said, "I hope you flushed first. L-O-L!"

"It's okay, Jillybean." Jeff smirked. "You've had your share of mishaps too."

"Oh, what about the time you dumped chocolate syrup on my head?" Jill asked.

"What's funny about this story, Marin—uh, Meredith." Jeff glanced over at his aunt and uncle, who didn't appear to notice his quick name correction. "What's funny is that Jill's the only one in the family who remembers it. Our parents swear it never happened."

Again, Hailey laughed out loudly, this time almost spitting out some lemonade.

"And what about you Hailey?" said Jeff. "Remember that summer your dad took us over to the lighthouse? You thought you saw a mermaid on the rocks far below." He turned to Marina. "We got Uncle Greg's binoculars for a closer look. It was a beach towel, no idea how it got there."

Jill and Hailey fell silent and slowly sipped lemonade through their straws as their eyes awaited Marina's reaction. She looked straight at Jeff, who had leaned in towards her. Her smile never faded as she said, "We all know how Hailey loves mermaids. I think they are pretty cool too."

Hearing Marina describe something as *cool* for the first time, Hailey gasped, almost choking on the lemonade she had sipped.

"What about you, Jeff?" asked Marina, taking Jeff's hand. "Do you like mermaids?"

He whispered, "If you like them, Marina, then I do too."

Before any mind-blowing revelations about Marina's true identity could be made, Uncle Greg announced that the food was ready. Marina tried a little of everything, all delicious foods she had never experienced. Hailey kept an eye on Jeff and watched his reaction to Marina's overindulgence with the food, but he continually smiled at her.

Their time outside lingered into the night, and scented insect-repelling candles illuminated the deck. Marina was captivated by Jeff's description of his summer jobs and how he would be studying business management when he went off to college, though she didn't fully understand everything he said. They stayed up late into the night and laughed, ate more food, told more stories, played games—even Aunt Susan and Uncle Greg joined in—and otherwise enjoyed their time together. Throughout the night, the gentle rumbling of the waves remained present in the background.

As Marina stared out to the ocean, dimly lit by the light of the rising semicircular moon, she thought back to growing up with Lorelei and her father. Though they had always been there and cared for her, that night on land was the first time Marina ever felt part of a real family.

~ Chapter Twenty-Three ~

Once Lorelei and Meredith had returned home, Meredith spent the rest of the day and into the next in the cavern. Lorelei's father tinkered about with various items he had retrieved from the shipwreck when he had scouted ahead. Occasionally, he asked Meredith what the gadgets were for, and she willingly explained the uses of the compass, the coffee mug, the smoking pipe, and the fork. Barney visited and also asked her a litany of questions about the objects, the human world, and being a human.

Lorelei, however, barely uttered a word to her. She came—listening politely when her father relayed the information Meredith had taught him about the items—and went—spending time with other mer-friends in the school that she hadn't seen since Meredith's arrival. If Lorelei's intent was to make her feel more like an outsider, then Meredith believed she was certainly succeeding.

Another three-quarters of a moon cycle receiving the cold shoulder from Lorelei was not what Meredith had planned. It almost made her consider leaving the ocean at the new moon, but her conscience quickly erased those selfish thoughts from her mind. She didn't want solitude, and as interested in her as Barney was, his questions could sometimes be a little overwhelming. She needed a friend, someone who wouldn't ask that much and just let her be. Lorelei was someone like that, but Meredith was having difficulty breaking the silence.

Until she remembered what day it was.

When Lorelei returned to the cavern from wherever she had been, Meredith swam over to her. "Lorelei, I know you're upset with me. I don't blame you, but please believe me that I wouldn't do something like that to Marina."

"You have apologized already," said Lorelei, avoiding eye contact with Meredith. "I forgive you, but that does not make us friends." Then she started swimming away.

"I understand, but I'd like to be your friend." Meredith gave her tail a big flick and shot forward until she caught up with Lorelei. "Imagine how difficult all this is for me. The changes to my body, having to master new skills, knowing I don't fit in. I'm like a fish out of water here, pardon the pun."

"Marina seems to be adjusting to the changes." Lorelei increased her speed.

Meredith flapped faster to catch up. "Of course she is. She has Hailey, who's obsessed with your species, to help her. You're interested in human customs and traditions, right?"

Lorelei swam faster and then turned around to face Meredith. "What do you want from me?"

"A truce. I want to show you something you may never have seen before. Can we get to the eastern side of the island before nightfall?"

Her curiosity piqued, Lorelei led the way. Occasionally, she doubled back to ensure that neither Calliope nor any other mers had followed them. For the duration of their trip, she and Meredith didn't speak much.

Shortly after sunset, Lorelei and Meredith found a secluded spot among some rocks at the base of a small cliff, no more than ten feet high, on the southeastern coast of the island. If Meredith had remembered correctly from Hailey's tour of the island's perimeter, she had brought Lorelei to an unpopulated location on the island.

As it grew darker, and the only sounds in the immediate vicinity were from the ocean, Meredith deemed they were safe from being spotted. Even though it was night, her vision was exceptional, and she could see the contours of all the jagged rocks. She reasoned that mermaids were adapted to see clearly in the dark depths of the ocean.

She found a relatively flat-topped rock jutting above the

water's surface. After swimming to it, she pulled herself out of the water and sat on one side of the rock. The upper portion of her tail was exposed to the night air, but the lower half and her fluke were invisible under the water. Patting the top of the rock beside her, and splashing the puddle that was there, Meredith gestured for Lorelei to join her.

"We cannot simply sit in view on a rock," said Lorelei, dunking down so all of her except her head was submerged. "What if we are seen?"

"We won't be." Meredith beckoned for her. "I thought you were adventurous."

Scanning the area and sensing no signs of humans, Lorelei joined Meredith on the rock, where they waited for some time until it finally was the darkest it was going to be. The moon, entering its waning crescent phase, was still a few hours from rising, so there was very little light where they were.

"How long must we wait?" asked Lorelei, her arms folded across her chest as she kicked her tailfin in the water.

"Probably not much longer," answered Meredith, a little perturbed that she was unable to pinpoint the precise time it was and unsure of the exact starting time of the event for which they were waiting.

Then a burst of bright colors appeared in the sky to the north, followed shortly thereafter by a loud banging sound. The unexpected sight and sound almost caused Lorelei to dive into the water, but Meredith reached for her shoulder to keep her in place.

The next explosion was made of different colors, and then there were more and more. Meredith watched as Lorelei sat transfixed at the display in the distance and its reflection on the water's surface. Some of the light twinkled off the scales of the exposed parts of her dark green tail.

"Beautiful," gasped Lorelei.

Each new shape amazed her. Some were a central eruption leading to colored lights cascading downward like waterfalls, with only a single bang being heard. Others were fast spirals of light, whinnying shortly after appearing. Then there were combinations of several different shapes and colors at once, glowing fragments of light seemingly colliding against the backdrop of the black sky. Occasionally, they could hear the collective reactions from the distant crowds along the beaches further north.

"They are spectacular." Lorelei was still attentively watching the sky. "What are they?"

"Fireworks," replied Meredith. "Small rockets are ignited and launched into the air. They contain a mixture of chemicals that combust. In the chemical reactions that follow, energy is released in the form of light. Different chemicals produce different colors."

Lorelei didn't take her eyes off the sky during Meredith's explanation. "I understand little of what you said, but I see that they are breathtaking."

~ ~ ~

Meanwhile, at the public beach nearest the ferry terminal, Marina was similarly awestruck by the fireworks display.

Uncle Greg had everyone pile into the SUV before sunset to find a decent place from where to watch. The beach and surrounding areas were crowded when they had arrived, so finding a parking space was difficult. Knowing that the teens probably wanted to watch without the adults, Aunt Susan and Uncle Greg let them go off on their own with the expectation that they return to the car not long after the display ended.

The girls and Jeff found an empty patch of beach, just large enough for them to sit in two rows of two. Jeff arranged it so he could sit beside Marina with Jill and Hailey in front of them. The first explosion startled Marina, and she shrieked and cowered against Jeff, who used the opportunity to put his arm around her.

Hailey peeked over her shoulder. Upon seeing them sitting that way, she grabbed Jill's knee and shook it while gleefully pointing at Marina and Jeff behind them. Jill chose not to look, as the sights of the budding romance were starting to nauseate her. Because one of them was her brother and the other was a mythical creature, Jill thought the situation was too sickeningly sweet, like a fairy tale.

With Jeff's arm around her, Marina felt warmth like she never had in the ocean. She grinned, no longer afraid of the loud, bright lights in the sky, not particularly afraid of anything at that moment. Looking toward the fireworks, Marina appreciated their beauty. Every color, including orange, mixed together in the sky and in the reflections in the sea.

Jeff was clearly more interested in watching Marina watch the fireworks. Her behavior, like a young child seeing them for the first time, enchanted him. As the lights twinkled in Marina's blue eyes, he realized that it was the perfect moment for another kind of first.

Marina turned to him, and their eyes met. Then before she knew it, his head leaned forward, and his mouth pressed against hers. She wasn't sure what was happening, but she knew she enjoyed the feeling. His soft lips were gentle, and she slowly opened hers and brought her arm up behind him to caress the back of his neck and tousle the scruff of hair there.

Hailey and Jill heard the tender sighs from behind and turned to see them kissing. Whereas Hailey was grinning, Jill stood up and walked away.

Marina and Jeff separated as an enormous burst of red filled the sky, low to the horizon. "Wow," panted Jeff. "That was some first kiss."

Blushing, Marina smiled coyly and nestled her head against Jeff's shoulder. She took Jeff's nearby hand in one hand and touched her other hand to her mouth, savoring the sensation. To compare the feeling on her lips to something familiar, she thought of home—wet and a little salty, yet extremely comforting. As far as Marina knew, Lorelei had never experienced something like that. Or if Lorelei had, she definitely hadn't shared details of the experience.

~   ~   ~

Eventually, the lights stopped, and a few lingering explosions could be heard in the background. At the rocks, Meredith turned to Lorelei and continued lecturing. "Though they occur at the same instant, we see the light from the explosion before we hear its sound because light travels nearly one million times faster than sound does."

There were cheers in the distance, and Lorelei applauded as well. "Is it over?" she asked.

Before Meredith could answer, the finale of the fireworks display began. It consisted of a rapid succession of explosions of light mostly colored red, white, and blue. The volume grew in intensity until the final few thundering blasts after the lights had disappeared. Lorelei applauded more excitedly than before, along with the howling crowd.

"Thank you for bringing me, Meredith," said Lorelei, still clapping her hands.

"I'm glad you enjoyed them." Hoping the trip was a positive step toward improving her relationship with Lorelei, Meredith took a deep breath and swished her tailfin in the water. "All over my country today, there are fireworks going off like these. My people are celebrating our independence that occurred on this day back in the year seventeen seventy-six." She paused, wondering if mers numbered years the same way as humans, and then she tried to remember what the mer term for a year was. "Anyway, over two hundred years ago…"

"May I ask you something? And please do not misinterpret my question." Lorelei clasped her hands and laid them on her lap as she turned toward Meredith. "You know much information about the moon cycle, about these fireworks, and about other human items and customs. What do you do with all this knowledge?"

"I study it." Meredith shrugged, unsure of the point of Lorelei's question. "I get good grades in school so I can be accepted by a good college and eventually have a good career."

"But do you need to know everything you know?"

Thinking about all the information inside her head, Meredith started classifying it all. Her intended career goal was in the sciences, but she wasn't sure whether she'd primarily focus on physics or chemistry or biology, and she would need to know whichever subject or subjects connected with her ultimate major in college. Being science-oriented, she knew she also needed a solid background in mathematics. Having an extensive vocabulary and understanding the rules of grammar would help her in presenting her findings. And knowing her history was important because people needed to know what came before them so they didn't repeat the same mistakes. Even though there was a possibility that she didn't necessarily need all the information, she believed that it was still crucial for her to know it.

"What's your point, Lorelei?" asked Meredith firmly. "I know a lot, and there's a lot I still need to learn in college."

Lorelei sighed. "I know much about the ocean by living there, and I have learned about humans on land by removing my tail and walking among your kind whenever I can. But I have learned none of this from memorizing and reciting. I have learned by experiencing. How much have you learned through experience?"

Before Meredith could answer, the sounds of car engines approaching were heard from the plateau above them. Lorelei instinctually dove into the water and disappeared under the dark surface. As Meredith followed, she grinned with the knowledge that she was learning and experiencing something that no other human ever had, regardless of whether she needed or wanted to learn and experience it.

~ Chapter Twenty-Four ~

Marina was standing on the beach and listening to the calm water when the sun rose the next morning. The moon was also visible, and the two celestial bodies coexisted peacefully in the dawn sky. She smiled as her thoughts drifted to Jeff, to the two of them leaning against one another the night before, to the warmth like sunshine she felt when he held her, and to the incredible sensation of his lips against hers—a kiss, he had called it. At last she understood what was happening in the painting she had seen in the shop. The boy and the mer were preparing to kiss, and she imagined Jeff kissing her again.

"You're an early riser," he said from behind her.

She turned and smiled at him. "This time of day is quiet, so I can think more clearly."

"What are you thinking about?" He took her hand and interwove his fingers with hers.

"You." She squeezed his hand. "And home."

"Speaking of homes, I'm up this early because I was supposed to leave on one of the first ferries. My mom hates schedule changes, but I texted her, and she's gonna pick me up tonight instead. I was wondering if you'd like to spend the day with me."

"I would like that."

As they walked along the beach, they swung their joined hands back and forth. Instead of worrying about what to tell Jeff or what not to tell him, Marina decided simply to enjoy the day.

The others joined them for Aunt Susan's big breakfast:

scrambled eggs and bacon with toast and a variety of fresh fruit and muffins. Jeff asked if he could borrow the convertible to take "Meredith" around the island, and Uncle Greg granted permission, but then Jill insisted that she and Hailey go with them. She explained they'd be able to stay out until Jeff's ferry and Hailey would drive back home, but it was an improvised excuse to keep a close eye on the couple. When Jeff tried to protest, Jill assured him that she and Hailey would keep their distance, but she was telling another little white lie.

They packed Jeff's weekend duffle bag in the trunk of the convertible, along with a bag filled with "emergency items" as Hailey had called them. Jeff chivalrously opened the front passenger door for Marina and closed it behind her before heading to the driver's seat, leaving Hailey and Jill to handle their own.

Their first destination was a carousel near the ferry terminal, one of the oldest in the country. Upon seeing it and how people rode the wooden horses, Marina mentioned that she had never been on one before. Though Jeff found her statement difficult to believe, he was charmed by her childlike glee when she rode it with him.

Hailey rode as well, choosing a reddish horse about a third of the carousel's circumference behind them, far enough away not to interfere, but close enough to enjoy the way they looked at each other and even snap a photo or two of them with her phone.

Choosing not to ride, Jill sat on the benches with parents of children old enough to ride by themselves. Though she felt like a chaperone, she thought it was better than Hailey behaving more like a stalking member of the paparazzi. Jill watched them circle around again and again, and on the rare instance when Jeff wasn't gawking at Marina and laughing, he glared in her direction. Jill knew the look on his face meant that he was displeased she was tagging along on his date. But she reminded herself why she was there; she knew her brother well enough to know that sometimes he fell too quickly and too deeply for girls. Despite there being plenty of fish in the sea, Marina was one that was going to throw herself back in a few short weeks.

Even though Jill was purposely keeping an eye on them, Hailey dragged Jill into a clothing shop to appear less conspicuous about following them down the sidewalk. Jeff seized the opportunity to snatch Marina's hand and take her to a nearby lot where bicycles were rented. After suggesting that they take a ride together, Jeff was surprised when Marina cowered away from the bicycles and insisted she had never been on one. Fortunately, the rental place had a few tandem bicycles, so Jeff explained he could do all the pedaling while she could enjoy the ride.

As they rode by Jill and Hailey emerging from the shop, Jeff rang the little bell on the bike's handlebars to get his sister's attention and to show her he was escaping from her supervision.

Jeff pedaled slowly, not only to make it easier for Marina to keep up, but also because they weren't in a particular rush to go anywhere. With Jeff controlling the bicycle's steering, Marina closed her eyes to imagine herself swimming in the ocean, the quick rush of air blowing over her almost like water. If not for the helmet on her head, she could imagine her long blonde hair flowing behind her.

They talked about the sights of the island that Jeff had pointed out along the way, including streets of uniquely shaped and painted houses. Marina was amazed by the variety of color, unlike the ocean being an expanse of bluish-green in every direction.

Returning the bicycle a few hours later, they found Jill and Hailey waiting in the convertible and starving, having expected to be joined for lunch. But during their ride, Jeff and Marina had stopped for sandwiches and had eaten them in a park—an impromptu picnic—where a jazz ensemble happened to be playing on a bandstand.

They spent the afternoon at the beach watching an older gentleman sculpt an elaborate sandcastle. Marina and Jeff were his first spectators, innocently talking there and sharing cotton candy, but a small crowd developed. Hailey pretended she was taking photos of the castle, but she was all-too-obviously taking more pictures of Marina and Jeff. When Jill chastised her, Hailey claimed she was taking them to preserve the memories for Marina.

As dinner time approached, Hailey whisked Marina away to the convertible to retrieve the bag of mysterious emergency supplies. When Jeff asked where they went, Jill told him she had no idea, and then he disappeared in the other direction.

The three of them returned at approximately the same instant, and Jeff was carrying a small bouquet of flowers. He froze when he caught a glimpse of Marina, who had changed into a short pink dress that Hailey had worn to her school's Spring Fling Dance. Feeling a bit underdressed in his polo shirt and khaki shorts, Jeff approached and gave her the bouquet.

"Thank you. They are beautiful." Marina smiled and sniffed the flowers—scents unlike any plants she had ever encountered in the ocean. They weren't dull and fluctuating in the current, but much more sturdy and vibrant. And mostly orange, as Jeff had remembered her saying at some point during the day the color had special significance to her.

They ate dinner at a restaurant with an open roof deck, at a table that had a flickering candle in a seashell-shaped glass jar as its centerpiece. "The view is beautiful up here off the ground," said Marina.

"Sure is," said Jeff, but he was gazing at Marina instead of at the scenery. "The candlelight makes your eyes twinkle, kinda like the way moonlight twinkles off the water."

Jeff had given Marina reasons to keep her smiling all day, but the compliment made her shyly turn away and look out at the ocean. Because the moon hadn't risen yet, the water was dark.

"Well, when the moon's out, anyway," said Jeff.

Becoming more crescent-shaped each day, the missing

moon acted like a ticking clock reminding her that in a few short human weeks, she would return home. She wanted to spend more time with Jeff, but she feared he wouldn't understand that after she returned to the sea, she could only spend time with him once a cycle.

"Jeff, before you leave, I must tell you that I am not like other girls." Marina stumbled on the last word, ensuring that she had used the proper human term.

"That's why I like you, Marina." Jeff grinned. "I think it's great that you're traveling on your own. Why'd you choose here?"

"A friend suggested I come up here. We were only supposed to spend a day, but…" Marina hesitated telling him her secret. She knew it was against the rules, but Hailey and Jill already knew the truth, and Jeff was part of their family. Would that be an acceptable exception to the rule? And what would his reaction be? Would he try to capture her as the legends about humans told?

During the prolonged pause, Jeff took her hand, and her anxiety disappeared. She could sense she was safe with him, but the restaurant wasn't the right place to tell him because of the other people around.

"The ferry's gonna be leaving soon," said Jeff when the waitress brought the check. "As much as I want to stay, my mom won't want to pick me up later."

They crossed the street to the ferry terminal. Hailey and Jill were waiting by the car after finishing their dinner from a significantly less expensive food stand. Hailey was excited that Jeff had taken Marina on perhaps the best first date ever, but Jill wasn't as enthused.

"I do not know when I will be able to see you again," said Marina.

"It's cool; I get it." Jeff took an orange daisy from Marina's bouquet and placed it above her right ear. "Long-distance relationships are tricky. In the fall, I go off to school."

Marina looked out to the ocean. "And I will soon travel

far with my school."

In earshot of their conversation, Jill gripped the dock's railing and keeled forward, looking straight down at the water—looking anywhere the lovebirds weren't. They were spewing out such sappy romantic dialogue, and though Jill could overlook Marina's half of the conversation due to her naivete, Jeff speaking that way made her want to throw up.

"But there are lots of ways we can stay in touch." Jeff handed her a slip of paper on which he had written his phone number and email address. "Too bad there wasn't a way—"

Jeff's words were interrupted by the final boarding call for the ferry. He turned toward the gangplank and then back at Marina, who took hold of his rough, unshaven cheeks while she stood on her toes to kiss him. His duffle bag slipped off his shoulder as he wrapped his arms around her tightly, not particularly wanting to let go.

Hailey's smile was wide as she made a clapping motion with her hands, keeping them from coming into contact with each other so as not to disturb the sweet goodbye kiss. Jill, however, had no qualms about ruining their moment by loudly clearing her throat and saying, "Mom's gonna be ticked if this boat leaves without you, Jefferson."

Jeff and Marina broke their embrace, and Jeff reached down for the bag with one hand, finding Marina's hand with his other. As he slowly backed away while she stood still, their joined hands rose until their arms were outstretched. When he finally stepped too far away, separating their hands, he said, "I won't ever forget you, Marina."

"Nor I, you." She continued raising her arm and waved at him, her hair blowing in the gentle sea breeze.

"Bye, Hailey," called Jeff as he waved at the girls. "Bye, Jillybean. Bye, Marina, call me!"

Marina stood there on the dock, swaying and waving goodbye until the ferry had left the terminal. When she eventually turned around, Hailey rushed at her. "O-M-G, he is, like, totally head over heels for you!"

As Hailey grabbed Marina's hand and led her to the car,

Jill dragged behind, grateful that Hailey hadn't gone on to ask if Marina had fallen head over tail for Jeff.

"So you're definitely gonna have to come back on land soon," said Hailey, opening the front passenger door of the convertible, its roof down. "He really wants to see you again, and I can tell you want to see him."

"I do." Marina sat and waited for Hailey to close the door and walk around to the other side. "But I do not know when that will be. Maybe we will both be better off cherishing the experience, but never able to see each other again."

"Oh, no you don't." Jill clutched the passenger door and glowered down at Marina sitting there. "You won't just leave and break my brother's heart like that."

"G-M-A-B, Jill," said Hailey. "All day you've been acting like you don't want them together. Admit that Jeff took her on an awesome date, and get in the car."

Jill opened the back door and slammed it shut as she sat behind Marina. Remembering the research they had done when Meredith transformed, she said, "Or maybe it's true what the legends say about mermaids teasing men and luring them into the sea."

Hailey gasped. "Jill, you apologize right now."

But Jill didn't say a word. She leaned back and wore a smug grin on her face, which Marina spotted in the exterior rearview mirror.

The tears that Marina wiped from her eyes weren't caused by Jill's insult; they came from the bittersweet goodbye with Jeff. Marina didn't want to break Jeff's heart as Jill accused, even though the pain inside her was coming from her own heart. She wanted to see Jeff again. And then again. And if there were a way she could see him every full moon, she would, but his school was further inland, and hers was near the island only during the northern summertime. Seeing him as often as she believed she wanted to would be a challenge, but she didn't feel the need to justify her thoughts or emotions to anyone, let alone Jill. So Marina sat there smiling contently with her eyes closed, feeling the wind rush by her like it had on the bicycle with Jeff. The three days she spent with him were some of best days she ever had, and as she once again sniffed the beautiful flowers he had given her, she was amazed that those days occurred on land without her tail instead of in the water.

"I'm sorry, Marina," said Jill when they were about halfway home. "I'm just looking out for my brother. He's family, and I know how he gets when he's interested in a girl. Kinda sickening, isn't it?"

"Endearing," replied Marina.

Hailey added, "Like, really, really cute, too."

"I was thinking." Jill rested her elbow on the back of Marina's seat as she leaned forward, her head in the space between the two front seats. "If you wanted to spend a lot more time with Jeff, you could always choose to stay on land."

Satisfied that she had at least planted an idea in Marina's head, Jill leaned back. The new moon was less than a week away, and if Marina decided to stay on land for good, Meredith could get out of the mermaid tail sooner than expected.

~ Chapter Twenty-Five ~

After their two excursions to the island—first to meet with Marina and the others, and later to see the fireworks—Lorelei suggested that she and Meredith keep a low profile for a few days in case they had been under surveillance by Calliope. They spent most of that time in the cavern or near enough to it to be seen by other mers in the school. When they came across Calliope and her friends, they received nothing more than the typical dirty looks and snickers, which they ignored. If they had been spied breaking the rules, they reasoned that action would have already been taken.

Meredith didn't talk much during that time as her thoughts often drifted to her conversation with Lorelei after the fireworks. She had completed eleventh grade, and she enjoyed learning and recalling the facts and information she knew, so she told herself there wasn't anything inherently wrong with her knowledge.

But then she began questioning her extracurricular experiences and her motives for doing them. She played on the field hockey team, not because she had any deep interest in the sport, but because the exercise was good for her health, and it looked good to have an athletic activity on her college applications. Jill had coerced her to be in the school musical so they could spend time together, but she didn't participate in it because she was particularly talented at acting or singing; again, it was for her college application. She was on the student council, not because she cared about government or planning school events she probably wouldn't go to otherwise, but because it looked good.

Ever since she could remember, Meredith wanted to study science, and during her time at school, she had studied several branches of science and excelled at all of them. She wasn't entirely sure which she intended to major in at college, but to get admitted to a prestigious school, she needed more than the knowledge. They wanted to see the experiences also, and Meredith felt ashamed that most of her experiences were somewhat fabricated.

Even since becoming a mermaid, she craved information. She wanted to know how she could breathe and talk, how she transformed, how she was going to transform back, and why she couldn't at the new moon, instead of simply appreciating the unique experience. If it wouldn't simply be dismissed as fiction, she could write her college essay on how she spent her summer vacation as a mermaid. Maybe a college or two would commend her creativity.

But first she needed to have some unique experiences.

When Lorelei snapped out of her resting period in the cavern, Meredith swam over to her. "Take me somewhere," said Meredith. "Show me something, anything that I wouldn't be able to see on land."

Lorelei raised an eyebrow and gave her half a smirk. "Are you asking to go on an adventure?"

Meredith nodded. "Just take me somewhere, and don't let me ask questions."

"There is nothing wrong with asking questions, Meredith."

"Then don't let me ask too many questions. I want to do something I've never done before and probably never will again."

"Never say never." Lorelei gave her fluke a little flick and started floating forward. Turning back to Meredith, she asked, "Sink or swim?"

"Swim," replied Meredith as she followed.

They swam above where most of the school congregated for the season. Meredith glanced below at all the other mermaids, their tails of almost all the different colors of the rainbow swimming in various directions. She could make out one group of three purple-tailed mers, most likely Calliope followed by her two lackeys who appeared exactly as their leader instead of choosing to stand out.

Lorelei didn't speak as she led Meredith closer to their destination. She had a particular experience in mind, and she wanted it to be a surprise. Understanding the silence, Meredith took the hint and didn't ask for information, instead savoring the anticipation. All Meredith knew from previous observations was that they were heading away from the island and thus towards open water. The blue water was getting brighter, so they were also rising closer to the surface.

After swimming for some time, Lorelei ultimately started slowing down. Meredith had been following close behind all along, and when Lorelei stopped, she also did and looked around. The sun was high in the sky above the surface, and its light shimmered off of the ripples of the ocean's gentle waves. But other than that, there was nothing else around other than a variety of small fish that Meredith had already seen.

Meredith resisted her urge to ask questions while Lorelei circled her several times, periodically stopping to listen. "There it is," said Lorelei, who darted toward the sound she had heard.

"There's what?" asked Meredith, swimming to catch up, but unable to hear the sound.

Lorelei didn't answer, but she waved her hand at Meredith in a gesture to stay quiet. She slowed down briefly but then abruptly changed her direction because the source of the sound had moved. They zigzagged a few more times until Meredith finally heard the distant chirping.

Meredith's eyes opened wide when she saw them up ahead. There were three of them, their gray skin color and streamlined shape—from their tails, their dorsal fins, and their bottle noses—easily identifying them. Meredith turned to Lorelei in overjoyed disbelief. "Dolphins? This is really cool."

The dolphins turned toward them, and Meredith could

detect three distinct voices communicating. She knew they weren't speaking human words, but it was clear that each of them had a slightly different sound, and she could perceive that they were talking to each other. Another interesting side effect of the mermaid tail, she thought.

"It is more than cool, as you say. This flows." Using both her arms, Lorelei beckoned for the dolphins. "They want to swim with us."

"Swim with us?" blurted Meredith. She had once seen a dolphin show at a water theme park on a family trip to Florida several years earlier, and even though she knew they were friendly animals, she was apprehensive, even a little afraid. "I...I don't know about that, Lorelei."

"Trust me. Here they come."

The three dolphins swam up to the surface to get a breath of air, and then they dove back down and swam towards Meredith and Lorelei. Two of the dolphins were slightly longer than the third, and it was the third that took the lead and arrived ahead of the other two.

Lorelei floated alongside the shorter dolphin's side and gently placed her hand on its back. "This is my friend Meredith." After the dolphin clicked and chirped, Lorelei turned to Meredith and said, "She says hello."

"She?" asked Meredith. "How do you know she's a she?"

The three dolphins communicated with each other while Lorelei swam back over to Meredith and said, "No questions, Meredith. Close your eyes and listen to them."

Following Lorelei's instruction, Meredith closed her eyes and concentrated on the sounds of the dolphins. There wasn't much coherence at first, but as she focused more and more, the noise became comprehensible. The dolphins were a mother and her two sons. Meredith's eyes popped open, and she turned to Lorelei, who nodded at her.

"How did I do that?" asked Meredith.

Lorelei waved an index finger, reminding Meredith not to ask questions.

While her eyes had been closed, Meredith lost sight of the

two other dolphins, until she felt one of them nudge her fluke with his nose, flipping her from a forward-facing position to a downward-facing position. Then she heard rapid clicking from their mouths. "They're laughing at me, aren't they?" Meredith chuckled.

"They are mischievous little males," said Lorelei, also laughing. "They want to play with you. They can tell you are different."

"They can tell? That's fascinating. Up on land, we've always believed dolphins were the second most intelligent species on the planet."

While the dolphins chirped together, Lorelei started laughing with them. Meredith's gaze bounced amongst them until she processed what had happened. The dolphins were asserting they were more intelligent than humans. She smirked, understanding them and actually believing they were correct.

The two sons flanked Meredith, and she knew they wanted to take her for a swim. She reached out to touch their sides, just behind their flippers. While they floated backwards, Meredith's fingers stroked their smooth, rubbery skin until her hands were on their flippers, which were held out for her as if they were chivalrously extending their hands for her to hold.

As she reached for their flippers, she felt the momentary panic that one would feel in the instant before the first drop of a rollercoaster. And then the ride started, and Meredith sped forward with the dolphins.

Water rushed by her and over her, but unlike when she skimmed across the surface with Lorelei, it was an exhilarating feeling. Since she was completely submerged, water wasn't splashing into her eyes, and she could watch the dolphins. It looked like they were smiling.

Occasionally, the dolphins headed for the surface to breathe, which felt to Meredith like she was going up and down smaller hills and bumps of the rollercoaster. The dolphins kept Meredith below the surface throughout because they must have known that it would hurt her if she belly-flopped on the water so often.

Right before they returned to Lorelei, the dolphins plunged rapidly straight down and then performed other maneuvers such as banked curves, corkscrew-style twists, and even a complete three-hundred-sixty degree loop. Meredith assumed that they had somehow read her thoughts since images of rollercoasters had flashed through her mind.

Lorelei and the mother dolphin joined in, but this time, they didn't swim as quickly as Meredith's first ride. Sometimes they swam together, holding hands and flippers in a row of five. Other times, Meredith and Lorelei propelled themselves to swim alongside the dolphins' heads. The dolphin boys performed some tricks for the mers; they jumped out of the water and did flips as they swam. After making sure there weren't any boats in the vicinity, Lorelei showed them she could also jump. Meredith didn't try, but she enjoyed being an audience member with the mother dolphin. While Meredith applauded, the mother dolphin chirped in approval.

When the dolphins told them it was time for them to leave, Lorelei showed Meredith how the dolphins said goodbye by touching the end of their closed mouths to Lorelei's cheek. Then the three dolphins, mother first followed by her two sons, kissed Meredith on the cheek. The second son chirped a thank you and goodbye afterwards, and then the three of them swam away.

"That totally flowed!" Meredith waved goodbye to the dolphins until they were out of view. The water had gotten darker as the sun had started setting. As Meredith looked around, she realized that she hadn't been paying close attention to which directions the dolphins had taken them. For all Meredith knew, they were much further out in the ocean. "Lorelei, you do know how to get back home, right?"

"Take pause, and use your instincts," Lorelei answered.

Meredith went through the motions of taking a deep cleansing breath, and then suddenly, she got the urge to start swimming. Lorelei followed her, commending her for choosing the correct direction.

The trip home took slightly less time, due to a combination of where their fun with the dolphins ended and Meredith's enthusiasm as she thanked Lorelei profusely and recalled the events of the day. Lorelei smirked and listened as Meredith talked all the way back to the cavern, proclaiming it as one of the most enjoyable experiences she had ever had and hoping that she would one day get another opportunity to swim with dolphins.

"Do you know that the way you are speaking, you sound just like Barney?" chuckled Lorelei, who then noticed that Barney was waiting for them outside her cavern. "Speak of the devil ray."

He was hovering upright, with his hands hidden behind his back. "There you are," he said when they were close enough. "You were not here. I was going to leave. But I waited. Are you all right? You were gone for a long time. I thought something happened."

"We are fine, Barney," said Lorelei. "We went exploring. Maids' day out."

Then Barney noticed the wide smile on Meredith's face, and he couldn't help but stare at it. "Where did you go? What did you do?" His questions were paced a little slower than usual as he watched Meredith approach, her scales sparkling brilliantly. "Did you have fun? I can tell you had fun. What did you do?"

As Meredith told him, she flitted about, reenacting the experience for him. Seeing how interested Barney was in Meredith's story, Lorelei slyly swam into the cave to leave the two of them alone. Barney had never spent that much time near the cavern during previous north seasons, so Lorelei knew Barney wasn't there to see her.

"I am happy you enjoyed yourself. Dolphins flow." Then Barney's speech slowed down further, as if he were carefully considering every word before he said them to Meredith. "Maybe sometime before you go back to land, we could go swimming with dolphins together."

Meredith did a double-take, unsure if her ears heard Barney ask her out on a date. During her three years of high school, a few boys had asked her out, but she usually turned them down because she didn't want a potential boyfriend to distract her from her studies. Again, she had placed her desire for knowledge above possible experiences.

Barney wouldn't be a distraction.

She was going to be leaving in two weeks anyway, she rationalized, and he was well aware of that. Inside her head, she could hear Jill's advice from the ferry, encouraging her to tell him yes. "Is that why you were waiting for me?" she asked.

"Not exactly." His face turned pink, and he started to quiver nervously as he brought his hands out from behind his back. "I came to give you this."

He held a pair of white seashells with waves of orange color. The shells were carefully punctured in specific places where strong seaweed had been threaded and tied off, and one laced strand connected the two shells together. There were four remaining strands, two on each shell, and Meredith could easily deduce that two were meant to be tied behind her back and the other two around her neck.

"I did not like the way Calliope was teasing you about what you wear." His fluke fidgeted forward and backward as he spoke softly and shyly. "I found the shells and thought of you, so I made you this."

Meredith took the gift from him and gently stroked the shells. They were smooth, and she had never before seen seashells with that color pattern. "This is beautiful," she said, looking up at his face, now completely red. "That was so sweet of you, Barney. Thank you very much."

"You are welcome." His whole body was trembling, so he quickly said goodbye and flitted away.

Meredith giggled at his anxiety and imagined that she'd behave the same way in such a situation. She held the shells in front of her and tied it around her like it was a bikini top. If she was going to consider the rest of her time in the water as a new adventure, she figured she could do the complete mermaid experience until the full moon.

She undid her tankini and pulled it out from under the seashells. Her bathing suit had covered the ring around her waist where skin turned into scales. As she looked down, past her exposed bellybutton, the boundary between human and mermaid was blurred, almost perfectly blended as if she had always been that way.

And Meredith wasn't terrified about it.

Even though exposing so much of her body was somewhat uncomfortable, she knew the polite thing to do was to use Barney's present. He had given it to her with such sincerity that she couldn't keep herself from smiling as her heart flipped a beat.

Having never received flowers or candy from a boy, and discounting those little Valentine's Day cards exchanged in elementary school, Meredith was truly flattered. Even though the giving of seashells was probably commonplace for mers, a part of her wondered if she should be insulted or creeped out that the first gift a boy had ever given her was, essentially, a bra.

~ Chapter Twenty-Six ~

The sun had risen, and Hailey and Marina were already in the convertible. As they backed out of the driveway, the sound of the tires crunching on the gravel carried to the open window of the guest room, where it was loud enough to wake the lightly sleeping Jill.

Groaning in frustration, Jill lay there and glanced at the alarm clock. It was the third consecutive day that they had left the house without her, but each day they had left earlier than the day before.

On the morning after Jeff had left, it was easy for Hailey and Marina to leave the house without her. They were upset by her behavior that evening, so they chose not to wake her up when they went to the public beach. Jill wasn't happy with them when they returned, but Hailey reminded her that she was traditionally a late sleeper, so it was her own fault that she missed them.

Jill was angry when they had purposely left not too long after sunrise on the second day. Marina was always awake by then anyway, so all Hailey did was set her alarm clock extra early. They sat in silence around the dinner table that night, and afterwards, Hailey and Marina retreated to Hailey's bedroom. Jill had heard them giggling behind the closed door, and she suspected that Hailey called Jeff for Marina.

Yawning, Jill rolled onto her side and stared out the window at the clear sky, which was orange from the rising sun. They had stranded her at the house once again, and she was getting tired of it. She supposed she could tell Aunt Susan or Uncle Greg, but then she'd feel too much like a tattletale. Almost done with one of her summer reading books, she could relax alone on the beach and finish it. But first, she decided to go back to sleep.

Hailey drove Marina to some cliffs on the southwestern corner of the island, where they sat and looked out at the water and listened to the waves on the rocks below. "I have never been this far above the ocean surface," said Marina.

"Are you afraid of heights?" Hailey grabbed onto Marina's hand, just in case. "We could go somewhere else if you want."

"No, this is quite exhilarating. I am sure that the sunset would be beautiful from up here."

"You are so right!" Hailey smacked herself on the forehead. "Why didn't I think of that? O-M-G, I can be so ditzy sometimes. We can come back here later then."

Hailey stood up to walk back to the car, but Marina pulled her back to a seated position. "No need, Hailey. I appreciate you showing me your island."

They sat to eat the breakfast that Hailey had packed. While Marina was thoroughly enjoying her blueberry muffin, Hailey was only picking at hers.

"Is something bothering you?" asked Marina.

"You know, it feels kinda weird not having Jill here. She comes out here every summer, and we do all sorts of stuff together, but I'm so mad at her right now. She shouldn't have said those nasty things to you, especially trying to convince you to give up your tail." Hailey quickly grabbed Marina's wrist. "Being a mermaid is probably, like, the coolest thing ever, and I don't want you to give that up just for Jeff."

Marina chuckled. "I will not give up my tail, Hailey. I promise you that. Even though your island is, as you say, really cool."

"I mean, G-M-A-B, big deal if you like her brother and he likes you, right?"

Thinking about Jeff, Marina shivered as she blushed. "I do like him. Jill claims she was looking out for him, and I can respect that because he is her family. I would probably do the same if I had a family." She looked out to the water stretching to the horizon. The ocean took up so much space, yet she was all alone inside it.

"What happened to them?" asked Hailey, but an immediate answer didn't come. "You don't have to tell me if you don't want to."

"I am not fully sure." For the first time Marina could remember, she openly mentioned her lack of a family to someone other than Lorelei and Finn. She knew she could trust Hailey, even though they were from two very different worlds. "Something happened when I was very young, and they had to go away."

"So, you're an orphan?" Seeing Marina's confused reaction to the word, Hailey defined it for her.

"Yes, and I have been with Lorelei and her father ever since. He was close friends with my parents, and he says he promised my mother he would take care of me."

"So she, like, knew she was leaving you?"

A few tears escaped Marina's eyes. While growing up, she had heard rumors in her school—especially from Calliope—that her parents chose to leave her behind. Marina had been too young to remember the events, and Lorelei wasn't much older than she was, so she knew very little as well. Finn told Marina she resembled her mother when he occasionally reminisced how her parents had been close friends with him and Lorelei's mother before she passed away. For reasons she didn't understand, no other mer in the school would talk about her parents or even mention their names. But they had names—Coral and Zale—though it seemed to Marina that some mers in her school wanted all memory of their existence erased.

"I do not wish to believe they left willingly." Marina stood, and a gust of wind blew her long blonde hair across her face. "What if something terrible happened to them? I did not want to join Lorelei on land because I feared whatever happened to them would happen to me."

The legends said that humans were evil and would capture

mers. Marina reasoned that her parents met a different fate because if they had been captured, the leader of the school would use their story as a warning. Instead, he refused to acknowledge her parents.

He had strict punishments for mers who showed their tails to humans, an because of those consequences, very few mers ventured onto land. Finn encouraged Lorelei to explore and gain new experiences, but Marina had always been reluctant to join her until this cycle. If only the other mers could meet humans like Hailey, then they'd see that the legends weren't necessarily true.

She turned back to Hailey and smiled. "Though I was afraid at first, I am grateful to have met a kind human such as yourself—one I can truly call a friend."

Clapping her hands, Hailey jumped up and threw her arms around Marina. "I feel the same way! You're, like, my new B-F-F!"

"B-F-F?"

"Best Friend Forever. And promise me you won't give up your tail. Okay, so I never saw it on you, but it looked so cool on Meredith, and it's such a pretty color." Hailey noticed Marina was wistfully staring out at the ocean again. "Oh, I'm sorry. I didn't mean to—"

"You did not say anything wrong. I wish the others did not taunt me because I am the only mer with an orange tail."

"Maybe you're looking at it all the wrong way," said Hailey. "Because I-M-H-O, being something that no one else is, well, that's really cool. You're unique, one of a kind."

"You sound like Lorelei." Marina stepped closer to the cliff's edge.

"Take me for example. I adore mermaids, like, really adore them. Have all my life. Do I get teased about it? Well, yeah, you've seen it. But that's who I am, and it's okay to be a little different."

Marina looked out at the water below her. The ocean was enormous; she knew that from traveling far with the school. Land was also enormous, and she was perched high on only a small island, so she couldn't fathom how much more land there was. Yet she was only one creature, somewhere between those two large realms—the only mer in the water with an orange tail, and the only girl on land who was a mermaid. But whether that made her an outsider or extremely unique, she wasn't quite sure.

They stopped for lunch after leaving the cliff, and Hailey decided to cheer Marina up the best way she knew how: by going shopping. It worked to some extent, not because Marina bought anything in particular, but because as they walked from shop to shop, none of the island residents or tourists gave Marina a second glance. For that afternoon, she and Hailey blended in like ordinary girls. As Marina thought longer about it on the ride back home, ever since she had been on land, an ordinary human-maid is what she had been.

After all her life of being one of a kind, she felt no pressure being nothing more than a face in the crowd. Maybe an extended stay on land was something to consider. There were people who would care for her like Hailey and Jeff. And if the rumors that her parents had left the sea to live on land were true, maybe they were still out there somewhere.

When they returned to the house late that afternoon, Hailey dashed inside to put away the new clothes she had bought on her shopping spree. Marina wandered toward the beach, stopping on the footbridge at the top step to gaze out at the ocean. Smiling, she took a deep breath and inhaled the refreshing air, and then she released a relaxed sigh.

"I'll bet you two probably had a great day," said Jill, lounging on a beach chair by the rocks at the base of the stairs.

"We did," said Marina. "Thank you for asking."

Jill stood, closed the book she was reading, and dropped it onto the chair. "After stealing away my brother, you're going to steal away my cousin too? Is that it?"

"Jill, it is not like that." Marina walked down the stairs and onto the beach to face Jill directly.

"I had this whole vacation planned to spend time with my

cousin and best friend, but you had to go and screw that all up."

"I will admit that I chose a poor hiding spot for my tail, but it was your friend who put it on. She and I are equally responsible."

"Yeah, Jill, lighten up." Hailey had come outside and was watching them from the top step. "Besides, you were the one who came up with the plan to—"

Jill turned to Hailey. "Marina doesn't need you fighting her battles, Hailey."

"But Jill—"

Keeping her eyes on Marina, Jill held up her hand to stop Hailey from speaking. "Let Marina stand up for herself."

Hailey's bottom lip started to quiver, so she ran back to the house before either of them could see her crying.

Marina took a step toward Jill. "I am sorry that you feel like I have ruined your vacation. That was never my intent. I have appreciated everything you and Hailey have done for me." Marina spread her arms outward. "But there is no need to be so mean to her."

"Mean?" scoffed Jill. "How am I mean to her?"

"Ever since I arrived, I have noticed that sometimes you mock her, or you move your eyes around when she speaks." Marina watched as Jill rolled her eyes. "Yes, you do *that*."

Jill put a hand on her hip and said, "Only when she says something silly. And I'm just teasing, she knows that."

"Does she?" Marina waited for an answer, but Jill stood there fidgeting. "I do not have a family of my own, but if I did, I would never treat them with disrespect."

With that, Marina left Jill on the beach.

Hailey was in her bedroom, lying on the bed with her face buried in a pillow. Marina sat beside her and put a hand on her shoulder. "Are you okay?" asked Hailey, her voice somewhat muffled.

"Me?" asked Marina. "I was concerned about you."

"I'm fine." Hailey sat up. "She's my cousin. I know how she gets."

Marina wanted to tell Hailey not to make such an excuse for Jill, but Hailey sauntered over to her dresser. After opening one of the drawers, Hailey removed something and kept it out of Marina's view.

"Now, don't freak out or anything when you see this, but I got this because it reminded me of you. As far as I know, it's one of a kind, so it's special, just like you are. I want you to have it."

Hailey revealed the orange-tailed mermaid figurine she had bought from the shop. Marina looked at it, remembering how much it had irritated her, but upon seeing it in Hailey's hand, she smiled.

"Thank you." She took it from Hailey. "What would you have done if I had, as you say, freaked out?"

Hailey shyly looked away and traced a circle on the floor with her foot. "Well, I really didn't think you were gonna freak out, but I would've kept it to remind me of you."

~ Chapter Twenty-Seven ~

Hoping the others wouldn't hear her leave, Jill quietly closed the sliding door as she stepped onto the back deck. As she walked towards the footbridge, she glanced back at the house, specifically at Hailey's bedroom window. The light was on, so Jill knew that the two of them were up there, probably combing their hair and having a private conversation about mermaids.

Or they were talking about Jeff. Shuddering at the thought, Jill knew that they had called him at least once since he had left the island. Marina hadn't yet mastered the use of a telephone, so Hailey could have called him again.

She really didn't care about what they were doing up there, but she was getting frustrated with them doing it without her. Even if she hadn't tried to be stealthy, they probably wouldn't even realize she had left. If their behavior over the previous few nights was any indication, it would probably take them a few hours to notice she was gone. And that was how Jill wanted it to be, for she hadn't told them about her plan to meet with Meredith.

To get to the designated meeting place, Jill stepped from the last step onto the sand and turned to the right directly towards the setting sun, which barely poked its way through clouds about two-thirds of the way below the horizon. Why mermaids—and here she included Meredith as one—were so obsessed with the sun and the moon, she didn't understand. But it would be good to see Meredith again, and hopefully she'd be bringing good news about the new moon and the possibility of returning to land.

The twilight sky was devoid of its usual bright, beautiful colors, and the clouds cast gray shadows over the shore. The remaining sliver of the waning crescent moon had already set beyond the clouds, and with rain in the forecast, it was predicted to be a dark, starless night.

When Jill arrived at the rocky inlet, the lowest set of rocks still above the water had little puddles atop them. Stepping carefully from rock to rock and trying not to slip, Jill stopped just around the bend from the main beach, out of view from the houses. The trees and bushes blocked sight of the area from the road, where there was a slow but steady flow of traffic.

As the sun finally set, Jill turned toward the open ocean, but there was no sign of Meredith, one of the most punctual people Jill had ever known. What if Meredith had been unable to sneak away from Lorelei, or what if Lorelei had found out about the meeting and prevented her from coming? Jill decided she'd wait until the first sign of heavy rain, which she hoped would hold off, but the clouds in the sky were moving closer to the island.

The air grew cooler and breezier, so Jill zipped up her hoodie and checked the time once again on her phone. Almost fifteen minutes had passed since the first time she had checked. But when she looked up, she saw the silhouette of a head and arm waving at her in the distance. Assuming it was Meredith, Jill waved back, and then the figure submerged.

A few quick seconds later, Meredith's head reemerged from the water beside the rock where Jill was standing. "I am sorry I am late, Jill," she said. "I miscalculated the time it would take to get here."

The voice down by her feet caught Jill off guard, for she was still looking out to where Meredith had waved to her. "Wow, you got here fast from there."

"Yes, I do swim more quickly now." Meredith hoisted herself onto the rock and sat there, the orange scales of her lap faintly twinkling.

Meredith's wet hair was mostly slicked back, but she smoothed it out to keep it off her forehead and away from her eyes. Jill gasped at the sight of Meredith fixing her hair, with her fluke visible as it floated just below the water's surface. She was behaving too much like a stereotypical mermaid and looking more like one as well, with the tankini top replaced by the seashells that revealed her bare midriff.

"Wow, Merri," said Jill, her eyes fixated on the slight ripples of Meredith's stomach muscles. "You're, like, pretty jacked right now."

Meredith glanced downward and chuckled. "I suppose I am. That must be from two weeks of swimming practically non-stop."

"You look great." As Jill said the words, she was carefully observing Meredith's appearance and demeanor. She didn't just look more toned, but also healthier and stronger. Sitting with her head up and her back straight, Meredith looked more secure, confident, and relaxed than Jill could ever remember. "Really great."

"Thank you." Meredith swung her tailfin back and forth in the water, creating little waves.

"So, other than swimming, what have you been up to?"

"I swam with dolphins, Jill. It was one of the most incredible experiences I have ever had. Lorelei knows of an anemone meadow and a coral garden not too far from where the school has settled, and I look forward to exploring with her. She says it is rare, but I had no idea that coral could thrive this far north."

Besides learning there was a scientific fact Meredith didn't already know, Jill couldn't believe what she was hearing. Why would Meredith have made plans with Lorelei, she asked herself, concerned that Meredith was seemingly planning to stay in the water for another two weeks. While the mermaid in the house was stealing away Jill's cousin and brother, the mermaid beside her was substituting her friendship with Lorelei's.

"What's up with that?" asked Jill. "You seriously want to

stay like that?"

"It is only two more weeks." Meredith looked up at Jill. "We have gotten this far. We can devise an explanation."

"Will you listen to yourself?" Jill knelt down and took Meredith by the shoulders. "Last week, you were all worried about losing yourself. Well, you've lost yourself, Meredith. We're supposed to be here to talk about you switching back tomorrow."

"Tomorrow? At the new moon? I could not do that. I would lose my tail."

"Forget about the tail! It's not yours, and it's not you."

Meredith didn't reply. She sat there and looked down at her tail, which wasn't sparkling, wasn't bright, and wasn't as visible under the water as it had been earlier. The sky kept getting darker as both night and the clouds had arrived. It wasn't her tail, Meredith reminded herself. She was a human, living an extraordinary fantasy, but she was still a human.

Jill sat beside her, not caring that the rock was wet. As the cold wind blew, she clutched her hoodie closer to her and shivered. "Are you cold?" she asked, glancing over at Meredith in only the seashell top.

Meredith shook her head. "I'm cold-blooded now, remember?"

Hearing the scientific explanation, Jill quickly turned towards Meredith's face. "Merri? Is that you?"

"Yeah, I think. I'm sorry, but I've been getting wrapped up in all this lately." She gestured down to her fluke as she lifted it out of the water and then let it splash the surface. "And it's not a bad thing, because I've done some amazing things that I would never have normally done."

Smirking, Jill turned away and shook her head, thinking back to how her advice to Meredith was to get out of her comfort zone and enjoy the vacation. Apparently, Meredith had done so, although Jill wished she had been able to enjoy the vacation with Meredith.

Suddenly, Meredith leaned forward and grabbed hold of the rock's edge, fighting an urge to dive into the water and flee. "Did you hear that?"

"Hear what?" Jill whispered. Between the occasional cars passing by, the wind whistling through the tree branches, and the waves crashing on the rocks, it was difficult for her to hear anything unusual. "What was it?"

"I don't know. I've noticed that my senses are heightened in the water. I can see perfectly without my glasses, and my hearing has improved." Meredith pointed toward the dark ocean. "It sounded like something was out there."

Once her tense muscles relaxed somewhat, Meredith asked about what had been happening on land, and Jill told her everything about Marina and Hailey's strengthening friendship and everything about Marina and Jeff's blossoming romance. Meredith smirked, thinking back to a crush she once had on Jeff. She knew he was attractive and was always nice to her, but she kept her feelings a secret and her crush unrequited because he was, after all, Jill's brother. She didn't want to do anything to jeopardize her friendship. Still, Meredith couldn't help imagining how cute a couple Jeff and Marina would be, even though their time together would ultimately end.

And then she started tuning Jill out as her thoughts drifted to Barney and how sweet he had been to her. What had started out as clinginess and dorkiness on his part had grown into something more. A friendship at least, she thought, but he had asked her out on what seemed like a date. And she wanted to go with him, which was a detail she wasn't ready to tell Jill.

"So you see, Merri," Jill said in conclusion, loud enough to get Meredith's attention back. "I don't think Marina would mind staying on land. You can transform back tomorrow."

"I won't do it, Jill. It's not my tail." Meredith folded her arms across her seashells. "If what Lorelei and her father say is true, the tail will disappear forever. I'm not willing to test the validity of their statement."

"But how can you believe it's true without scientific proof?"

"This is one thing I'm going to take without proof."

There was a flash of lightning, and for that instant, the tail glowed bright orange. The thunder faintly rumbled several seconds later, telling Meredith how far away the lightning had struck—one mile for every four and two-thirds seconds, as she remembered from her physics class. Then the rain started.

"You should head back," said Meredith. "Before the rain gets much worse."

Jill covered her head with her hood. "So two more weeks like this? Until the full moon? How are we going to explain that? We were only staying here another week."

"We'll think of something. Maybe we can meet back here three nights from now after the new moon has passed. Bring my phone, and we can ask our parents to stay another week." Even without access to a calendar, Meredith was almost positive that her parents had returned from their anniversary safari trip that afternoon.

There was another flash of lightning, followed by a much louder thunderclap occurring sooner than the previous one. The rain started falling much harder. The friends said goodbye to each other, and Jill carefully started climbing over the rocks, which were difficult for her to see in the darkness, until she made it safely to the beach. Soaking wet, she ran back to the house and saw the light still on in Hailey's bedroom just as it was when she had left. She figured Hailey and Marina probably hadn't left the room, and they probably hadn't realized she had left the house. Neither car was in the driveway because Uncle Greg had gone off-island that afternoon, and Aunt Susan had probably gone to her book club meeting.

Meredith waited until Jill was out of view before diving into the water. At that moment, there was another flash of lightning, followed a few seconds later by the accompanying thunder, its sound muffled by the water. She could hear the loud pattering of the raindrops striking the ocean's surface above her, but they softened as she swam deeper and further away from the island.

From the lightning and thunder pattern she observed, Meredith predicted the storm would pass over the island and then go out to sea. Though people were advised to stay out of the water during a thunderstorm, she knew from physics class that electricity flowed along the surface of a conducting material so she'd be perfectly safe at the depth of Lorelei's cavern.

But what Meredith didn't know was that Calliope was rushing through the water far ahead of her.

Having seen Meredith swimming away from the school, Calliope had secretly followed her to the water near the land. She had been peering above the water far enough away not to be spotted or hear what they were talking about, but close enough to see Meredith associating with the human-maid and blatantly showing her tail. At that moment, Calliope had to get back to the school to tell her father immediately, so she swam back, hoping her fluke breaking the surface hadn't been heard.

There were rules against Meredith's behavior, and all the mers knew those rules and were required to obey them. And there were consequences for breaking the rules, especially for revealing one's true form. Calliope was going to gather up some of her friends so they could catch Meredith and bring the orange-tailed rule-breaker to her father. As the leader of the school, he was the one who could issue punishments for such severe offenses.

And her father's punishment for mers who exposed their tails to humans was immediate banishment to a deserted island.

~ Chapter Twenty-Eight ~

Holding the phone to her ear, Marina sat on Hailey's bed and dangled her feet over the edge of the mattress. She was talking to Jeff, who had called to say hello. It was their second phone conversation, and though Marina didn't comprehend how the device worked, she enjoyed using it to listen to Jeff talk. He talked about how his favorite baseball team was playing and about his job at the country club, neither of which she fully followed, but she liked simply listening to his voice.

Unlike their first phone conversation, which had been mostly one-sided, Marina spoke as well. She talked about the places Hailey had taken her on the island and things they had done together, but she didn't tell him much about Jill. He had said he didn't want to hear about his sister because he thought it would be too weird, so Marina was relieved she wouldn't have to tell him how she and Jill weren't getting along.

Hailey was sitting cross-legged on the floor, painting Marina's toenails orange. She had just finished Marina's fingernails when Jeff called, so to give them privacy, Hailey put on her earphones and bobbed her head up and down to the rhythm of her favorite songs. When she finished with Marina's toes, she went to her desk and flipped through the pages of the mermaid picture book she had bought at the new shop. Outside, the gray sky grew dim, as the sun had just set.

After a few strange beeps on Hailey's phone interrupted what Jeff was saying to her, Marina politely excused herself to get Hailey's attention. Marina had to speak loudly to be heard over the music, but Hailey eventually removed one of her earphones and took the phone from Marina. There was an incoming call from a number she didn't recognize.

"Got another call, Jeff. Marina will B-R-B." Then Hailey switched over to the other line and said, "Hello?"

"May I speak with Hailey, please?" The woman on the other end spoke slowly, and continued after Hailey identified herself. "This is Isabel from *The Mermaid's Lagoon*. You and your friends came into my shop last week. Please forgive me, dearie, but I got your telephone number from the mailing list card you filled out. I'm trying to get in touch with one of your friends, the girl with the sad blue eyes. Would you know how I can contact her, dearie?"

"Yeah." Hailey skeptically drew out the word because she didn't want to reveal too much about Marina. "Like, what is this about?"

"I've been unpacking the rest of my inventory, and I came across an intriguing print that she might be interested in. A picture of a mermaid with an orange tail."

"O-M-G." Hailey held the phone in place as she turned her head toward Marina. The woman was still speaking, but Hailey's ear was too far from the phone to hear her clearly.

Marina had rolled onto her stomach and was smiling as she lay on the bed. Her knees were bent such that her feet, crossed at the ankles, were swinging up in the air to dry the nail polish. Hailey watched, picturing Marina's legs and feet replaced by her orange mermaid tail, the fluke flipping back and forth.

Hailey wondered why out of all the prints and posters in the shop, either on display or still packed, did the old woman choose to contact her about that particular one. Her psychic reading of Marina—or whatever it was that rainy afternoon— was accurate in Marina was mourning the loss of family members. Could the woman know that Marina was really a mermaid, and could she know the precise color of the tail?

"We can be there in thirty minutes," Hailey said slowly.

"How late are you open?"

Curious, Marina looked up at Hailey. She was even more confused after Hailey switched the phone back to Jeff's call and said to him, "Say good night to Marina. She'll have to T-T-Y-L."

Hailey held the phone by Marina's cheek so she and Jeff could say good night, and then she told Marina about the old woman's discovery. Out in the hallway, Hailey stepped towards the guest room to invite Jill to come along with them. As she held up her fist to knock on the door, she froze, figuring that Jill would probably think the trip to the shop was a waste of time. Hailey wanted at least to make the offer, because she missed hanging out with her cousin and felt guilty for not including her, so she knocked once on the door and politely said, "Marina and I are going out, K? Wanna come?"

But there was no answer. They hadn't realized that Jill had left the house.

Hailey's father had gone back off-island for work that morning, and he wouldn't be back for a few more days. Her mother had left for her book club, picked up by her friend as usual, so the convertible was parked alone in the driveway with its roof already closed.

As they drove across the island, the sky grew much darker from the combination of usual nighttime and the heavy cloud coverage. There were already raindrops falling when they parked the car and crossed the street to the shop.

A "Sorry, We're Closed" sign hung behind the window on the front door. The blinds were drawn on all the windows, including the one in the front door, and there was only dim light inside, but Hailey knocked anyway. They heard someone unlatch the door, and then it creaked open slowly and rang the bell above it. Seeing Hailey and Marina standing there, she smiled wide enough to show she was missing a few teeth.

"Get yourselves out of the rain, dearies," she said while gesturing them inside. Then she closed and bolted the door behind them.

Wearing a floor-length black dress similar to the one she wore when they first met her, the old woman waddled over to Marina. "It's you, dearie." She reached up and squeezed Marina's cheeks. "I knew it was you."

"What are you talking about?" mumbled Marina, her lips scrunched up like a fish's mouth.

The woman released her hold on Marina's face and walked towards the counter where the cash register was. "I was rotating my inventory, and I came across a print of a painting. I've had it for some time now. Not sure where I got it, on the mainland somewhere, I believe. But when I came across it today, I recognized the face and the sad blue eyes. I knew it was you, dearie."

Worried about the information provided by the woman, Hailey and Marina turned to each other apprehensively. Over the phone, she had mentioned that the picture was of an orange-tailed mermaid, and in the store, she declared that it was Marina. If this weird woman knew Marina's true identity, Hailey worried that she'd try to capture Marina, especially since she had told them about the mermaids granting wishes or their blood and tears having healing powers. Hailey glanced over her shoulder at the locked front door with its blinds drawn, and fearing for her friend, she clutched Marina's hand as they finally reached the cash register.

Resting flat on the counter was a matted print inside a standard eighteen-inch by twenty-four-inch wooden frame. As they peered down, their eyes instantly focused on the orange-tailed mermaid in the bottom right quarter of the image. Hailey sighed in relief upon seeing that though the mermaid in the picture appeared to have blue eyes, she was a baby girl—a mere infant—and clearly not identifiable as Marina.

"L-O-L, lady." Hailey's hand was at her chest, feeling her beating heart slow to a normal rhythm. "You really had us going there, thinking my friend here was a mermaid."

"Oh no, dearie, don't be silly," said the woman. "Look at the other face."

Marina had already pulled her head back to see the image in its entirety. The baby was being cradled in the arms of a woman who was standing barefoot on a rock near turbulent waters. Other than the mer's bright orange tail, the remaining colors of the picture were muted, suggesting a somber scene. Reaching up from the water was a pair of arms, their owner obscured by the waves. The woman's dress, billowing in the wind, was colored a dull shade of peach. As she looked down at the baby mer, her face was sad and unbelievably familiar; long blonde hair, blue eyes, and a pure white complexion. The woman in the picture had Marina's face, almost as if Marina were looking into a mirror.

"Quite an uncanny resemblance, wouldn't you say?" The woman had come out from behind the counter and was standing behind Marina. "I knew it was you, dearie, but the question is how could it be you? According to the date on the back of the print, the painting is seventeen years old."

Marina didn't take her eyes off of the image, and she traced her fingers along the glass of the picture frame to follow the contours of the woman's face. *Seventeen years old,* she thought, remembering that her age in human time measurement was only one year older.

There was a flash outside that briefly lit up the store's interior, followed quickly by a loud crash of thunder, which startled Marina out of her trance.

"It could just be a coincidence." Hailey took Marina's arm to get her away from the woman before her questions became more personal. "We should get home before the storm gets too bad."

Marina turned to Hailey and said, "Yes, we should leave."

As they stepped towards the door, the woman called them back. "Dearie, you're forgetting something. I believe you may need this to find what you've been looking for."

There was another lightning flash, but the thunder that followed wasn't as soon or as loud. The girls turned back to see the old woman holding the print out to them. Hailey reached for her purse, but the woman refused the payment, offering the picture as a gift to aid in Marina's search.

Other than the raindrops pounding the car's exterior and the occasional thunderclap, the ride home was quiet. Hailey kept her concentration on driving instead of talking. Many of the island's roads didn't have street lights, and even with the car's windshield wipers on their highest setting, visibility was low. Marina held the print in front of her, catching a glimpse of it at each lightning flash and trying to memorize the complete image.

During the darkness between lightning bolts, Marina's memory flashed back to her early childhood. She could only remember living with Lorelei and Finn since she was orphaned as an infant. She couldn't remember what her parents looked like, and she certainly didn't know why they left her. For much of her life, she doubted she even had parents, except whenever Lorelei's father would occasionally comment how much Marina looked like her mother.

At the next flash of lightning, Marina saw the face in the picture once again, and she believed the woman had to be her mother. And she was the baby mer with the orange tail. And her mother was sad that she had to leave her baby in the sea with another mer. The picture told part of her life story, and she knew where the plot went from there, but she wanted more than anything to know her story's beginning and why her mother had to give her up. The only reason she could think of was because her mother could no longer live in the water, and the only way that could happen was if her mother lost her tail at sunrise on the morn of no moon.

After Hailey had parked the car in the driveway, they dashed inside through the pouring rain. Hailey was completely drenched. Only Marina's back was soaked from running hunched over to shield the picture from the rain.

When they got upstairs, the door to the guest room was still closed, with a thin sliver of light shining underneath the door. Assuming Jill hadn't even left the room while they were gone, Hailey decided to leave her cousin alone. Hailey opened the door to her bedroom, only to find she had left the light on, and she and Marina went inside.

Once they were in dry pajamas—Marina having opted for a flannel nightgown—they sat on the bed facing each other with their legs crossed and the print between them. Marina told Hailey everything she had thought about in the car, stating that the picture was proof that her mother was somewhere on land.

"Let's find out more," said Hailey as she turned the picture face down and carefully opened the frame.

The picture stayed secure in its matting while Hailey removed the cardboard backing to the frame. Printed on the bottom left corner of the blank white back of the picture were the words "*Coral*, acrylic on canvas" and a date seventeen years earlier, but no mention of an artist's name.

"So the painting's title is *Coral*. W-T-H does that mean?" Hailey curled both her hands into fists and gently tapped them against her forehead as she leaned forward and thought aloud. "There's coral under the sea, right? Ooh! Her dress is a pretty shade of coral, don't you think?"

But Marina's eyes had widened and she was sitting straight and smiling. "My mother's name is Coral."

"That's another awesome mermaid name." Hailey bounced off the bed and grabbed her laptop.

After booting up her laptop, Hailey started an internet search for the painting. Unfortunately, the search parameters of "coral mermaid" were far too vague, and hundreds of unrelated websites and images were listed. Hailey tried a variety of different word combinations, but there were still too many pictures, and the painting they were seeking was not among the first few pages shown.

But Hailey diligently scrolled through the search results while Marina stared at the print and tried to imagine the circumstances behind her mother giving her up. The tears in her mother's eyes told her that it was a reluctant choice, but it also gave Marina hope that she had family out there somewhere. All she wanted to do was find her mother, not even to ask her what happened, but just to meet her and embrace her and no longer feel so alone.

The storm continued, and about an hour later, Hailey turned away from the laptop screen and blinked her strained eyes. "I can't find it. O-M-G, like, *everything's* supposed to be on the internet."

"I need to know why you left me and why no one in the school will tell me your reason." Clutching the frame in her hands, Marina spoke to the face in the print. "Mothers should not keep secrets from their daughters." A few teardrops fell from her eyes and splattered on the glass of the picture frame.

Upon hearing Marina's words, Hailey's shoulders slumped as she stared guiltily at the floor. *Daughters shouldn't keep secrets from their mothers either*, she thought. "I've been lying to my mom. I know I've been doing it to protect you and Meredith, but O-M-G, what will she think of me?"

Marina took Hailey's hand. "If you feel you must tell her the truth, then tell her."

Sniffling, Hailey shook her head. "But that means more people will know about your kind. I want to keep you all safe, but I don't want to—"

"You do not want to lie to your mother. That is admirable. I have trusted you to keep my true identity safe, and you have proven yourself worthy of that trust. Perhaps she will also be so worthy."

Hailey believed that protecting the merfolk was just as admirable as telling her mother the truth. As the lightning flashed outside, she bounced on the bed and said, "Maybe my mom can help. She's a librarian, and even though that's about books, she might know how to find an artist."

"The woman said she believes it came from the mainland," said Marina as the thunder rumbled in the distance.

"Well, yeah, my mom might be able to take us off-island." Hailey wiped away her last few tears and grinned. "She's got to work tomorrow, but maybe this weekend—"

"Remember that it is halfway through the moon cycle." Marina stood and looked out the window at the cloudy, moonless sky. The rain was pouring down fast and heavy. "Time is running short, so I should leave soon if I want to search for my mother."

It was at that moment when Susan was about to knock on Hailey's door to check on the girls, but when she heard Marina's final statement, she backed away and returned downstairs to make a phone call. When the voice on the other end greeted her, she said, "I know you just got back from your safari yesterday, but Meredith's acting strangely. If you can, you might want to consider coming to get her."

After Susan revealed what she had overheard, Meredith's mother's mind was made up. It was too late and stormy that evening, so she and her husband would be arriving on the first ferry the next morning to bring their daughter home.

~ Chapter Twenty-Nine ~

Unable to believe the terrible news he had just heard, Barney was swimming as fast as he could back to Lorelei's cavern to warn them.

Before the sun had set, he had gone to the cavern to visit Meredith, but she wasn't there, and Lorelei didn't know where she had swum off to. Not wanting to be alone, he had found a pair of maids that were friends with Calliope, though they weren't with her at the time. The maids were usually nice to him when she wasn't around, so there had been no need for him to be afraid to swim with them.

Sometime after the sun had set, Calliope returned and gathered up the maids. Barney had dashed off almost immediately, but not before he had overheard why Calliope was there. She was going to bring Meredith to her father, and Barney knew that the only reason mers were brought to Calliope's father was because they had broken rules. Fearing that Meredith's secret had been discovered, Barney took off to warn her.

"Lorelei? Is Meredith here?" asked Barney when he saw Lorelei outside the cavern. "Bad news. There is bad news. I think Calliope knows. But I do not know how she knows. Or why she knows. How could she know? I did not tell. Did you tell? No, you would not tell. How could she know?"

"Calm down, Barney." Lorelei took hold of his flailing arms. "What do you think Calliope knows?"

"About Meredith. Why else would Calliope want to bring Meredith to her father? And she has friends to help her! They will take her away. Where is Meredith? We have to protect her."

Lorelei hadn't seen Meredith all evening. Earlier in the day, it had appeared that Meredith was resting, so Lorelei had gone out for a swim. When she had returned to an empty cavern, she assumed at the time that Meredith had gone out to find her. Even though Barney was often prone to exaggeration, he wasn't a liar, so she knew there was truth in his information. Meredith was in trouble.

If Calliope knew the truth about Meredith and planned to tell her father, then the punishment would be exile—not just banishment from the school, but being left washed ashore on a small unpopulated sandy island far off the coast of the main island. With the day of no moon starting at the next sunrise, it wasn't just Meredith that was in trouble; Marina would be in danger of losing her tail.

Whether the timing in the moon cycle had something to do with Meredith's unexplained disappearance, Lorelei couldn't be sure. But if it did, she didn't want to wait to find out. She had to protect Marina's tail above everything else.

"When you saw Calliope, do you know which direction she came from?" asked Lorelei. After Barney nodded, but before he could speak, she commanded, "You swim that way, and maybe you will find Meredith to warn her. I will try to stop Calliope. This is sink or swim time, Barney."

As Barney swam away, Lorelei hoped she could talk some sense into Calliope before she could speak to her father since he could be even more stubborn. Not even Lorelei's father, the school's trusted advance scout, would be able to sway him once he had made a decision. Lorelei prayed it wouldn't come to that.

She stopped when she saw Calliope in the distance swimming at the front vertex in a triangular formation with the two other mers. It was clear that they were swimming with purpose, so Lorelei propelled herself forward to intercept them.

"Get out of my way," growled Calliope.

Lorelei ignored the demand and floated right in front of

their path, causing them to break formation as they swam either over, under, or around her. They kept swimming, but Lorelei had slowed them down for a few seconds at least. She blocked their path two more times before Calliope finally stopped and shrieked, "Will you stop that?"

"You do not need to do this," said Lorelei.

"Your new friend has exposed her tail to a human."

Lorelei took the underwater equivalent of a deep breath. Though Calliope had accused Meredith of a severe violation, Lorelei was relieved that Calliope hadn't discovered Meredith's true identity. "She is new to our school. She has not yet learned all of our rules."

"That does not matter. Meredith has placed all of us in danger." Calliope circled around Lorelei. "I hope you are not hiding her, or I shall have to report you as well."

"She would have no reason to interact with humans." Lorelei held her arms before her in a gesture to calm Calliope down. "You may be mistaken."

"I saw her sitting on a rock beside a long-haired human-maid. She must be punished, and then our school must leave these waters. There is no other option."

Calliope's eyewitness account confirmed for Lorelei that Meredith had gone to visit her friend Jill, probably to discuss sacrificing Marina's tail and transforming back to human form at sunrise. Though angry that Meredith had made such plans in secret, Lorelei couldn't turn Marina's tail over to Calliope and her piranha-like friends.

"It is suspicious that Marina has been absent so long. Could Meredith have taken her tail?"

Lorelei gasped but quickly said, "Marina would never let that happen."

"I knew when this Meredith first arrived that she would be a problem. I should have alerted my father then. He always said orange-tails were not to be trusted." Calliope turned to her minions, who were nodding their heads and muttering their agreement. "At least all Marina did was follow you blindly."

"How dare you speak that way of my best friend," said Lorelei through clenched teeth. She swam toward Calliope, and at the last moment before colliding with her, she sharply turned away and upward. With one forceful swing, Lorelei's fluke slapped Calliope across the face.

As Lorelei swam away, she heard Calliope reprimanding her, but she didn't look back. She doubted Calliope would chase after her but hoped that she had provided Meredith with enough extra time. More importantly, she hoped that Barney had succeeded in his task to find her and warn her.

Barney was swimming as fast as he could towards where Calliope had come from. He muttered to himself, hoping that he was going the right way and that he wasn't too late. He was still in relatively deep ocean water, but he knew he was getting closer to the island. If Calliope had seen Meredith near or even on the shore, would he have to go that far himself? He had never been so close to land without his parents, and he was terrified.

The ocean was dark, and even though his eyes adjusted to it, Barney wasn't exactly sure where he was. He slowed the flapping of his tail and glided into a vertical position to better look around, but all he saw was dark blue in every direction, sprinkled with glowing dots of green. As he frantically spun around, he was no longer sure which direction he had come from or which direction he was headed.

Just when he had almost lost hope of saving Meredith, he heard a voice ask, "Barney, what are you doing out here?"

The familiar voice came from behind and above, and when he turned toward it, he smiled upon seeing a mer calmly swimming downward towards him. Her orange tail, pale and appearing almost colorless in the water, didn't identify her as Meredith as easily as her slicked-back short hair did.

"You must not return to the school right now. There is trouble," said Barney, without pausing much between sentences as usual. "Calliope is coming to find you. She wants to bring you to her father. Lorelei went to try to stop her.

You must hide."

Abruptly stopping, she deduced that it must have been Calliope she had heard in the water while she had been talking to Jill. Since Calliope was after her, Meredith knew that she had been spotted with Jill, and she would be in trouble for that. She feared that if Calliope had heard any part of the conversation, then the truth was known. "Where should I go?" she asked.

"I do not know these waters." Barney looked around. "I do not think I can get myself back home."

"Home is that way." Without even thinking about it or how she knew, Meredith pointed in the direction she had been swimming before noticing Barney. She wiggled her fluke and floated off in one direction a bit and then turned around as if she were pacing while she thought out loud. "I don't know where there's a safe place to hide. Lorelei might know, but that won't help right now, and I can't stay here right now."

In one fluid motion, she brought her arms to her side, arched her upper body forward, and flipped her tail upward. Jetting ahead, she headed neither for the island nor Lorelei's cavern.

"Where are you going?" asked Barney, struggling to catch up with her. "How will we know where to find you?"

Meredith slowed down to allow Barney to swim beside her. "You won't know where to find me. You can't know. It's the only way to protect you and Lorelei. I'm going to have to be on my own until the full moon."

Barney reached out for her hand and said, "I could stay with you."

For the first time since she had transformed, Meredith felt warmth inside her, both from Barney's sudden touch and his sincere offer. Her fluke stopped flipping as she slowed and turned to him, the two of them soaring into face-to-face vertical positions. "That's so sweet of you, Barney," she said, wiping her eyes with her free hand. She felt a few heartfelt tears float off into the ocean. "But I can't let you do that."

"I want to." He squeezed her hand gently. "Sink or swim."

Meredith looked into his eyes and noticed for the first time how their gray color sparkled a little silvery, matching his tail. *Sink or swim*, she thought as she reached around his neck and pulled his head close enough to kiss him.

Her eyes closed, and she felt his hand let go of hers as both of his arms fell limply from the surprise. Her other arm free, Meredith reached up for his cheek and held him closer to her. She had never kissed a boy before, and she only barely knew what she was doing from young adult romance books she had read. But she knew she was enjoying the experience as her entire body, from head to tail, tingled. She felt as if she was floating.

Unfortunately, she knew she couldn't let the kiss linger too long, for she had to hide. When she backed away and looked around at the slightly lighter water, she giggled upon looking up and realizing they were a little closer to the ocean's surface. The kiss had caused both of them to float. Literally.

She had to nudge Barney to rouse him from the wide-smiled trance he was in, and then he didn't barrage her with the usual series of quick questions and comments. Meredith took his hand and gestured in the correct direction home. "Maybe we'll see each other again," she said, reluctantly letting go.

Still rendered speechless, Barney waved goodbye and then swam away. Meredith watched for a fleeting moment before having to flee herself.

Passing many smaller fish, she headed in the general direction she had been pointing, but she angled herself downward to swim towards the ocean floor. If there was going to be a safe place to hide, Meredith reasoned it would most likely be there. As she descended, she couldn't help but feel guilty. All she had wanted to do was follow through on a promise she had made to Jill, but she embroiled Lorelei and Barney in her problems. As much as she was responsible for sitting with part of her tail above the water, she couldn't be held responsible for Calliope's devious spying on her. That mer had been out to get her since they first met, and she couldn't understand why. Maybe it was jealousy; Calliope had a purple tail like many other mers, but there was only one orange tail.

One orange tail that Meredith needed to preserve at all costs.

Having shorter hair than other mers caused less fluid resistance, so that helped her speed, but she sensed something large and threatening nearby. Over the two weeks, she hadn't encountered any sharks, and hopefully, it wasn't one. She glanced below her and casually to each side but saw nothing. She couldn't look too far to either side or above and behind her at all without drastically changing the angle of her head, which would either alter her course or reduce her speed.

Whatever it was she sensed, it was behind her off to one side and approaching quickly. "You cannot outswim us," said Calliope from behind.

Meredith kept her arms tightly by her side and her head tucked down to keep a constant speed, but what she sensed pursuing her was larger than one mermaid. Calliope must have brought along her friends—or maybe a full herd, pod, or whatever a group of mermaids was called. While contemplating the correct vocabulary word, Meredith suddenly felt fingertips brush against the very edge of her fluke.

Calliope had reached for her, but by bringing and stretching her arm forward, she slowed, which allowed Meredith's fluke to flap right out of her grasp. She cursed herself as she brought her arm back to her side and kicked forward, knowing they would have to overtake her.

Meredith could sense Calliope slowly rising behind her and gaining on her. Whatever advantage her short hair gave her was washed away by Calliope's swimming ability, having spent her entire life with a tail as opposed to Meredith's two weeks. If she couldn't outswim Calliope, she'd have to use her brains to outwit her, so Meredith thrust her head backwards and arched her back.

Hovering over Meredith's fluke, Calliope was poised to reach down and grab Meredith at the base of her tail, but Meredith suddenly curved upward and over them, twisting herself around and taking off in nearly the opposite direction. As Calliope turned to follow Meredith, her two friends, who weren't paying close attention, passed by her and jabbed her hips with their flukes. Wincing in pain, Calliope grunted. The delay had put some distance between her and Meredith, and she took off to catch her.

While she had flipped over them, Meredith saw that Calliope was accompanied by only two other mers. Her aquatic acrobatics fooled them once, but she doubted it would fool them again. She didn't look back to see how far behind they were; she only knew that they'd eventually catch up unless she devised a method to swim faster.

She reminded herself that she had gotten an A in her physics class, where she had learned a little about airplanes and aerodynamics that she could apply to submarines and hydrodynamics. They were shaped the way they were, with a nose cone, to reduce drag. Her head and her wider shoulders weren't shaped that way; she needed to be more streamlined. She had the knowledge inside her, and she desperately needed the accompanying experience.

Bringing her arms forward and stretching them ahead of her, She clasped her hands together tightly, such that they were slightly rounded like the nose of an airplane. Though she slowed down while getting into the position, once she was in it, she shot forward faster than she had before.

She hoped she had been far enough ahead of them that they didn't see what she had done, but she didn't dare look back. Flapping her tail as quickly as she could, Meredith just swam forward. She didn't know where she was or where she was going anymore, and she didn't care, allowing her instincts to lead her somewhere safe.

Calliope was angry that she and her friends were only maintaining a constant distance behind Meredith instead of gaining on her. But she wouldn't relent until they had captured their prey. No mer was going to flaunt her tail to humans while her father led the school.

Meredith's muscles strained to keep her arms in place, especially as the water became more turbulent. When a sudden flash illuminated the waters above her, Meredith realized that she was swimming directly into the storm. But she didn't want to change direction. Maybe the others wouldn't follow her.

Calliope's two cohorts opted out of the chase and headed for home, but Calliope continued forward. As Calliope and Meredith swam further and closer to the surface, the frequency of lightning flashes increased, and the sound of thunder reverberated under the water. They both were unexpectedly pushed sideways by the force of the waves, and then again in the other direction.

Drive into the skid, Meredith told herself, thinking back to lessons in her Driver's Ed class. She turned, and she was caught by the wave, which propelled her forward further away from Calliope. But then without warning, a new wave pushed her into another direction.

From behind, Calliope watched Meredith get thrashed about by the waves. She stopped flipping her tail and turned around, deciding that any punishment her father could give Meredith would be minor compared to what the storm was doing to her, if she even survived the storm.

Losing all sense of direction and time, Meredith was flipped upside down and spun around as if all the scariest thrill rides from amusement parks were combined into one. She couldn't keep her eyelids open as water sped past her face. She tried to get away by flipping her tail, but the waves were much stronger than she was, and they carried her far away.

Sink or swim, she told herself, doing her best to swim with the waves. Eventually, the storm would have to subside, and she could use her instincts to go somewhere safe afterwards. She wondered if Lorelei had ever had such an experience.

The storm didn't relent, and the muscles in her tail grew sore and weary from her continued necessary flapping and the waves pounding against her. As she got more and more tired, she found it more difficult to focus in the dark and fierce waters. Once she stopped flipping her tail, a large wave grabbed her and flung her into something hard, where she was knocked unconscious.

~ Chapter Thirty ~

She awoke with the sensation of having crash landed from a terribly high fall, but with very little recollection of what had happened to make her feel that way. She was lying on her stomach with her arms splayed outward on either side of her. Slowly, she lifted her right cheek off the dry sand, some of which had gotten into her mouth. The gritty granules stuck to her tongue like barnacles, and she tried to spit them all out.

In the distance behind her, she could hear the sounds of the ocean echoing inside her aching head. The waves were roaring, and some gulls were squawking, but there didn't seem to be anyone else around. As far as she could tell, she was alone.

She was able to raise her upper body with little difficulty, but everything below her waist wouldn't budge. As she flexed and contracted her lower muscles, hoping to lift the heavy mass, she glanced over her shoulder to see an orange fish tail flapping. Every time it flopped, she could feel the nerve impulses course all the way up her body, and she could hear the light smack it made against the sand. Faintly sparkling in the pale light, scales of various shades of orange covered her from the end of her fin to the small of her back.

She was clearly a mermaid.

Memories whirled around in her head. It had been dark. The waters had been rough and the waves large. She had tried to avoid the undercurrents—her instincts were leading her somewhere safe—but the stormy waters were too strong for her. Her tail wouldn't flip fast enough to escape, and she was caught. She had been violently thrown around in the storm until she blacked out.

Sometime in the middle of the darkness, she had washed ashore. Faint red light in the cloudless, sunless sky suggested to her that it was either dawn or dusk. Based on how deserted the beach was, she could only guess that it was before sunrise. Humans could appear any minute, she told herself, and mers weren't supposed to be seen by humans when in their true form. That was the rule. She had to get back to the water before she was spotted and easily captured.

She was facing away from the water where the receding tide had deposited her. The only way back to the water was to crawl or roll, but she had to turn herself around first, and both tasks were difficult when lacking legs. Heaving her upper body up as high as she could, she pivoted clockwise about her hips almost a quarter turn before her arms gave way, and she collapsed back onto her stomach.

When she repeated the process, she saw the red house. With the footbridge. That spanned over the rocks. The stairs leading down to the beach. It seemed strangely familiar, like déjà vu, or the remnants of a previous life. There was something about that house.

Then Meredith remembered. It was Hailey's house, on a private beach, on an island about an hour by ferry from the mainland.

And she was *not* a mermaid. She was a human girl who had unintentionally transformed into a mermaid on the day of the full moon and had lived amongst mermaids for two weeks.

Two weeks and a day from the full moon. Which made that morning the day of the new moon.

The new moon?!

She turned to the east, the way she was already rotating herself towards the ocean. The sun hadn't appeared yet. There was still time for her to get back into the water.

With a great heave, Meredith spun herself until she was facing the correct direction. The tide was out, so she still had a great distance to traverse. As a human, she could run to the water in only a few seconds. As a mermaid, the quickest technique she thought of was to flip herself onto her back and then onto her stomach, repeating the process until she reached the water.

A single roll took tremendous effort, as her tail wasn't light or buoyant on land. Due to the tapered shape of her tail, narrower near her fluke than at her hips, she curved a little with every flip. The constant course correcting wasted time, and once Meredith was on her stomach and facing the water, she devised a new plan. Digging her arms and elbows into the sand, she pulled herself forward in an army-style crawl with her tail dragging behind her.

She kept her eyes focused on the water ahead. She needed to get there before the sun appeared. Though the sun shining on her dry tail would finally return her to normal, it came with a great cost. Even if she had to be alone because she had been banished from the school, spending two more weeks underwater was a small price to pay compared to Marina spending the rest of her life on land.

Her arms were strained, and she wished she was on a surface more solid or graspable than beach sand, but she didn't stop moving forward. She looked up and saw Lorelei's head and shoulders above the water's surface, at a point deep enough for Lorelei to be treading water. Though Lorelei was still a great distance away, Meredith could clearly see that Lorelei was glaring right at her.

"When you did not return after the storm, I searched for you. I cannot believe you would come here to perform such a selfish act." Lorelei turned her back to Meredith and dunked her head in the water to swim away, her green tail flipping above the surface before it also went under.

"Lorelei, wait, it's not like that!" While still pulling and squirming ahead, Meredith reached forward to beckon Lorelei back. "I need your help! I don't know if I can make it to the water in time!"

When Lorelei didn't immediately return, Meredith thought of the one person left who had always been there for her. She no longer cared about mermaid rules forbidding her to be seen by humans, and she was somewhat grateful that she hadn't washed ashore behind the house where Hailey's nosey neighbor lived. After taking as deep a breath as possible, she bellowed, "Jill! I need you!"

Inside the guest room, Jill was awakened by the sound of a thump, one after another. When her eyes opened slightly, she saw Marina removing heavy textbooks from Meredith's suitcase and stacking them on the nearby dresser.

"What are you doing?" asked Jill, tossing the bedcovers aside and sitting up.

Marina started filling the suitcase with Meredith's clothes. "I am taking a ferry to the mainland today."

"You can't just pack up and leave." Jill sprung from the bed and tried to wrestle some of Meredith's clothes from Marina. "And you can't just take my friend's stuff with you."

"She has had my tail since the full moon. I think it is fair to borrow her clothes for the same length of time."

"You can't do this, Marina. That wasn't part of the plan."

"For all of my life, I have been without my parents, and now I may no longer be alone. Someone on the mainland once saw my mother. I need to find that someone." She placed the orange-tailed mermaid figurine that Hailey had given her into the suitcase. As she glanced at it, she remembered how Hailey had said it looked like her. But not any longer, because that mermaid was small and complacently sitting on a rock instead of taking a stand. "This is the first time in my life where I will follow no one other than myself. Please, let me go."

"What about Meredith? What's going to happen to her if something happens to you out there, and you don't come back before the full moon?"

"If she does what Lorelei tells her, she will transform back at sunrise at the full moon whether I am here or not." Marina closed and zipped the suitcase, and then she lifted it off the bed. "You will have your friend back."

"What about Jeff? You're gonna leave him on the hook, aren't you? And you're gonna do the same thing to Hailey now, right? Well, that's not fair to either of them."

"It is not like that, Jill." Marina reached for the doorknob and slowly opened the door. "With only half a moon cycle remaining—"

"Enough about the moon!" Jill's long arm reached out and slammed the door shut. Standing straight and tall, she loomed over Marina. "Look, I tried to be nice to you at first, but let's admit that you and I haven't been getting along lately. Last night, I told Meredith she should just do it, come ashore today and do the whole new-moon thing, even if it trapped you out here on land forever."

Marina backed against the door, slowly sinking downward in intimidation.

"Meredith refused. She stood up for you. She told me we'd figure out a way to keep this going another two weeks. She did that for *you*, Marina. So walking out that door is not standing up for *her*. I guess that makes you half the mermaid she is."

There were four knocks on the door, the secret signal. Marina stepped out of the way to allow Jill to let Hailey inside.

"O-M-G, you two are loud." Hailey stood there, yawning and blinking the slumber from her eyes, but she was otherwise fully dressed and holding the handle of her own suitcase.

"You're going too?" scoffed Jill, one hand on her hip and the other with its index finger pointed at her cousin. "Don't expect me to improv an explanation to bail you out of this sinking ship."

"No need," said Marina. "We are going to tell Aunt Susan the truth."

Jill laughed. "And you think she'll believe you? If I hadn't seen it with my own two eyes, I'd think you're both crazy. You're gonna need proof."

Something on the beach outside the window caught Hailey's eye. She leaned forward until she recognized the orange tail, barely noticeable atop the sandy surface. "Oh no, we have some proof. Nine-one-one, there's a beached mermaid who needs our help."

Keeping her eyes just above the surface of the water, Lorelei carefully watched Meredith crawling towards the ocean. She couldn't believe what she was witnessing. Meredith wasn't doing something for herself; instead she was sincerely sacrificing the opportunity to revert to human form two weeks ahead of schedule.

Lorelei swam to the beach, allowing the incoming waves to propel her faster until her stomach slid to a halt on the wet sand. She turned to the horizon—no sun yet—and then back to face Meredith, who was still struggling.

"Sink or swim?" Lorelei asked.

Using whatever energy that hadn't yet drained from her, Meredith hauled her tail, which only seemed to grow heavier and heavier. Meredith's upper body was hunched over from fatigue. She could barely look up when she heard the familiar phrase. "Swim," she wheezed. "I don't...know...if I...can make it."

Lorelei glanced eastward. The red in the sky had grown brighter. "The sun is soon to rise. I cannot leave the water." She flopped her fluke and heard it splash, verifying that she was still sufficiently submerged. A wave rolled over her, soaking her shoulders before it receded. "You will have to reach for me, and I will pull you in."

Meredith stretched her right arm, but there was still a distance of several feet between her and Lorelei. The pace of her crawling had slowed as she became more and more physically exhausted, but she lunged forward. Remembering Lorelei's strength while dragging her out into the open water for her first swimming lesson, Meredith extended her arm further.

"You are almost here." Careful to keep her tail in the water, Lorelei had inched forward as the rising tide slowly inched up the beach.

All of the muscles in Meredith's upper body ached, and all she could do was belly-flop forward. On her third flop, the tips of her fingers finally brushed Lorelei's, but before Lorelei could yank her forward, Meredith's arm jerked back as she squealed and writhed in severe pain.

Her tail curling, she keeled over onto her side and clenched her throbbing stomach. She wailed and flopped onto her back, her fluke thumping down on the sand before it started tingling.

The sun had pierced the horizon, and Meredith's transformation had begun.

~ Chapter Thirty-One ~

Meredith's tail was overcome by the stabs of pins and needles, which increased in their intensity. Then without warning, she felt as if the two ends of her fluke were wrenched in opposite directions, violently ripping the tailfin apart in the middle.

Clamping her eyes shut, she screamed in excruciating pain. Whether due to the transformation itself or the timing of it happening on the morning of the new moon, Meredith didn't care. She just wanted the torture to end as quickly as possible.

She tried to flap her fin, but the two halves jiggled independently from one another like they were bags of jelly. They didn't feel like feet, but they were sore at the edges from where she had been torn apart.

It took all her might, but she lugged herself up into a seated position. The vibrant colors of her tailfin had faded, and she watched as the two residual flippers shrank in length but inflated in thickness. As five little buds sprouted from the tips of each half, she felt more solidity and less floppiness. After two weeks without them, she finally had her two feet back, each with its complete set of toes.

The jagged sides of overlapping scales, from her ankles up to where her knees would be, were separating as if the two halves of a zipper were being violently pulled apart. Orange gave way to pinkish flesh, and each half slowly started reforming into her shins as scales disappeared from her knees.

A herd of footsteps clopped on the footbridge, and the volume grew louder until it abruptly ceased. Meredith forced her eyes open, and tears blurred her vision of the three figures rushing down the beach towards her. The two girls in front were taller than the third girl, who lagged behind with some sort of large case hanging at the end of one arm.

"Jill! Hailey!" Meredith tried to kick her feet or even wiggle her toes, but she was numb from the waist down. "I can't move my legs. Get me to the water, quickly!"

"But why? You're almost human again!" Jill jumped back and grabbed the suitcase from Marina's hand. She opened it and rifled through the contents until she found the one dress that Meredith had brought with her to the island.

"We have to save Marina's tail!" Hailey had run all the way to Meredith's back and reached under her arms to start dragging her backwards toward the water.

Jill turned toward Marina, who stood teary-eyed in shock as she watched Meredith's knees reappear. The only part of her orange tail that remained was still wrapped around Meredith's thighs and hips, but those scales were melting away into human skin.

Barely budged by Hailey, Meredith called, "Jill, please. Being a mermaid has been too incredible an experience. I can't just let this tail disappear."

"You can be really stubborn sometimes, you know that?" said Jill, who tossed the dress over her shoulder and ran towards Meredith.

Facing the water, Jill and Hailey stood on opposite sides of Meredith, and each reached under one of her arms. They lifted her up but only barely because of the dead weight of Meredith's immobile legs. They lurched forward, and Meredith's dragging heels dug two parallel paths into the sand.

"Do not enter the ocean," commanded Lorelei from the water ahead of them, her tail safely submerged.

"We're trying to save your friend's tail," said Jill. "Don't you want to help?"

"There may be another way." She beckoned for Marina. "If Meredith removes the tail as soon as she reverts to human

222

form, there may be enough time for you to put it on."

Marina stepped forward. "I must stay on land. I need these legs."

"Do not be foolish, Marina." Lorelei smacked the water's surface with her fluke. "Your tail will soon be gone forever."

"My mother, Lore." As she walked toward the water's edge, Marina passed by Meredith. "She is out here. I may find her with legs, but not with a tail."

Lorelei said, "Then you would no longer be a mer, and you will remain human."

Marina hung her head. "I know."

Jill and Hailey lowered Meredith back onto the sand. Meredith looked down at her legs, which were still numb but fully formed. The translucent skirt that she had found and put on over two weeks earlier was reappearing, but it was firmly adhered to her skin by a band of pale orange scales around her waist. "We're running out of time!" Meredith suddenly felt some movement in her feet. "I can wiggle my toes."

"I must find my mother," said Marina sternly.

Jill put her hand on Marina's shoulder. "I think it's very brave to take this kind of stand, but don't let it stop you from being who you are."

"You promised," said Hailey. "At the cliff, you promised that you wouldn't give up your tail. You're the coolest mermaid ever."

"There will be many more full moons," pleaded Lorelei. "We can search on land together. I will let *you* lead the way."

Marina looked out to the ocean, where a smiling Lorelei lay on her stomach in the shallow water, protecting her tail. Her fin curled up above the water and waved at her. Lorelei's lovely green fluke, its veining translucent in the bright sky, flopped gently in the breeze. Marina thought back to her first moments on land and how reluctant she had been to join Lorelei, but if it hadn't been for Lorelei's encouragement, she would never have found the painting. It was as if she were meant to spend the time on land as if something had brought her there, guiding her a few footsteps closer to her mother.

Then Marina remembered the image of her mother sadly returning her to the sea, and an alternate interpretation of the painting streamed into her mind. For whatever reason, her mother hadn't been able to come back but wanted her to be in the ocean. Marina hadn't been abandoned; she was being protected, perhaps preserving her orange tail—the only one in the school, maybe even the only one in the entire ocean.

"Make a decision quickly!" Meredith had regained some control of her knees but required Hailey's help to get to a standing position. Only a thin strip of faded scales connected the skirt to her waist, and then Meredith felt it separate from her. "It's time. I'm fully me."

Jill threw the dress over Meredith's head at the same moment Meredith stumbled and allowed the disguised mermaid tail to slide down her legs to the sand. After slipping her arms through the short sleeves of the dress, Meredith relished the sensation of wearing human clothes once again. Since Marina's tail was still in contact with her ankles, Meredith hoped it was safe to pick it up off the beach.

In the sunshine, it shimmered with every color of light. Transfixed by it, Hailey reached for it and slowly said, "O-M-G. It's so beautiful."

"Do not touch it!" called Lorelei, and at the same time, Jill pulled Hailey away.

A sparkling mist surrounded the skirt, and as Meredith examined it more closely, she concluded that the mist wasn't just around it; the mist was emanating *from* it. "It's evaporating." She staggered forward, her brain and body still reconfiguring themselves to operate two legs instead of one tail. "Marina, you need to get this on now."

If the painting showed her mother wanting her to stay safe in the ocean, Marina was going to follow her mother's wishes. Two human weeks later, she could come back on land at the next full moon to continue her search, and then at every subsequent full moon—however long it took to find her mother. She dashed from the water and met Meredith halfway to retrieve the tail from her. It had lost some of its iridescence, and it looked more flimsy than she remembered it being. When she took it from Meredith, it felt slimy and wet, not how it was supposed to feel.

Marina slid her tail-skirt up her legs underneath her sundress. Some of the mist from the dissolving tail spritzed her skin. Once it was around her waist, she stepped out of her flip-flops and darted for the water, but she could feel her tail losing its substance.

She splashed in the shallow water towards Lorelei until the level of the cold water reached above her knees. There she plopped downward and sat slumped until her shoulders were underwater. As the skirt of the sundress floated on the water's surface, Marina gathered it close to her stomach and stretched her legs out in the water in front of her. She wanted to watch them merge into her tail.

But nothing happened. She knew the tail was soaked because she could feel its wetness clinging to her thighs, but she couldn't feel any part of her body changing. "Lore, something is wrong." She shuddered as she spoke. "I am not transforming."

Lorelei peeked under the water, and then her head came back up. "It is fading away. None of your scales are appearing."

On the beach, Hailey started sobbing. Jill tried to put a consoling arm around her shoulders, but Hailey pulled away and headed for the house. Jill could feel tears welling up in her eyes just from watching how badly Hailey was taking the unfortunate news about Marina's tail.

With her balance mostly restored, Meredith stepped forward and into the water. "I am so sorry."

"Do not blame yourself," said Marina. "You tried to save it. I was too late."

Soon Marina would be a human forever, her tail slowly becoming as invisible as a new moon in the night sky.

~ Chapter Thirty-Two ~

Hailey sprinted to the footbridge and jumped over all three stairs at once. The strides of her long legs brought her quickly past the empty driveway and to the house. Inside, she ascended the stairs two at a time, until she was on the second floor and inside her bedroom.

Without slowing down, she plowed through the blankets and pillows strewn about the floor. Bracing herself for impact, she crashed into her closet door.

"Please, Mom," she anxiously muttered to herself. "Please don't have organized in here."

She jerked the door open and crouched down to rummage through all the clutter on the floor until she uncovered her sewing basket. It sat against the wall underneath where her sequined mermaid costume hung. She whisked it off the floor and leapt to her desk.

When she yanked open her top desk drawer, some water spilled over the edge of the glass dish inside and dampened some papers, pens, pencils, and other items. The office supplies didn't matter to her; only the contents of the dish mattered. Carefully, she lifted the heart-shaped container out of the desk, and the orange scales from Marina's tail sparkled vibrantly inside the water.

Maybe the old shopkeeper's comment about the restorative power of a mermaid's tail was true, or at least Hailey hoped and prayed it was.

Although she knew time was running out, she descended the stairs slower than she had ascended them. Any bounce or stumble could jostle the container and scatter the scales all over the place, wasting what little precious time there was left.

When she returned to the beach, she breezed by Meredith and Jill, who were huddled together with their heads bowed as if they were mourning. Marina sat still in the water with her face buried in her hands and her head cradled by Lorelei, who gently stroked her blonde hair. A ring of glittery sea foam— remnants of her slowly dissolving tail—circled Marina's waist. It appeared as if the four of them had lost hope.

But Hailey hadn't.

She knelt in the water beside Marina and plunged her sewing basket onto Lorelei's lap, not caring if its contents got drenched. Before Lorelei could protest or even question, Hailey handed the dish to Lorelei and commanded, "Don't drop this."

Jill stepped forward. "Hailey, what are you doing?"

Hailey didn't even turn around. Opening her sewing kit with one hand, she thrust her other hand far behind her, the palm fully outstretched. "T-T-T-H, Jill!"

Upon realizing what was in the dish, Lorelei nudged Marina. Slowly, she looked up, her shoulders and head rising as her eyes widened upon seeing the scales glistening in the sunlight.

Marina turned to Hailey and asked, "Are those…mine?"

Hailey nodded while threading a needle from her sewing basket

"But how? Why?"

"I collected them off the floor when they came off Meredith." Hailey looked up, and her eyes met Marina's quizzical stare. Hailey shrugged and smiled. "They were mermaid scales. Of course, I'd keep them."

"Thank you." Marina stood and lifted the hem of her soaked sundress just above her knees, revealing the transparent skirt underneath. Its glimmer was almost gone.

Quickly, Hailey reached for a scale from the dish and pierced it with the needle, drawing the silver thread through the hole. Then she held up the lower edge of Marina's tail-skirt. The fabric, or whatever it was, was extremely thin and sheer, almost non-existent. "I don't know if this'll hurt, but it's worth a shot."

She pushed the needle through Marina's skirt, but there was very little material to keep the thread in place, almost as if she was sewing through mesh. Searching her basket, Hailey needed something stronger to stitch the scale to, something to use as an inner lining.

Something human-made in her kit wouldn't solve the problem, and she realized that what she needed was already in the heart-shaped dish. She started sewing a chain of scales, alternating between the inside and outside of Marina's tail-skirt. With each new scale, Hailey pulled the thread tightly to keep the chain in contact with the skirt.

Once they had realized what Hailey was doing, Meredith and Jill approached and were impressed by the diligence and speed of her work. Once believing the old shopkeeper's words to be fictitious, Jill hoped that they were indeed true. Meredith watching Marina's legs, longing to see the dazzling orange tail that she had grown attached to over the previous two weeks.

Lorelei looked toward the horizon and announced, "The sun has almost fully risen."

As Hailey sewed the final scale in place, she backed away and crossed her fingers. Between the rising tide and an incoming wave, Marina was suddenly submerged to her waist with the chain of scales fully immersed. She hoped that contact with the water would activate them, but still nothing was happening. Another glittery ring from her dissipating tail bubbled up to the water's surface as light from the full sun illuminated them.

Then Marina's knees buckled.

She fell backwards into the water, and her entire body sank. Seconds passed, but nothing was happening. Then suddenly, bright light radiated from the spot where Marina had plunged into the water, so bright that everyone else averted their eyes and backed away.

And then an orange tailfin broke through the water's

surface.

Hailey was the first one there, ready to wrap her arms around Marina's shoulders when they floated up and above the water. "That was incredible, Hailey," said Marina. "I have no way to repay you."

"You don't have to repay me. This is one of the flowiest things I've ever done! I just saved a mermaid." A smile stretched across her face, and she bobbed her head up and down. "And not just any mermaid. I saved my B-F-F."

"B-F-F?" asked Lorelei.

"Best Friends Forever," replied Marina.

"Nuh-uh." Hailey shook her head and giggled. "Best Friend with Fins."

"I promise I will return on the next full moon," said Marina. "We can spend the day together."

"Till you come back, I'm gonna do as much searching as I can, on the internet and stuff, to find out where that painting came from. Your mother's out there, Marina, somewhere. I know it. You'll find her."

Jill approached her cousin. "Hailey, what you just did...well...that was brilliant. And what you're going to do for her now, I'm so proud of you." Jill looked over at Marina, who nodded in approval. "And I'm sorry if I ever made you feel like you were—"

"Silly Jillybean," snickered Hailey, standing and putting her arm around Jill. "You're, like, the best cousin ever."

Hailey took her glass dish and drenched sewing basket from Lorelei. Then, the cousins started walking up the beach to leave Meredith and Marina alone for a moment. Even Lorelei floated a short distance away.

Walking through the water toward Marina, Meredith observed that it was difficult to move forward with her legs. "Your tail is stunning, right back where it belongs."

"Thank you for taking such good care of it." Marina swished the water with her fluke.

"I tried to get back in the water. If I hadn't met up with Jill last night, I wouldn't have gotten washed ashore, and you wouldn't have almost lost your tail. I'm so sorry." Once Meredith felt Marina's hand on her shoulder, she calmed herself, and somehow she knew that the apology she was issuing was both unnecessary and unconditionally accepted. "If I had known you needed the time to start searching for your mother, there wouldn't have even been a question. I would have willingly spent two more weeks—"

"You did everything you could, Meredith. Thank you for trying to preserve my tail."

"But if I had spent two more weeks down there, I would have been able to learn…" Meredith glanced back at Lorelei, and they smiled at one another. "To *experience*. I would have been able to experience so much more. Thank you for sharing something so special with me. You are one fantastic girl, Marina."

"You and I hardly spent any time together, Meredith, yet I feel I know everything about you. Back on that first day, Jill made sure I did." Marina smirked. "You are a true and loyal mer."

As they hugged, Meredith standing chest-deep in water and Marina floating, the sound of car tires on gravel could be heard from the house. Wondering who it could be, Hailey turned to see her mother pulling the convertible into the driveway. While swinging her arms widely toward the ocean to shoo Marina and Lorelei back into deeper water, Hailey shouted, "All mers need to hide immediately! T-T-Y-L, and T-T-F-N!"

Marina and Lorelei disappeared into the water, reemerging shortly thereafter some distance away. They waved and then dove back under, their tailfins—the orange and the green side by side—flipping above the surface before their silhouettes vanished from the horizon.

Meredith started trudging her legs through the water, but decided instead to ride an incoming wave to the sand.

Hailey and Jill had dashed ahead, hoping they could direct Susan into the house instead of towards the beach. But when they reached her, she eyed their wet clothes and asked,

"What's going on? Taking an early swim?"

They heard two more car doors shut. They weren't alone. Jill turned and recognized the man and woman as Meredith's parents.

On the beach, Meredith had stopped to gather her suitcase, which had been left there by Marina. When she finally reached the footbridge and saw who had arrived, she dropped her baggage, ran to her parents, and practically jumped into her father's outstretched arms.

"Morning, Sweetie," said her father. "You're soaked."

But Meredith squeezed him so tightly that the bikini's seashells under her dress dug into her skin. "I love you so much."

She moved to her mother, who asked, "And in that dress? Are you feeling all right?"

"I feel great. How was your vacation?"

"We'll get to that," said her mother. "Susan called last night to say she overheard you wanting to leave and come find me. Is something bothering you?"

Meredith's father retrieved the suitcase. "Already packed? Sweetie, please tell us what's wrong."

"Nothing's wrong, Dad. Just a little homesick." Meredith sighed, happy to be with her family. "Mom, I know I was supposed to stay another week, but since you're here, can we go home today?"

"Of course, Meredith." Her mother tapped her foot on the gravel driveway. "But first I'd like an explanation. Susan says you've been acting suspicious and secretive."

"You can tell us, Sweetie," said her father.

Without thinking, Meredith blurted, "I've decided what major I want to study when I go to college. Marine biology."

"Is that all, Sweetie?" Her father hugged her again. "If that's what you want."

Her mother put her hands on her hips. "Naturally, we support your decision, but Meredith, you don't like the water."

"I do now." With that, she wrapped one arm around her

mother and pulled her closer.

Jill and Hailey had been talking to Susan, distracting her and keeping her positioned to avoid seeing Meredith's face. Once Meredith and her parents embraced, the two cousins sighed almost inaudibly and made what they thought was secretive eye contact.

As she smiled and waved at Meredith's mother, Susan spoke quietly through clenched teeth to the girls flanking her. "Meredith's no longer a blonde, I see."

Hailey's eyes bulged while Jill quickly said, "Nope. She got it dyed and cut yesterday at the place where Hailey—"

"And a full facial too? Her parents recognize her, but she looks very different than the Meredith we've been harboring here for the past two weeks." Susan raised an eyebrow as Hailey and Jill turned to her. "I'll play along until they leave, but then you two have *a lot* of explaining to do."

Glancing at each other and gulping, Jill and Hailey respectively wondered whether improvising or telling the truth was the best way to get themselves out of some seriously deep water.

~ Chapter Thirty-Three ~

On the ride to the mainland, Meredith stood on the top deck at the back of the ferry, the ocean breeze blowing through her hair. Her parents had gone one deck below to get some coffee at the snack bar. She was leaning against the railing and staring out onto the ocean, reminiscing about the most bizarre and enlightening vacation she had ever had. Other than Jill and Hailey, she couldn't tell it to anyone. There'd be no *How I Spent My Summer Vacation* essay for school. No one would believe her anyway, but she would always remember her two weeks as a mermaid, perhaps the greatest adventure she would ever experience.

Or maybe the first of many great adventures. She had been swimming with dolphins and, without learning how, had communicated with them. Deep in her heart, she wanted to do it again and learn everything else there was to know about aquatic life—both through studying it *and* experiencing it. There was room for both. She would find the college with the best marine biology program, one with hands-on learning opportunities. After living underwater for two weeks, she believed a part of her belonged there to preserve and protect all life in the oceans, including keeping the mermaids' existence a secret.

Among the white-capped rippled water in the ferry's wake, Marina swam as fast as she could to keep up. Lorelei was home with her father, so Marina was taking the lead on her first adventure. A ferry just like the one in front of her would someday take her to the mainland, or maybe she would swim there herself. It would be a fascinating experience on the mainland with humans, many of whom were sweet and helpful and loving, like a family should be.

Her mother was out there somewhere; she could feel it in her heart. It would take much time and patience and research to find her, perhaps lasting several moon cycles. She could spend the days of the full moon traveling on land, and then the remainder of cycles hiding in various bodies of water along the way. But she would stand on her own two feet and search, no matter how long it took her. Her mind was made up.

Marina maintained a safe distance from the back of the ferry, but when she looked up, she noticed Meredith on the uppermost deck. Meanwhile, Meredith saw Marina's familiar shape gliding through the water, her orange scales shimmering just below the surface. The Friday late-morning ferry heading away from the island was practically empty, but Meredith looked around to make sure no one was watching her. Then she waved at the mermaid in the water, who flipped her tailfin above the surface to wave back.

Meredith and Marina held their gazes on one another, knowing that no one else would ever fully understand what they had experienced. The new journeys they were about to start could never have happened if they had never switched places, and yet they realized that they had been everlastingly transformed for the better. As they looked at each other and ahead to their futures, they could feel deep inside them that they would forever be connected—their lives, minds, and hearts.

And tail.

Sneak peek at
Skipping the Scales
~ Chapter One ~

"Marina, you should *not* be doing this!"

She didn't have to turn around to know her best friend Lorelei was following her. Without responding, Marina flapped her orange tail even more vigorously than before. Water streamed around her as she glided through the ocean, her long blonde hair flowing behind her to halfway down her back. She knew that it would only be a matter of time before Lorelei caught up with her because while Lorelei wore only her typical seashell top, the human covering that Marina wore created too much water resistance.

As Lorelei gained on her friend, she noticed Marina's tail sticking out from under a pink sundress, presumably taken from the sunken yacht they had borrowed human clothes from before. "I know what you are thinking, and this is *not* the proper way to go about it."

"I have made up my mind, Lore." Marina caught a glimpse of Lorelei's red hair in her periphery and realized she was now swimming alongside her friend. "Though I appreciate your offer, this is something I must do on my own."

"You have only been on land twice before. I go almost every cycle."

"Lore, you forget that I spent half a moon cycle amongst the humans. In that regard, I could say that I have more experience than you."

"You may be correct, but you did not plan it back then."

Lorelei took hold of Marina's hand and then slowed the motion of her own green tail, thus decelerating both of them. "You must carefully consider the choice you are about to make. If the consequences are the same as others who have made that choice, then—"

"Sink or swim, Lore." As they drifted into a vertical position, Marina used her free hand to keep the dress from floating upwards while she looked into Lorelei's eyes. "I understand what you are trying to do, and I truly appreciate your concern, but I must not follow anyone other than myself."

Lorelei quickly surveyed the surrounding area to ensure no one had followed them. Since they had returned to the north, Calliope, the purple-tailed daughter of their school's leader, had been keeping careful watch on them. She had grown suspicious when the disappearance of the odd mer Meredith had coincided with Marina's return to the school, especially because they were the only two mers with orange tails. Her father's decision to migrate early was due to Calliope revealing that Meredith had interacted with a human-maid.

Fortunately, the early departure was the only consequence of those events, but Lorelei remained cautious when she and Marina ventured away from the school. Seeing no other mers around, Lorelei said, "I am willing to follow *you*, Marina. Please let me share the experience."

Marina glanced upward and caught glimmers of faint red light dancing on the ripples of the undersides of the waves. She was not only closer to the water's surface, but also closer to the desired time of day. "You will share it, just not the way you think you will." She turned to Lorelei and smirked. "Remember, there are two of us, but only one on the other side."

Dropping her arms limply by her side, Lorelei stared quizzically at Marina. During the awkward pause that followed, Marina seized the opportunity to kick her tail forcefully and thrust herself forward to her destination.

~ ~ ~

Sitting cross-legged on the private beach behind her island home, Hailey stared out at the eastern horizon and watched for the sun to rise. Awash with fiery colors, the cloudless sky was waiting to change to a beautiful light blue on that Wednesday morning. Waves rustled calmly as they rolled onto the shore, and the seagulls flying by called to each other. For the early time of day, the air was unusually humid, even for late June. Her straight dark hair frizzed a little bit, almost as if there were some static electricity around her. But she hoped that the sensation was a precursor to something much more fantastical.

There was going to be a full moon that night.

She had spent her entire senior year paying close attention to the calendar and circling the date of each and every full moon with orange magic marker. On each of those days, she had written the precise time the sun would rise—information she had easily obtained from an online almanac. She would go to bed as early as possible on the nights before so she was wide awake and outside before the sun came up. As she sat on the footbridge connecting the beach to her yard, Hailey would hope it was *that day*—the day that a mermaid would come back to visit.

Marina had appeared one other time during the previous summer—on the morning of the first full moon after Hailey had helped her return to the ocean—just as promised. And just as promised, Hailey had spent the two weeks researching the painting they had received, but information about it was practically non-existent. Even the strange old shopkeeper at *The Mermaid's Lagoon* who had given them the print wasn't entirely sure how or when it had ended up in her possession.

The painting depicted a baby mermaid with an orange tail being handed to outstretched arms in the ocean. The woman giving the child away, with her blue eyes and long blonde hair, bore a striking resemblance to Marina, and the painting's title, *Coral*, matched Marina's long-lost mother's name. It wasn't a far stretch of the imagination to assume that the baby was Marina, and the arms belonged to Lorelei's father, who had become Marina's adoptive guardian so long ago. The painting was enough evidence that Marina's mother— and maybe even her father—had once been somewhere on land, but no one knew where.

Though she and Hailey spent from sunrise to sunset together, it was a bittersweet reunion. After almost eighteen years of being orphaned, Marina's first glimmers of finding at least one of her parents had been washed away.

When the waterlogged translucent skirt transformed her legs into a single iridescent orange tail, Marina warned Hailey that she wouldn't be returning again that summer. After rumors surfaced that the mer named Meredith had exposed herself to humans, the leader of the school decided to migrate away earlier than usual. Regardless, Hailey vowed to be sitting on her beach at sunrise on the same day of every moon cycle in case Marina ever wanted to visit.

On the marked days, Hailey awoke to witness the sunrise but sulked away when it was time to head off to school. As the months passed, and summer turned into fall, the sun rose later, and she spent less and less time waiting on those full-moon mornings.

Even through the cold winter, she'd sit outside bundled up. There were some rainy days in the spring, where she sat under an umbrella on the steps of the footbridge connecting her yard to the beach. On one occasion, the morning of the full moon coincided with a birthday slumber party at a friend's house, and she faked being sick to drive home in time to be on her beach at sunrise.

But Marina never came back.

A full year passed. Hailey had graduated high school and received an athletic scholarship to a smaller state university on the mainland to join their swim team. Although she wasn't sure what her major was going to be, she had accepted. Anything that kept her swimming regularly would get her one step closer to her ultimate career goal of becoming a mermaid performer at an aquarium or a water theme park. There were other wonderful developments—and a little bit of information about the painting—that Hailey wanted to share with Marina. Hopefully, that early summer morning would be the day they'd see each other again.

A warm breeze blew as Hailey watched the sun in its entirety hanging low in the sky, and some of her long hair blew into her face. She wove her fingers between the fine dark strands and stared at their colorless tips. For a long time, she had kept the last six inches or so dyed, but due to the additional time spent underwater in chlorinated pools, the color had faded away into bleached streaks.

Sighing dejectedly, Hailey stood and walked towards the wooden footbridge. When she stepped on the first stair, a voice in the distance called, "Hailey! Is that you?"

She turned, and in the distance was a girl with blonde hair wearing a pink sundress that clung to her body. She was skipping towards Hailey, one hand in the air waving and the other hand by her side with a rainbow emanating from it. Only one object could produce such vibrant colors, and Hailey immediately smiled when she realized what it was and who was carrying it.

"Marina?" Hailey took off towards her mermaid friend. "O-M-G, it's really you!"

They met and hugged on the stretch of sand behind Hailey's neighbor's house. Fortunately, Mr. Dobbins wasn't awake yet, and even if he were, Marina had legs, so all he'd do was complain about them being on his part of the private beach.

"I am sorry that I have not visited before now," said Marina. "The school has only recently returned here."

"Don't worry about it." Hailey jumped up and down and clapped her hands. "I'm just so happy to see you again."

"So much has happened, and I—"

Before Marina could say anything further, Hailey took her hand and started leading her to the footbridge. "So much has happened here too. Let's go inside, and we can give each other the four-one-one. I can't wait to show you what I've got! And you're gonna totally freak out when you see what I use it for!" Remembering that Marina didn't always understand human expressions, Hailey abruptly stopped and turned to her. "And I don't mean freak out in a be-angry kinda way. I mean freak out in an O-M-G-that's-really-awesome kinda way, K?"

"Hailey, there is something important I must ask you first."

"Marina!" called a voice from down the beach. "You *cannot* do it this way!"

Approaching them was Lorelei, her wavy red hair blowing behind her as she sprinted across the beach. Unlike Marina, who had removed the tail-skirt, Lorelei was still wearing hers around her waist and was wearing her purple seashell bikini top.

"It is the most sensible solution, Lore," said Marina firmly. "And I have done it before."

"That time was an accident. This is—"

"This is my choice, and it is the only way I may fulfill my dream."

While the two mermaids continued debating in her presence, Hailey's eyes bounced back and forth towards whichever one of them was speaking. In the brief pauses between their statements and responses, Hailey tried to interject but couldn't time herself well enough. All that she uttered were scattered *ums* and *ers* and *buts* until finally she flailed her arms and exclaimed, "I-D-K what you two are even talking about! Can one of you please clue me in?"

Marina took Hailey by the hands and answered, "I have learned more about the disappearance of my parents, so I am going to the mainland to do whatever it takes to find my mother."

Hailey's face beamed. "That's awesome news! I've got a folder with printouts of everything I found out about the painting. It's not a lot, but it's better than nothing."

"I truly appreciate your help."

"I'm sure Jill and Meredith—and maybe even Jeff—will help too. Whatever you need me to do, Marina, I'll do it. You can count on me."

"That is reassuring to hear. My search may take some time, and I do not know how long I will need legs. I do not wish my tail to disappear like it almost did last time." Marina withdrew her hands, leaving the translucent object in Hailey's grasp. "So will you keep it safe until the next full moon?"

ACKNOWLEDGMENTS

I started writing this book during the summer of 2013, so I must thank the kids and staff of the 2013 SMARTS Summer Institute and director Sherye Weisz for listening to me drone on and on about how my writing was going. But hopefully, my writing inspired the creative writing students to write.

Thanks to Tatiana Vila for the beautiful cover design. It is a pleasure working with you, and I'm impressed by your talents. I can't wait to see what the sequel's cover looks like.

Thanks to Becca Lopez and Jeanine Swatton for all the help setting up my social media sites and blog. I enjoy writing about *All Sorts of Stuff* there almost as much as I enjoy writing stories like this one. Thanks also to John Barker for designing the flippingthescales-thebook website.

Special thanks to my beta readers who gave me tremendous and necessary feedback, comments, questions, spell-checks, and everything else in between and beyond. In no particular order, thanks to Nancy Tella, Meredith Silva, John Barker, Chris Jones, and Sabrina Rucker.

And finally, extra special thanks to Susan Soares, the greatest beta reader of all—so great that she should be called the alpha reader, and not only because she read it first. I think back to the email I sent you with the basic premise of this story along with three others, and you insisted that this one was the one to write. All I had was a basic idea—a girl and a mermaid switch places due to this shimmery skirt-thing—when you made me write a novel that summer. I started without an ending, but I found one, and then I found that there were more stories to tell with these loveable characters. I couldn't have done it without your encouragement. Thank you, and keep on writing.

ABOUT THE AUTHOR

Pete Tarsi graduated from MIT with a degree in Creative Writing and Physics, and he considers himself fortunate that he still gets to do both. When he's not writing, he can be found teaching high school science, directing theatre, or spending time with his three lovely daughters. He grew up in a small town north of Boston and still lives in Massachusetts.

Visit Pete online at **petetarsi.com**

Made in the USA
Charleston, SC
18 January 2015